W9-ASX-622

Passion's Passage

"Poke fun at me if you will, but I would gladly take the raft to staying here on your ship and submitting myself to you."

"You can't be that angry simply because I made love to you last night."

"There was no love between us, Captain Rikkar, only lust."

His laughter rang out, his eyes dancing with humor. He leaned forward, his warm breath grazing her cheek. "Even in my state of intoxication, I remember the events of the evening very clearly," he said softly. "I remember enjoyment on both our parts." His voice was a husky whisper and one finger stroked her cheek. "When something is so enjoyed by two people it should be repeated, don't you agree?" Lainie trembled beneath his touch.

DESIRE'S DREAM

PEGGY HANCHAR

PINNACLE BOOKS NEW YORK

ATTENTION: SCHOOLS AND CORPORATIONS

PINNACLE Books are available at quantity discounts with bulk purchases for educational, business or special promotional use. For further details, please write to: SPECIAL SALES MANAGER, Pinnacle Books, Inc., 1430 Broadway, New York, NY 10018.

This novel is a work of fiction. Names, characters, places, and incidents are either the product of the author's imagination or are used fictitiously. Any resemblance to actual events or places or persons, living or dead, is entirely coincidental.

DESIRE'S DREAM

Copyright © 1985 by Peggy Hanchar

All rights reserved, including the right to reproduce this book or portions thereof in any form.

An original Pinnacle Books edition, published for the first time anywhere.

First printing/July 1985

ISBN: 0-523-42567-8
Can. ISBN: 0-523-43511-8

Printed in the United States of America

PINNACLE BOOKS, INC.
1430 Broadway
New York, New York 10018

9   8   7   6   5   4   3   2   1

To Bob, who provided the ribbon, and to Laura, who baked the cookies, and to Steve, who kept believing even after I stopped.

Prologue

One ship stalked another upon the great ocean. It rode just over the rim of the horizon, out of sight, its sails billowing above its sleek, dark hull like some deadly bird of prey. Indeed the ship's bow carried the name *Sea Hawk,* and on its prow sat a great hawk, its fierce beak and eyes no less menacing though they were carved of wood.

Men scurried about the deck, silent and purposeful in their actions as they readied cannons and ammunition. Each was armed with his own cutlass and short pistol. Little direction was needed for they had been through this many times before. The captain stood tall on the rolling deck, his steely eyes intent on the horizon, scanning for his prey.

Just over that gray horizon was the *Southern Moon*, a fleet merchant ship with a rich cargo. It was swift, but not as swift as the *Sea Hawk*.

The men on the *Southern Moon* were unaware of the menace that stalked their ship, but their captain was uneasy. Deep within the bowels of his ship was a fortune in cargo, barrels and crates of silks, spices and myriad other goods greatly in demand in the new world. Anxiously the captain paced the deck, raising his nose to sniff the ocean wind. His unease grew.

Something else was also in the hold of the merchant ship, hidden among the crates and barrels. A stowaway stirred restlessly in sleep. Dreams of sunlight sparkling on the water and the slap of wind in the sails brought a soft smile to the stowaway's grimy face. Soon, it would be time to leave behind the darkness of this place and climb to the deck and daylight again.

As the mauve shadows of dawn began to give way to the first golden rays of day, the sea grew choppy. The captain of the *Sea Hawk* ran his hands through his dark hair as he strained to see through the dim, early light. A glance at the open deck told him that all was ready. A flag lay nearby, waiting to be run up the pole at the last moment, its white skull and crossbones stark against its black background. The time was at hand.

"Let's go get her," the pirate captain said quietly and his men smiled gleefully as they leaped to put out more sails. The sleek ship skimmed across the water toward its quarry.

Chapter 1

"I won't see him! I hate him!" Lainie exclaimed. Her chin was set determinedly and the wings of her eyebrows drew down in a scowl over the nearly black depths of her eyes. The sunshine spilling through the window caught in her golden curls, causing their bright splendor to contrast sharply with the darkness of her eyes and somber gown.

"Lainie, you must," Elsa said softly. "He's your father and he's come a long way to see you." Her voice was gentle and persuasive as she spoke. It seemed to suit her subdued coloring and quiet, calm air.

"Oh, yes, he's come a long way," Lainie stormed and whirled about so the dark skirts of her mourning gown swirled about her slim figure. "But he is too late, eight years too late."

How dare he come now, she fumed, when it was too late and Mama was already dead. Why hadn't he come at any time during the past eight years to take them both back to Belle Fleur where they belonged. If he had, Mama might still be alive. A sob caught in her throat as she thought of her mother. Marie Gautier had been like a rare, delicate butterfly, but underneath that gay exterior, Lainie knew her mother's heart had been breaking for her home and the husband who no longer wanted her or their daughter.

3

"I won't see him," Lainie muttered, looking at Elsa Marchand. Elsa had been her friend and confidante for the past few years they had spent here at Mademoiselle Françoise's l'Ecole des Jeunes Filles. Without Elsa, Lainie was sure she would never have been able to last here at the school.

The school had been her prison from the first moment her mother had brought her here at the age of ten, and she had spent the eight years since passing her days in these rooms, leaving the school only for brief, unsatisfactory visits to her mother at the chateau of some friend, or for some school outing to the small shops in the village. With each passing year the walls of these rooms had seemed to close more tightly around her.

Lainie glanced about the room she and her friend shared. It was one of the larger rooms with a window that faced south and caught most of the afternoon sun. Everything was in creamy whites and pale golds with delicate yellow rosebuds sprinkled across the pale papering on the walls. Even the furniture was a creamy white with gilt edged trim.

Sheer ruffled curtains hung around the high four-postered bed with its thick, downy mattresses and pillows. The sheets on the bed were soft and clean and scented with lavender. In a small, white marble fireplace a fire burned cheerfully, chasing away any spring chill that might still be in the air. It was a pleasant room, feminine.

Throughout the years, Lainie's every comfort had been anticipated and attended to, the result of the large sums of money her father settled on the school each year. But it was not Belle Fleur, the plantation in eastern Florida, where she had lived until she was ten. After the tropical beauty and the freedom of Belle Fleur, the cloistered atmosphere of the school was stifling.

Never a day went by when she didn't think of the St.

John river plantation located in the northeastern portion of the Florida Territory. Her memories of Belle Fleur had been her heartbeat, her sustenance during these years of exile.

The sights, smells and sounds of it had been a special part of her growing awareness of the world around her from early babyhood. How she'd loved the graceful, two-storied house with its stately wings and balconies, the barns and sheds which held such delightful mysteries, the stables, the slave quarters where she'd often preferred to share the slave's simple fare, falling asleep as she stared into the roaring campfires and listened to the slaves' ghost stories.

She'd loved the beautiful, spacious rooms of the main house with their gleaming dark woods and cool shadows, the secret hiding places only a child could know, the sheer curtains at the tall windows letting in lemon yellow sunlight, the sparkle of glass chandeliers and hand-rubbed silver. She'd often sat at the top of the stairs, straining for a glimpse of the beautifully gowned and jewelled ladies who danced in the ballroom, imagining herself there one day when she was grown up.

On long afternoons when supper seemed an eternity away, she had often stood outside the kitchen door, where an indulgent cook passed out slices of pink ham still dripping with grease from the frying pan, tucked between two halves of cold biscuits. No French cuisine had ever pleased her palate as much.

How special the dew misted mornings when the land seemed enchanted and she, delighting in the cool, slippery moisture beneath her bare feet, had set out to explore it. Often she would sit on the side of the river bank watching the boats passing to and fro on their way to St. Augustine.

She remembered it all and her heart contracted with pain

and longing. One day she would return to Belle Fleur and when she did, no one would ever send her away again!

Lainie paced about the elegant room, her face pinched and wan as she paused in front of a small portrait of a beautiful, smiling woman.

Silently Elsa watched her friend, her blue eyes filled with concern. Although Lainie and her mother had not seen each other often, Lainie's love for the beautiful French woman had been fierce and blindingly loyal. Marie's death had been a painful blow to Lainie.

"Perhaps your father has something important to tell you about your mother," Elsa suggested softly, trying a new tact and was rewarded by a flare of hope in Lainie's eyes. Quickly it faded and Lainie wandered like a lost child to the window. Her shoulders slumped, her dark eyes large and waif-like in the pale oval of her face.

"Why don't you change your clothes and go down to greet him. It will be good to see him and to hear what he has to say." Lainie did not answer and Elsa went on. "If he goes away again, you'll be left with nothing." Elsa touched her friend's shoulder gently.

"Even if I go down to see him, he'll still go away," Lainie said softly, tears gathering in the corners of her eyes and sliding down her cheeks. "He did once before."

Her thoughts turned back to that time when her world had fallen apart and she was taken away from Belle Fleur. It was her tenth birthday and there had been a party. She had been so happy until afterwards, when all her guests had gone, and her mother called her to her room. Boxes and trunks were packed, and her mother announced that Papa had left them, and they were sailing to France where Lainie would be placed in Mlle. Françoise's school. It was the worst birthday of her life.

A few weeks after her arrival at school, Lainie was summoned to the main parlor by Mlle. Françoise and there she'd found her father. Tearfully, she'd flung herself into his arms pleading with him to take her home.

"Lainie, my precious girl, my good little girl," he had murmured over and over again. "Come now, smile for me," he'd coaxed and hopefully she'd forced a smile through her tears. She would do anything for Papa, especially if he would take her home again.

"Are we going back home soon?" she'd asked.

"Lainie, you won't be going back to Belle Fleur with me—"

"Papa, please," she'd cried.

"Not yet, not for awhile. The school is a good idea. Someday you'll be a great lady, mistress of Belle Fleur. You want to be a good mistress, don't you?"

"I can learn how at Belle Fleur."

"There are some things you can't learn on the banks of the river or in the slave quarters. You must stay here and work hard to be a lady so I'll be proud of you, so Belle Fleur will be proud of you."

"No!" Lainie had cried rebelliously.

"I'm afraid you have no choice in the matter, Elaine Marie. Now act like a big girl and kiss me good-bye."

"No, I won't! I hate you! I'll never love you again. I won't stay here. I won't!"

He'd tried to reason with her and at last had given up and left.

"I hate you," her childish voice had rung out, full of her anguish and pain.

Mlle. Françoise's school became her prison. Occasionally her mother had invited her to join her at the chateau of some friend, but Lainie had felt awkward and out of place. Marie had done little to ease Lainie's feelings of not belonging. As the invitations grew fewer and farther apart, Lainie missed her mother deeply, her only link to home in this foreign land. She grew even lonelier for those days when they'd all been together at Belle Fleur.

The laughter and sunshine of her early childhood echoed mockingly through the bleak loneliness of her years at school. She longed to reach out and find a friend, but some newly developed shyness held her back. Her aloofness, as well as her emerging beauty, did not make her popular with the other girls.

While they agonized over each little blemish, Lainie's complexion remained clear and delicate as a newly opened rose petal. While the other girls dieted to keep their figures slim, walking with books on their heads for a graceful carriage, Lainie moved with a natural grace that could never be acquired or improved upon.

Even Lainie's hair curled naturally in springy, vibrant tendrils while other girls stood for hours in front of mirrors, the smell of singed hair rising above them. The color of her hair seemed to bring the greatest envy to even the kindest girl's heart.

Then Elsa had arrived and had become Lainie's roommate and, more importantly, her friend. For the first time Lainie had someone to talk with, someone to laugh with and to share thoughts and dreams.

Elsa was a gentle, generous girl who had recognized the hurt Lainie felt and through her own steadfast friendship did much to overcome the wary reserve Lainie had built up toward others. Her cheerful kindness acted as a buffer with the other girls as well. At last Lainie was acceptable to the other girls. She had been heard to giggle and seen to blush and somehow seemed less formidable. Out of her shell at last, the charm of Lainie's personality and her irrepressible humor enchanted her school mates.

With a sigh, Lainie turned from the window. She'd spent enough time on memories, she must now face the reality of her father's presence.

"All right," Lainie murmured at last. "I'll go down to see him."

"Good," Elsa applauded her decision. "I'll lay out a more suitable gown for you."

"No." Lainie's sharp tone halted Elsa's footsteps. "I'll go down as I am. I am in mourning."

"But Lainie, it's been three months since your mother's passing. Perhaps you should wear the gray gown or the lavender. It would not be inappropriate—" she paused as her friend continued to shake her head from side to side.

"I wish my father to see that I mourn for my mother," she said.

"You wish to shame and embarrass him," Elsa retorted.

"Yes, I do," Lainie flared, "if it is possible for such a heartless, uncaring person to feel shame or grief." Quickly she walked toward the door.

"Lainie," Elsa called after her and when Lainie turned back, her face a cold mask, Elsa merely shook her head regretfully. "Remember he is your father," she said softly and sighed as Lainie turned without answering. There was too much hurt for Lainie to put aside her anger and bitterness for her father and try to meet him halfway. It would be a difficult meeting.

Lainie's eyes misted over as she stood in the doorway of the great parlor where guests were received. One hand tightened around the ornate knob of the heavily carved door, her mouth parted in surprise as she looked at the man seated in the room.

She'd last seen her father eight years before and she was shocked by the change in him. His hair, once as dark as a raven's wing, was now white and his thin face had aged considerably. The blood pounded in her ears and she blinked back the tears that threatened. She stood, torn with a longing to rush into his arms as she had as a ten year old or scream out her pain and anger at his abandonment of her.

Jean Gautier looked up and caught sight of her. He got to his feet and stood looking back at her, his dark eyes overly bright.

He was not nearly as tall as she remembered. Where once she had thought him strong and invincible, she could now see the fraility of his body. Still, he carried himself proudly. His thin shoulders beneath the rich broadcloth of his coat were thrown back, and he stood ramrod straight. Although one would never think of him as a dandy, the fashionable cut and style of his clothes, from the fineness of his linen to the immaculate press of his long trousers and the shine of his well-cut boots, identified him as a gentleman of substance.

He carried a cane of richly polished wood with a carved brass head. As he walked toward her, Lainie could see the cane was not a mere affectation for he walked with a slight limp. For a moment her lips parted as she thought to ask him of the injury, but she pushed down the urge. It no longer mattered to her, she told herself.

"Lainie," her father said in wonder, looking at her with surprised eyes. "You are so grown up. I left a little girl and return to find a lady." As he embraced her fiercely, she caught a whiff of tobacco on his clothes. Numbed by the unexpected embrace, Lainie stood stiffly in his arms until he drew away, a hurt look in his dark eyes. Her flush of shame was quickly stifled as she reminded herself that the years of their estrangement had been caused by her father. How dare he return now and expect to find the same adoring little girl he had left behind those long years ago.

These bitter thoughts in mind, Lainie strove to maintain a stiff, restrained decorum. Silently she dropped a formal curtsy to her father, then stood before him, eyes lowered.

"It is good to see you again, Lainie," he said gently.

"Thank you, Monsieur," Lainie responded in a low, even voice.

"Monsieur?" Anger flared for a moment in Jean Gautier's dark eyes, then was replaced by sadness. "You used to call me Papa," he said. "Won't you do so again?"

"If you wish," Lainie said stiffly, then paused for a moment before adding, "Papa."

"Come and sit," Jean directed her to one of the ornate parlor chairs. Obediently, Lainie settled herself on the edge, hands folded demurely in her lap, eyes lowered to study the intricate design of the rich, tapestry rug.

"Lainie, I have come to take you home," her father began without preamble.

"Home?" There was a bitter edge to Lainie's voice.

"To Belle Fleur," Jean Gautier continued, a smile flashing in his brown eyes.

"I no longer think of Belle Fleur as my home," Lainie replied, keeping her voice even. "I have been so long here in France, I now think of it as home."

"But you always loved Belle Fleur."

"I do not love her now," Lainie cried passionately, her eyes flashing as she raised them to meet her father's.

Jean Gautier studied his sullen daughter, not knowing how to reach through the barrier of all the years. Squaring his shoulders he adopted a stern tone as he began to speak.

"You are to return to Belle Fleur," he said firmly. "I have made arrangements for you to be married within the year."

"Married!" Bright spots of color stained Lainie's cheeks as she leaped to her feet in outrage. "I won't," she cried. "I'm staying here in France."

"If you stay in France, it will be without the benefit of any money from me. I will not make the same mistake twice." Jean Gautier's voice had risen and Lainie was reminded of his anger when she had been a child at Belle

Fleur. Her gentle kind-hearted father had seldom raised his voice, but when he had, everyone obeyed, even Mama. The thought of her mother made her jut out her chin in rebellion.

"I won't go back and you can't make me," she insisted. "You have no right to tell me what I must do. You gave up that right years ago."

"Lainie," her father began moving closer to her, but she jerked away.

"You haven't changed, have you, Papa?" she stormed. "You move people about as if they had no will of their own. You expect them to do exactly as you say and if they don't you just get rid of them."

"Lainie, don't be too harsh," her father tried again.

"Why not, Papa, after all, aren't I your daughter? Don't you think you were harsh when you sent Mama and me away? Now you decide you want me back and for what? Out of love, because you missed me? Of course not, you covet a neighbor's lands, no doubt, and suddenly remember you have a daughter, a marriageable daughter who might get you those acres. I'm glad you've finally found some measure of value in me, Papa."

"Lainie, stop this, you know what you're saying isn't true," her father cried, but she couldn't stop now.

"How many acres are you getting in return for such a bothersome daughter, Papa? I hope your price was high. And if I truly am my father's daughter, I must ask you, what's in it for me? What will I receive in return for submitting myself to the pawing attention of some fat, old crony of yours?"

"Lainie, I insist you stop this instantly," Jean Gautier roared at his daughter. "You're hysterical. I won't have you throwing childish tantrums like your mother simply to get your way."

"How dare you speak of my mother like that!"

"I dare," her father shouted, "because I know your mother for what she was." Black rage filled Lainie's heart at his words. He really was as cruel as her mother had said. Funny how as a child she'd never recognized this. Now she looked at his thin face with the stiff angry lines and the snapping eyes, and she hated her father all the more. How could he speak of his dead wife in such a manner.

"Then you won't want me, for I am very like my mother," she said, her voice quiet, deliberately cold and haughty. She expected her words to be met with another outburst of rage, but her father was silent for a moment and his voice calm when next he spoke.

"You will do as I say, Lainie. You will return home to Belle Fleur and you will conduct yourself in a manner befitting a young lady of virtue and breeding. I won't tolerate any disobedience or any of these tantrums. Is that clear?"

His eyes were unyielding as they glared into hers. His words sank through her angry rebellion. She knew that she had no home or family here in France. The truth was she had little choice but to return to Belle Fleur with her father.

"If you insist," she said, "but I go against my wishes."

"I am truly sorry to hear that, Lainie," Jean Gautier said, visibly relaxing now that she had agreed to his wishes. "I had hoped you would be as happy about your return to Belle Fleur as I am." He moved restlessly about the ornate room. "I am sailing on the *Southern Moon* which leaves in a fortnight," he continued. "It may ease your mind a little to know that you will stay here until the term is finished, then you will follow on the *Delta Queen* in three months time. Mlle, Françoise has been instructed to find a suitable traveling companion for you when the time comes."

Lainie raised her eyebrows in astonishment. "I am not to sail with you?" she asked.

"No." For the first time during their confrontation, her father avoided her eyes.

"Why? I can be ready to leave when the *Southern Moon* sails."

"But I don't want you on this voyage," Jean Gautier said. "I want you to finish this last year of schooling, Lainie. There are no schools of such high repute in the territories."

"I've had sufficient schooling," Lainie said. "If I must return to America, though it be against my wishes, I prefer to do so now."

"And I prefer you stay and complete the term," Jean said sternly. "Besides," he added in a softer tone, "I want you to see to new gowns." He crossed the room and stood looking down at her. Reaching out a hand, he touched the black crepe sleeve of her gown.

"I am in mourning," she said stiffly, regretting for a moment that she hadn't followed Elsa's suggestion and changed to a different gown. Then anger flared within her and she raised her eyes defiantly to her father's.

"I understand," he said gently and his hand came up in a loving gesture to brush the hair from her temple. The lines that creased his cheeks and forehead seemed to deepen and Lainie looked at him in astonishment. Had he been grieving for Marie, too? she wondered.

"The time for mourning is past," he said. "I want you to see to new gowns suitable for a trousseau. You needn't worry about the cost of them. I want them to be very lovely as befits a young woman of your beauty."

"I see," Lainie said, pulling away from his touch. "Am I to get a wedding gown as well?"

"Yes." The reply was terse. He turned away and walked

to the fireplace. His shoulders were slumped as if in defeat.

"Have I no choice?" Lainie asked.

"No." Again the terseness.

"Then, if I have no choice in this matter, I had better see about a dressmaker," Lainie said stiffly and turned to leave the room.

"Lainie," her father cried halting her hand on the knob of the closed door. "I know I've done you wrong by leaving you here when you were so young, but I did it because—" he paused for a moment before continuing. "We haven't much time left to get to know each other. I pray we don't waste it in anger."

Lainie looked at her father's ravaged face and felt a thrill of triumph at the beseeching look she found there.

"I am not angry," she said with mock gentleness. "I am indifferent. Now, if you'll excuse me, there are duties to which I must attend."

Quietly she closed the door behind her and walked sedately along the hall to the stairs, her heels beating a steady rhythm against the polished floor while inside her chest, her heart beat its own erratic message. At last, at last, she was leaving Mlle. Françoise's l'Ecole des Jeunes Filles. She was going home to Belle Fleur! A smile spread across her face as she ran up the last few steps and raced down the hall to her room. She was going home to Belle Fleur and although she didn't yet know how she would go about it, she intended to return on the same ship with her father.

"I tell you, Elsa, it *will* work," Lainie said, her eyes aglow as she thought of her plan. Nearly two weeks had passed since that painful interview with her father and the days had been spent in a flurry of feverish activity.

A dressmaker had been summoned and with Mlle.

Françoise's influence had completed several gowns and undergarments in record time. Elsa and Lainie had talked of nothing else for days but the right colors, fabrics, and laces. Their room had been turned topsy turvy with every chair and chaise covered with completed gowns and petticoats in a silken rainbow of colors.

They had just returned from an outing, their last, for the *Southern Moon* sailed on the evening tide and with it, Lainie's father. At Lainie's request, Jean Gautier had taken them that afternoon to the dock for a view of the ship and as she walked beside her father, Lainie had quivered with barely suppressed excitement. Elsa had sensed her friend's mood, but had not understood the reason for it, until now. She looked at Lainie with wide, dubious eyes.

"It just won't work," Elsa repeated. "Your father will have you put off the ship. He isn't taking any passengers this voyage."

"Yes, and that's rather strange, isn't it? But he has to have a crew and that is what I shall be, at least until I get aboard, then I'll hide."

"But where will you hide? What will you eat and drink?"

"I'll hide in the hold and steal food from the galley." For a moment Elsa was silent, although Lainie could tell her lively mind was working furiously.

"Even if you get away with it," Elsa said finally, "your father will be very angry."

"Oh, fiddle, I'm not afraid of his anger," Lainie said brightly.

"Won't you be frightened?" Elsa asked, her eyes searching the other girl's determined face.

"Of course not," came the quick reply and Lainie tossed her golden curls to emphasize her words. "Why would I be? After all, it is my father's ship. I'll just sneak aboard and hide and when the ship is far enough out to sea, I'll come out of hiding. What can they do?'' She gave an eloquent shrug of her shoulders and an impish gleam appeared in her eyes. ''They won't turn back,'' she said positively.

''No, they won't,'' Elsa agreed, ''but chérie, how will you sneak on board? They'll see you and your father will send you right back here.''

''I'll disguise myself,'' Lainie told her. ''I'll dress like a cabin boy and carry on some trunks and valises which a certain Mlle. Eugenia Marcell is shipping to her sister in Savannah. That's *you*, my dear friend!''

''I shall miss you very much,'' Elsa murmured in a voice that caught in her throat. It had suddenly occurred to her that Lainie was really leaving and they might never see each other again. The same thought seemed to have struck Lainie for she flew across the room to embrace the girl who had been such a good friend. The two girls sobbed on each other's shoulders while memories of the things they'd shared swept through their minds.

''I must make ready,'' Lainie soon said, looking at the dark shadows outside their window. ''I want to be gone before dinner.''

A sense of adventure coursed through her as she pulled a pair of tattered trousers and shirt from a chest. Part of the money meant to be spent for ribbons and hats had gone to bribe a street urchin into getting the clothes for her. Another sum had been saved to pay a man to pick up Mlle. Marcel's trunks and take them to the *Southern Moon*.

Lainie slipped out of her gown and pulled the boy's shirt over her head. Its voluminous folds hid her full bosom. In the dark she might pass, she thought, looking at the garment critically.

The scuffed seaman's shoes were heavy and much too big on her feet, but she donned two pairs of heavy woolen stockings. The thickness would help protect her soft skin from the chaffing of the stiff leather. Securing her long, golden curls in a severe knot on top of her head, Lainie covered it with a sailor's hat.

"Well, how do I look?" she asked, pushing at the too long sleeves.

"You look like a cabin boy, except for your face. It looks like that of a very pretty girl," Elsa said. Crossing to the fireplace, she picked up a piece of coal and returned to Lainie.

"Hold still," she commanded and applied the charcoal to Lainie's cheeks and forehead. "Now your hands," she said and rubbed the black coal across the palms and around the fingernails. Then she stood back to admire the results.

"Now you'll do," she approved. Lainie went to the mirror and stared in astonishment. She did indeed resemble those young boys she had seen on board ship.

"Well, wish me luck," she said and moved to hug her friend, but the sight of her grimy hands stopped her. They looked at each other in surprise then laughed before sobering at the thought of their parting. The sound of wagon wheels on the cobblestones was loud and startling in the quiet room.

"The wagon is here for your trunks," Elsa said reluctantly.

"Yes," Lainie's voice broke on the single word, then she rushed on. "Go down and bring the man up," she then said.

Elsa met the burly man in the great hall and showed him upstairs.

"My boy will go with you and see that they are properly loaded," she said, nodding her head toward Lainie who hovered nearby.

"Here now, are ye' sayin' ye' don't trust me to git ye'r trunks there?" the man asked belligerantly.

"No, it's just that I don't trust the captain to store them in a dry place," Elsa returned quickly.

"Well, me boy," the man growled at Lainie, "grab hold t'other end."

"Wh-What?" Lainie asked, startled, then remembered and disguised her voice.

"I said, grab hold," the man ordered.

"Ah—he's not supposed to lift," Elsa quickly intervened. "He's been ill."

"Ill, huh?" the man sneered. "Looks healthy enough t'me, but if'n you say so." The man hoisted the trunk onto his shoulders. "At least ye' kin bring some o' the smaller cases," he growled and turned toward the door.

Hastily Lainie grabbed a small portmanteau and followed the burly figure. They made several trips before all the cases were loaded on the wagon. Finally, Lainie climbed aboard and gazed up at the window of her room. The dearest friend she'd ever had stood in the window waving goodbye, her figure outlined by the lamplight behind her. Lainie twisted on the seat as the wagon rolled away and waved even after Elsa could no longer be seen.

Getting aboard the ship was easier than Lainie had anticipated. She simply took one of the bags and followed the burly man on board and into the hold. Once the trunks were stashed below, Lainie, in her disguise, bade the man goodbye and headed for the stairs.

"Wait a minute, lad, what's ye'r hurry?" the man leered at her.

"I have to go," Lainie said and hurried back toward the ladder. She could hear the heavy steps of the man scurrying after her.

"Hey, sonny," the man called, but Lainie sped up, then darted behind some kegs. Crouching in the dark shadows, she waited breathlessly while the man paused and peered into the darkness.

"Aye, laddie, come on ou'. I'm not goin' ta hurt ye'. Did I make ye' carry those heavy trunks, huh? No, old Mac did it. Nawh, ye' owe me a li'l consideration. Right? Right!" the man bellowed.

Lainie drew farther back into the shadows, hardly daring to breathe. The silence closed around her. Then she heard the scuffle of feet as the man turned toward the ladder.

"They's others more willing. Don' have to beg no brat," he muttered under his breath. Lainie listened to his ponderous progress up the stairs then breathed a sigh of relief as he reached the top. Her breath went out of her as she heard him close the hatch and bolt it.

She was exactly where she wanted to be, and so she tried to tell herself she really didn't mind the impenetrable darkness. Cautiously, she crawled back to the oaken planking that ran between the storage areas and groped her way toward her trunks. Inside one of them were candles and a flint as well as some food filched from the dining room earlier that day and wrapped in one of Mlle.'s fine linen napkins.

Lainie lit her candle, feeling like an explorer as she crawled around the hold looking for a place to sleep. She found barrels of rum and molasses and hard tack. Other barrels held pork and coarsely ground grain. There were a few trunks like hers, which she didn't open, but the hold seemed strangely empty for a merchant ship of this size; some of the barrels and caskets stored there were actually empty. How could a ship pay for its operation if it took no passengers and little or no cargo? she wondered.

At least her immediate problems were solved, Lainie thought, turning her attention back to her own needs. There were casks of water and food and with the supplies she had stashed in her own bags, she could easily last until the ship was too far out at sea to turn back. Her biggest problem would be early discovery if someone came into the hold.

Digging once more into her bag, Lainie drew out a heavy cloak. Holding her candle high, she moved among the barrels and trunks until she found what she wanted: a case of cloth. She struggled to pry the top off and when at last a board was free, she used it to pry the rest of the top off. Climbing up she spread her cloak and lay down. Yes, that would do quite nicely for the time being. She blew out the candle and pulled the cloak about her. The sway of the ship at anchor soon lulled her into a fitful slumber.

She awoke in the dark, startled out of sleep by the sound of bells. The pitch and roll of the ship told her they were at sea. She felt a leap of joy. They were on their way. Soon, she would leave this dark place and climb out to the sunshine and her father.

Despite her carefully thought out preparations and plans, the next few days were not pleasant ones for Lainie. A storm at sea caused the boat to lurch and roll until she was too sick to move. Finally the day came when she was well enough to go above and face her father. She couldn't bear to spend another day in this dark, dank place. At the next sounding of the bells, it would be morning and her father would be on deck. It would be the best time to make her presence known. Resolutely, she folded her cloak and sat huddled on the crate waiting for the signal she'd set for herself.

Suddenly the bells began to clang, sooner than she'd expected, louder and more urgent, too. Taking up her last candle, Lainie made her way to the ladder and began her ascent to the hatch. She knew they were open, for several times during the past few days, seamen had gone up and down from the hold to get supplies.

Suddenly, a sound like thunder split the air and the ship lurched and shuddered. Lainie was caught unaware. Her feet slipped from the ladder and she dangled helplessly, trying to regain her footing. Cannons thundered above her and the smell of gun powder filled the air.

Pirates, thought Lainie as she struggled for a foothold. Again the thunder and again the ship shuddered and rolled. The momentum swung her further out from the ladder. Unable to keep her grip, she fell into the dark, yawning hold, her head slamming against the oak planking. The sounds above dimmed and a roaring darkness filled her head. The stowaway lay unconscious, oblivious to the noise and death above her.

Chapter 2

Slowly, Lainie opened her eyes and tried to focus in the dark. Above her was a square of light. How strange that she'd never noticed a window in her ceiling before. She wondered if Elsa had noticed it and turned her head to see if her friend was awake. The movement was so painful she was stunned, but behind the pain was the the memory of where she was. Above, the gunfire had stopped but the shouts of men and the clang of steel against steel still rang out on the morning air.

The sound of the booming cannon brought her fully awake. She didn't want to be below desk if the ship were going to sink. No one knew she was here. Ignoring the pain and nausea she felt, she crawled to the ladder and pulled herself up the first rung.

"Help me, please, someone help me," she called, but her voice was lost in the fury of sound from above. Painfully, Lainie pulled herself up the ladder one rung at a time trying not to brush her bruised hip against the wood. The closer she drew to the square of light, the sharper the pain behind her eyes. Lainie felt sure she would never make it to the top, but the thought of the dark hold yawning below spurred her on. She winced at the pain in her hip and climbed the next rung and the next until finally her head emerged into the sunlight.

She stood on the top rung of the ladder half in and half out of the hatch. The sunlight was like a flashing explosion against her eyes, so she closed them to ease the pain. Around her the voices of jubilant men mingled with the groans and curses of those in pain.

"For God's sake, man, have mercy on my men," the voice was that of her father. She opened her eyes against the glare of the sun, but sunspots darkened her vision. Through multi-colored sun spots she made out her father as he spoke to a tall man. The man's features were obscured and blurred, but she could see that he was taller than her father and his hair was dark.

"I beg of you," her father said. "My men are good men. Leave them their lives. Take mine if you must, but not theirs."

"Oh no," Lainie whispered, struggling out of the hatch.

"You heard him, Captain," one of the sailors shouted, approaching her father menacingly. Raising a belaying pin he brought it down over the head of Jean Gautier who crumbled to the floor.

"Let's finish him," the other pirates yelled.

"No, wait," the tall, dark pirate said, moving to stand over the helpless man. He held a pistol in one hand.

"This man is mine to kill, I have an old score to settle with him."

The pirates moved back. The man cocked the pistol and aimed it at the unconscious figure on the floor.

"No, no," Lainie screamed but her cry was lost in the blast of the gun. The pirate captain turned to his men, the pistol still smoking in his hand.

"Now we're even," he said and his laughter rang out. "Let's get back to our own ship," he ordered. The pirates gathered up the last of the booty and began to follow their captain.

At first no one seemed to notice Lainie, who sat against the hatch, her eyes unfocused and staring, her face streaked with soot and blood. Her mind was numbed by what she'd seen. Her father was dead, killed by a pirate. It couldn't be true. It had to be a dream that would soon disappear from her mind. She sat limp, waiting for the nightmare to end, but it was only beginning. Her long golden strands caught the glint of dying sun and the greedy restless eyes of one of the pirates.

"What have we here?" he said to his mate as the two men approached the dazed girl.

"We got us a wench," one of them said as Lainie shrank back from them.

"Come on out here, girlie, let's look you over." The other man grabbed her long hair and dragged her forward.

Dazed and shocked, Lainie offered no resistance as the man pulled her to him and raising her chin with one blood-grimed hand, planted a wet kiss on her soft mouth. The stench of the man's body and breath invaded her apathy and with a cry of disgust, she turned her head away. He only laughed and threw her over his sweaty shoulder and carried her to his ship.

"No, please," Lainie cried out in protest as the man's hard fingers scraped across the soft flesh of her bodice.

She struggled as his hand caught at her shirt and ripped it down the front. His small cruel eyes showed no mercy as he grasped her thin chemise and ripped it away. Lainie screamed and flailed at him, her back arching away from the repulsive body until her hair nearly touched the deck.

By now the couple was encircled by pirates. "Look what Monty's got," one of them yelled.

"Hurry up, Monty, it'll be me turn next," called another.

"Want me to hold her down for ye?" one jeered.

The pirate's face reddened at these jibes and he doubled up one fist and hit the defenseless girl such a blow that she lay on the deck, stunned and unresisting. Kneeling above her prostrate body, the pirate ripped away the canvas pants she wore.

"Gah, she's a beauty," one man cried.

"Ten shillings down she's a virgin," said Lainie's attacker.

"Go on, how'll you prove it to us?" one young pirate jeered.

"By the blood of 'er, idi't," another called, pushing him derisively. Ribald laughter followed.

"What's the joke, lads?" It was the voice of the captain who had now approached the group.

"We got us an extra prize, Capt'n," one man said, moving aside so the captain could enter their circle. He grimly surveyed the scene before him.

"Montgomery," he barked. The pirate paused, his slack lips thinning in anger.

"Spoils, Capt'n. It's our right," he said.

"Leave her alone." He knelt beside the girl and raised one eyelid to gaze into her eye.

"Ah, she's okay. I just back-handed her to quiet her down a little," Monty said. "I don't like me wimmen to struggle that much."

"Leave her," the captain repeated. "Jenson, get a robe to cover her."

"Look here, Capt'n," Monty protested, "she's mine, I found her."

"She's no ones, least of all yours," the captain said.

"You're not on one of your merchant ships now, Capt'n," the man said, rebuckling his pants and rising to meet the challenge. "On a pirate ship, all spoils are shared equally. I'll share her with you, but I get her first. I ain't had me a virgin in a long time."

"We're not sharing her." The captain squared his shoulders and stared at the man. He was very much aware of the danger of the situation. By tradition all things were shared equally among the pirates, with the captain not getting much extra consideration in spite of his title. All these pirates were woman hungry and expected to vent their desires on the lovely young body that lay before them. The captain knew he must handle this carefully or he would be chucked into the sea and a new captain elected.

"All right, mate," the captain said relaxing his stance and smiling a little, although his eyes remained cold. "She's your prize."

Monty grinned, casting a triumphant look at his shipmates. The captain let him savor his moment of victory, then said softly, "I'll fight you for her."

Laughter died away as the pirates turned to stare at the captain. A fight. This was getting better. The pirates turned expectantly to Monty.

Suddenly the jubilant pirate felt the loss of their support. Monty outweighed the slim captain, but he had no misconceptions about the other man's strength and agility. None of them had.

"Why should I fight you for what's already mine?" Monty asked belligerantly. "What's in it for me?"

"My share of the ship's loot," the captain replied easily. His steady gaze never wavered from Monty's face. His half smile remained. Monty felt a surge of fear sweep over him.

On the deck the girl moaned, and her dark eyelashes fluttered against her dirt smeared cheek. No roll was worth it, Monty thought, but he knew there was more involved now. He couldn't back down or his life would be hell; his shipmates would see to that.

"Done," he said to the captain. The pirates cheered. "But I choose the weapons," Monty quickly added.

The captain nodded agreement.

"Knives," Monty said.

Warily the two men circled each other, each looking for the other to relax his guard. Monty's bulk was impressive, but the tall, lithe form of the captain made some of the crew hesitate a moment before placing their wagers.

The captain grinned and this infuriated Monty, who abandoned caution and rushed to attack.

The captain gracefully sidestepped, using his own blade to knock Monty's knife aside. The sound of steel against steel rang out, then the captain lunged, puncturing Monty's shoulder. The sight of his own blood further enraged Monty and he leapt at the captain but missed, landing with a thud on the deck. The two men struggled, rolling over and over; finally they came to a stop near Lainie. The captain was astride the fat pirate, each intent on holding off the deadly knife of the other.

One of the crew edged forward to drag the helpless girl out of the way, but Lainie, half dazed, didn't understand his motive. She screamed and lashed out with her legs. Startled, the captain looked up, momentarily relaxing his guard. Monty quickly took advantage of the lapse. Lunging upward against the captain, he sent him sprawling across the deck, at the same time wrenching the knife from his hand.

Monty scrambled to his feet and stood, a knife in each hand, looking at the prostrate captain.

"This is going to be a real pleasure," he sneered, confident now that the battle was won and the girl would be his.

The captain lay propped on one elbow and quietly watched the man approaching him, then swung his legs into Monty's feet, tripping him. The fat pirate's eyes opened wide in surprise and he staggered, trying to regain his balance. But he fell heavily to the deck next to Lainie, one arm flung across her. His short hoarse cry and death rattle was lost among Lainie's terror-filled screams.

"Be gawd, he fell on his knife," one pirate cried out.

"Move him away from the girl," the captain ordered, as he approached Lainie.

Through her tears Lainie saw him unbuttoning his shirt, a dark silhouette against the glaring sun. "Oh God, no more, no more," she whispered to the cloudless blue sky above her.

For a moment, as she stared at the untroubled sky, she felt as if she had been lifted away from the horror around her. She felt the warmth of the sun as she soared closer to it, and she saw the laughing waves of the sea below her. There were no ships with billowing, black smoke tainting the clear air, no harsh, raucous sounds of men's voices and the clang of steel to sunder the quiet, no stench of blood and death, only the seawind, the sky and Lainie.

Suddenly, she was no longer afraid. To die could not be worse than what she had seen and felt in the past hour. When she felt them lift the pirate's arm from across her body, she tightened her muscles in readiness. The captain knelt above her, his bare, tanned chest blocking her vision of the sky. He smiled at her and held out his hand, his shirt clutched in the other. What was he doing? Was he trying to befriend her? She looked into his eyes, steel gray and cold. No! There was no friendship there. His approach was different, but the result would be the same.

Perhaps she could use him, make him think she trusted him. Tentatively, Lainie smiled at him, not realizing its devastating effect on the man. He was touched by her grimy, tear-streaked face and brave smile as much as by the perfection of her bare, taut breasts and slim hips. Her golden pink skin caused a stirring in his loins. What she had been doing on that ship, dressed in those rags, was a mystery he intended to unravel.

Jean Gautier had said no passengers would be taken aboard the *Southern Moon* for this trip. Maybe she had been smuggled aboard by a friend in the crew. Well, there was no taking her back to the other ship. The wind had widened the distance between the two ships. He couldn't have gone back anyway, the crew would have asked questions. Questions he couldn't answer. He was stuck with a female on board and a ship full of randy men. Damnation!

His irritation flashed in his eyes and caused Lainie to cringe. She must do something. She grasped his hand and felt herself pulled to her feet as the pirate rose smoothly from his squatting position. As Lainie regained her feet, he let go of her hand.

"Now," a voice inside Lainie hissed and without further thought she leapt for the railing, ignoring the coil of rope that tangled about her ankles. There was no time to extricate herself. Her bare feet found footholds and she lifted one slim leg over the rail, then the other. Behind her, she heard an outcry. One quick look at the dark sea below her, one last anguished look of hope behind her and Lainie pushed away from the railing.

She fell through space, weightless and free. It wasn't so bad to die this way, she thought, before the water came up to meet her. The impact stunned her. She sank deep into a green watery world. Her lungs began to burn and there was a pain in her chest. She needed air. The cold sea numbed her. She couldn't fight her way back to the top. Something was pulling her downward and she couldn't fight the force of the swirling water.

She could feel a darkness closing over her, but she didn't want to die yet. Frantically she fought toward the light and air. There was so much she wanted to see and do, so much to say. She wanted to tell her father that she loved him and forgave him. Then she remembered that her father was already dead and she stopped struggling. Cold blackness settled over her.

The next time she opened her eyes the sky was gone, but a golden glow came from one corner of the darkness. Lainie saw a shadow move restlessly at the perimeter of the light. She slept and woke again.

She was in a room, the room moved and the circle of blue sky was a porthole. She was on a ship. Lainie turned her head to follow the sunlight; the movement brought a man to her bed. He was the shadow she had seen during the night.

"So, you're awake?" he said gruffly. Lainie opened her mouth to speak, but couldn't get any sound out, so she said nothing, simply staring back at the figure before her. Something about him, silhouetted in the sunlight, tugged at her memory, but his face was in shadows. She looked about the room, her glance falling on a sea chest and the pitcher sitting there. She was overwhelmed by thirst. She ran her tongue over parched lips and turned back to the man.

"Do you want water?" he asked. At her painful nod he poured a cup.

Lainie's hands trembled as she reached for it. The man raised her shoulders and supported her against him as he guided the cup to her lips. She drank deeply, draining the cup.

"More," she croaked. He took the cup and refilled it. As he turned back to her, Lainie sat up and the coverlet fell away, exposing her bare bosom. Concentrating only on the cup of water, Lainie ignored the dropped coverlet and her nakedness. Instead she reached her arms upward for the water.

Finally refreshed, she took a deep breath and looked up at the man who towered above her. Her tangled golden curls fell about her shoulders and down her back. One curl lay along one tender breast. Her eyes, raised in innocence and gratefulness, were enormous in her pale face. The man felt a stirring at her innocent beauty, while at the same time, an anger flared at her artful display of herself, her lack of modesty, and most of all her candid scrutiny of him.

Before her, Laine saw a tall, slim man, deeply tanned, his long legs encased in a soft brown material which seemed to cling to each ripple of muscle and bulge of masculinity. Lainie raised her eyes to his broad shoulders and chest covered with a soft white shirt opened almost to his waist. Dark curly hair swirled across his chest. Thick, black hair fell across his high forehead. It was a strong face, Lainie thought. The mouth was slightly parted and his white teeth made a stark contrast against his tanned skin. She noted the straight nose and dark arching eyebrows. Her examination was arrested by his eyes. Something in their steely gray depths made her shiver. She had seen those eyes before in her shadowy nightmare world. Something about this man frightened her, but she couldn't say why.

With a sardonic lift of an eyebrow, the man leaned forward and lifted the strand of golden hair lying against her bare breast. Lainie gasped in fear and drew the coverlet around her. The man's smile took on a cynical twist.

"Now she'll play the innocent," he told himself and felt suddenly weary of all the artful, well-worn games of women. "Do you know where you are?" he asked.

Lainie shook her head, the movement causing the tendrils of her hair to dance and brush against her pale skin.

"You are on the *Sea Hawk*. It is a pirate ship," the man enunciated each word, giving them added import. "You were taken from the *Southern Moon*. Do you remember?"

Again Lainie shook her head, while dismay filled her. She had left the nightmarish, watery world of her dreams for another nightmare, much worse for this one was real. Before her stood a man whose very eyes showed her there would be no mercy, no kindness.

"What were you doing on that ship?" he asked. Lainie looked at him dumbly, searching her mind for an answer, but none came.

"I don't know," she said.

"Were you with some one?"

"I-I don't know. I don't remember," Lainie cried, closing her eyes against the fear she felt.

"How convenient," the man sneered.

Lainie's anger flared. He didn't believe her! She'd never lied before in her life. Her head hurt and the pain, as unrelenting as the pirate who stood questioning her, brought the blood pounding to her temples in a rush of fury. With a cry she suddenly launched herself at him and before he could stop her, her nails raked along his cheek, drawing blood. Quickly he grabbed her wrists.

"Let me go!" she cried. She spat at him and arched her body back. Her legs, entangled in the sheet, flashed as she kicked at him. The pirate bent her over the bed until she thought her back would break. Her knees gave way to the pressure and she fell onto the bed, the man falling heavily on top. Still she struggled, her arms flailing to get free, and wherever she could, her nails raked his skin, bringing blood.

"Hold still, you wild cat," he said.

"Let me go," she cried.

The pirate worked one leg between hers to pin her wriggling body. Suddenly, Lainie became aware of his hard body pressed along the length of hers. The wiry, curly hair of his chest brushed against her nipples as she struggled, and she could feel too a hard bulge pressing against her inner thighs as he pinned her legs down. Frantically she struggled not only against him but at the strange new sensations she felt within her own body. Sobs tore from her throat as hysteria rose within her.

"Stop it," the man commanded harshly. His fingers were steel against her flesh as he grasped both of her hands in one of his.

Lainie was past hearing. She heaved her body against his in an attempt to throw him to one side. Swiftly the man raised his hand and slapped her cheek. The stinging pain that followed had little effect on Lainie. She continued to cry out and struggle. The man grasped a handful of hair and pulled her face toward him.

"Stop it, you little fool," he said icily.

Now he held her arms above her head and rested for a moment, thinking. She had acted like a brazen hussy, allowing the cover to fall so he could fully view her beautiful breasts. Even now as she struggled, her legs parted still further, allowing his body to fall against her moist heat. It had been too long, and she was too desirable. He brought her face to his, ignoring her cry of pain and ground his mouth into hers. His tongue expertly parted her lips. His kiss was long and ardent. He could feel the girl's struggles cease and the stiff resistance leave her body. Ah, so this was what she wanted after all.

Lainie thought she was on fire. The pain of his sudden kiss gave way to sensations she had never before felt. She ceased struggling. She felt her body swell against the man. His tongue probed her mouth until her head was reeling. When at last the kiss ended, Lainie could only lie quietly beneath him, her eyes closed. The man loosened her hands, but still lay on top of her and caressed her breasts. Lainie opened her eyes and looked into the cynical eyes above her. She found only ruthlessness there. She turned her head away and cried quietly, the tears running silently down her cheeks.

"What is it?" the man asked. Lainie couldn't answer,

but her quiet crying continued, the tears unchecked as she made no attempt to wipe them away. As it had before her mind moved backwards, toward the welcoming shadows, away from confrontation and pain. She couldn't tell him who she was. She didn't know and the thought frightened her, just as the fierce, gaze of the man did. Where was she? Who was she? What was she to do? Even more frightening were the strange feelings inside herself as this man touched her.

"What sort of woman are you?" the man asked. "You change from one mood to the other and back again." He searched Lainie's face, but she refused to speak or look at him. Desire died in him at the sight of her tears.

What a fool I am, he thought. He rolled to one side and covered her body with the coverlet.

"You'll be all right," he said roughly.

"I'll never be all right again," Lainie sobbed.

"Sure you will, you need some food and you'll regain your strength." Gently he placed a pillow beneath her head. "I'll have food brought to you."

Lainie lay with her face turned to the wall. The man felt a twinge of regret mingled with shame at his behavior. You're becoming as barbaric as your shipmates, he told himself, turning away. The girl's quiet sobs followed him down the hall and up the stairs, and haunted him throughout the day.

Chapter 3

Fatigue took its toll on Lainie and soon she fell into a deep sleep. Too weary to dream, Lainie's underwater world did not return to her. Her rest was untroubled and she awoke refreshed.

"I wake you up?" a strange, dark-skinned man asked.

"No, no," Lainie murmured and tried hard not to stare at him. He was obviously Indian, but not Seminole as Lainie was familiar with from her early years in Florida. This man was taller and wore his dark hair cropped just below his ears. He was dressed much the same as the other sailors except that his clothes were much too small for his massive frame.

"Of what tribe are you?" she asked.

"Me, Caloosa," he said pointing to his chest. "You eat now." He brought forth a small iron pot and, placing it on the table, began to ladle broth into a bowl.

"I'm not hungry," Lainie began but her protests died as the rich aroma of the soup reached her. Suddenly she was ravenous.

"Many days since you eat," the Indian said. "You very sick. You swallow much water."

"Water?" Memory of her water filled nightmares flooded back. "Why?" she asked.

36

"You jump in the ocean," the Indian said surprised that she asked.

"How did I get out?"

"Foot in rope, drag you behind ship. Rikkar go in and pull you back to real world," Caloosa said.

"Rikkar?" Lainie was puzzled.

"The captain. He is very brave and kind. He nurse you back to the world of living." Caloosa brought the soup to her. "Now you eat and be more better."

As Lainie sat up to reach for the soup, she became aware of her state of undress. Quickly she grasped the edge of the cover and blushed as another memory surged back. That of a tall, lean man with hard, cynical eyes who had stared at her contemptuously. Her eyes opened wider as she recalled the man's hard body pressed against hers. Color stained her cheeks.

The Indian noticed her dilemma and held out a shirt to her. Murmuring her thanks, she rose to her knees and quickly donned the shirt while the Indian turned his back.

The shirt fell midway down her thighs and the sleeves were too long, but at least she was covered. It was designed to open deeply at the throat and chest so that even with the top buttons closed, too much bosom would be exposed if Lainie moved quickly. Gathering the loose folds of the shirt forward to help compensate for the too low opening, she sat on the edge of the bunk.

"I'm ready," she called to Caloosa who once again brought the broth. Lainie ate with gusto. No food had ever tasted so good to her, but after only a few spoonfuls she was too full for more.

"I am finished," she said to Caloosa just as the door swung open. The pirate captain, Rikkar, filled the doorway as he entered the room and Lainie felt his overpowering presence in the small cabin. Involuntarily she shrank back against the bunk. The man's eyes flicked over her, then dismissed her as he turned to Caloosa.

"Isn't she eating?" he asked.

"Yes, a half bowl," the Indian replied. "She will eat more later. It will take time for her stomach to grow again. She did not take nourishment for so long."

Lainie stared at Caloosa. Where was the pidgin English he had used with her? He was now speaking beautiful English. Lainie watched as the two men spoke in low tones, then Caloosa turned to pick up the dishes and the pot of soup.

"No, don't go," Lainie cried out as he turned toward the door. The Indian paused, surprised at the outburst. The tall pirate looked at her and narrowed his eyes speculatively. Something flared behind his lashes. Anger? Laughter? Lust? She turned to avoid his gaze.

"Please stay," she begged of the Indian. He turned to his captain, his eyebrows raised questioningly. The movement of the head was barely perceptible, but the Indian responded instantly, closing the door behind him as he left the room. Lainie choked back a last protest. This smug, overpowering man wouldn't see her beg, she decided. Proudly she raised her chin. Whatever she must endure, she would do so with so much courage and dignity that this barbarian couldn't help but be impressed, and would leave her alone. She felt disconcerted to see a grim smile about his lips and eyes. The heat rose to her cheeks and her eyes flashed fire.

"Are you frightened to be alone with me?" the pirate asked.

"Shouldn't I be?" Lainie retorted.

"No." He held her fierce gaze for a moment then turned to pull a stool closer to her bunk.

"What is your name?" he asked. The question startled her. She sat silently concentrating, trying to drag forth an answer to his question. From beyond that watery night-mare world the sound of whispered voices whirled through her head.

"Why do you refuse to answer?" he demanded.

"I don't," Lainie protested. She sank back against the pillows. Tears ran down her cheeks, quenching the fiery anger of moments before.

"Then what is your name?" the pirate insisted.

"I—I don't know."

"Come now," the pirate said disbelievingly. "Do you remember where you are?"

"Yes," Lainie said eagerly, glad to be able to say so. "I'm on a pirate ship, your ship."

"Do you remember how you got here?"

"No. I only remember the water."

The pirate frowned. "How convenient. Do you remember why you were on the other ship?"

"The other ship?" Lainie echoed.

"The other ship," he repeated, irony in his voice. "The *Southern Moon*."

"The *Southern Moon*?"

"Why were you on that ship." The pirate's voice had become hard.

"I—I must have been a passenger."

"The captain took no passengers. The crew had been warned. They wouldn't have brought on anyone. Why were you on that ship?" The pirate's voice rose as he spoke and he moved menacingly nearer Lainie.

"I don't know," she cried shrinking away. "I don't know why I was on that ship. I don't even know my own name."

"Who is Elsa?" The pirate tried a new tack.

"Elsa?" Lainie shook her head.

"You called out Elsa when you were delirious."

"Elsa. Perhaps that is my name," Lainie said hopefully.

"You wouldn't call out your own name. Besides Elsa doesn't fit you. It sounds nordic, and you're not from lands of ice."

"I'm very tired now. Please, will you leave?" she said. Through her lowered lashes she saw the pirate's strong, tanned hands clench into fists, then the ripple of muscles as he rose from the stool.

"Certainly," he said. "You will, of course, remain in the cabin at all times."

"Have I any choice?" she asked.

"No, you haven't," the pirate turned and left the room.

Lainie lay for a long while trying to sort through the shadows that filled her mind. They seemed just out of reach, teasing and taunting her. Was her name Elsa? She repeated it several times, but the name brought no images, no sudden spark of awareness. Why was she on the *Southern Moon*? Had she been a passenger? Perhaps the pirate was wrong, perhaps she had been travelling to join her family. Perhaps they would miss her and inquire about her and someone would rescue her. She forced her mind to picture herself being put aboard the ship by loving friends and families, the waves of good-bye, the farewell hugs, but no familiar images burst upon her consciousness.

Where was she going? she wondered. Who was waiting for her at the other end of the voyage? Finally, exhausted by her efforts, she fell asleep.

The shadows moved away and in their place were bright sights and sounds. There was a lawn party where the ladies danced in wide-skirted gowns of jarring colors, their bosoms bared. Lainie also wore such a gown and a man with a gentle, sad face reached out to touch her, but then his eyes turned hard and steel gray, his smile contemptuous, so Lainie covered her bare breasts and ran away across the green lawn. As she ran, the dancers parted and she saw a faceless man draw his pistol and shoot another man. The dancers laughed gaily and began to dance again. A woman's laughter turned to sobs and Lainie began to cry too, not knowing why she grieved. Something tugged at her mind. Suddenly she was falling and the green lawn turned to green water, filling her mouth and nostrils. She fought against the water, but she couldn't breathe. Dark shadows surged back and Lainie sobbed in her sleep.

When she awoke hours later, the dream had receded and she had forgotten most of it. The room was dark, a single lantern burning low. The roll of the ship caused the flickering light to sway and jump. By its light, Lainie could see the pot of broth left on the table along with a bowl.

Gingerly she rose. The room spun around for a moment. Grabbing the post of the bunk she hung on until things settled into place, then slowly made her way to the table.

She managed a whole bowl then drank a cup of water. Her body had begun to function more normally now and she felt a pressing need for a chamber pot. She searched about the room and was dismayed when she found none. Perhaps there was one outside. Lainie made her way to the door and tugged at it. It was locked. Panic gripped her.

"Let me out," she cried. "Is anyone there? Please open the door." She heard the soft sound of cloth brushing against wood outside the door.

"Is anyone there?" she called again. No one answered, but the latch under her hand moved. "Please open the door. Hurry." Suddenly an outraged bellow sounded from the other side of the door.

"Get away from there," a man shouted and the door shook as two struggling bodies fell against it.

Lainie backed away, listening to the enraged men beyond. Finally the door was flung open. The tall pirate captain stood there chest heaving and nostrils flaring as he sucked in air. Beyond him sprawled a huge man.

As Lainie stared, he rolled his head and sat up. Involuntarily, Lainie screamed. The man sparked terror in her, but she didn't know why. The captain stepped into the room and shut the door.

"So you do remember," he said. Lainie turned her stricken eyes to his face.

"That man," she said, "who is he?"

"That's a good try, but it won't work," he said, approaching her. "We are going to talk."

The fear aroused by the unknown man outside and the manner of the pirate before her was too much for Lainie. Bursting into tears she turned and flung herself across the bed.

"When all else fails, resort to tears," the captain said derisively. He stood over her, his gaze following the lovely lines of her long legs and delicate ankles.

"Come on, my lovely," he said, catching her shoulders and turning her over. Leaning his weight on one knee upon the edge of the bed, he loomed above her.

"No," Lainie cried, flailing out with her arms. Roughly the captain caught her wrists in one hand.

"We've gone through this once before," he said. "This time I may not be able to control myself. Now do you want to continue this or do we talk?"

"Talk?" Lainie asked. "That's all?"

"That depends on you and the answers you give."

"Will you let go of my hands and get off me?"

Without a word the pirate released her and moved to the side cabinet where he poured a cup of rum. He held the cup toward Lainie inquiringly, then drank deeply from it when she refused.

"Now, tell me. What were you doing on that ship?"

"I don't know, I told you."

"You don't know?" The pirate's eyes blazed with anger.

"I don't remember," Lainie said.

"You remembered that man outside that door."

"Not really," she said. "I just knew he was someone who frightened me. Why is it so important to you?"

The pirate narrowed his eyes as he stared at her. "I live a dangerous existence," he said. "I need to know everything about everyone to stay alive." Lainie shivered at his intensity.

"Yes, I can see that," she said. Anger flickered in her. "You kidnap people, hold them against their will. You show no mercy, so you can't expect any."

The pirate laughed. "No quarter given or sought," he agreed. "Doesn't that frighten you?" One eyebrow raised mockingly.

"Only for a moment," she replied honestly. "Then I feel anger at you because you have no right to hold me against my will. No right to lock me in."

"Perhaps I'm not concerned so much with locking in as I am with locking out," he replied. "That man outside the door," he continued in answer to her questioning look. "What do you suppose would have happened if he had opened the door?"

Lainie shrank back against the bed. Patches of memory flashed before her, images of another burly man, the feel of his rough hands on her flesh, his laughter ringing in her ears, his foul breath suffocating her as he forced his mouth on hers.

"For your own safety I wanted him and the others to think you were still near death. You shattered that image today. You made it very clear you are once again strong and healthy."

"I'm sorry," Lainie said contritely. "It's just that being locked in a room frightens me."

"Why?"

"I don't know."

"Why were you at the door?" the pirate asked.

"I was frightened, confused, I thought it was someone who could help me."

"Why would one of my men help you?" the pirate asked, his angry gaze holding hers.

"I don't know." Lainie turned away in anger. "I was at the door because I—I have need of a—a—" she hesitated, not wishing to request a chamber pot from this hateful man.

"You have need of what?" the pirate asked impatiently and as she continued, her lashes lowered, her cheeks suffused in color, his quizzical look gave way to one of amused understanding.

"Ah, of course. I'll see to it right away. In the meantime, you are not to go near that door or make any more attempts to talk to any of the crew."

"Why would I try to talk to any of your crew?" Lainie asked indignantly "They're all cutthroats and pirates."

"Why indeed?" the captain said enigmatically and turned away. It seemed he had hardly closed the door behind him when Caloosa returned with a chamber pot, followed a discreet period later with a wash bowl, clean towel and a bucket of heated water.

"Not like Mlle. Françoise's specially scented soaps, but it does the trick," Lainie said aloud, lathering up and scrubbing enthusiastically. She paused as the realization of what she had said hit her. Mlle. Françoise!

She was remembering! She paused and stared intently at the wall, trying to glean more facts from that pitiful shard of memory. Scented soap and lavender and Mlle. Françoise. Now there were two names from her past, Elsa and Mlle. Françoise, but who were they? she wondered. Friends, maids? What did they look like? Were they young or old? Trying to remember only made her head ache. But this was a start, and soon she would remember everything. Then she would demand the pirate release her!

Her toiletry completed, she found herself with nothing

to do. The day was long and Lainie greeted Caloosa enthusiastically when he brought her midday meal and later her supper, but the tall Indian was strangely aloof and non-talkative. Once she smiled as he gathered the dishes and thought she caught a spark of sympathy in his eyes.

The captain didn't return to the cabin at all. Caloosa brought a rope at Lainie's request and she was able to tie up the pants she had found earlier in a chest. With her legs covered she felt more comfortable. She perched on a stool and watched the waves through the porthole until she felt seasick.

Toward evening Lainie fell to brooding. Her thoughts turned to the pirate captain. What had Caloosa called him? Rikkar! What a strange name, but somehow it fit him. He was very handsome. A pity he had chosen to become a pirate. What had made him do it? Perhaps a love gone wrong she mused. His love had died or been stolen away by another man leaving him bitter and angry, so he turned to pirating. Her mind painted romantic pictures of his life before he became a pirate. He was very strong, Lainie thought, remembering their struggle when he kissed her and the hardness of his body on hers. Lainie's thoughts whirled together and soon she slept, her dreams filled with a handsome pirate captain.

Her rest was ended by wood slamming against wood.

"Who's there?" she called out in the darkened room, fear making a lump in her throat. A shadow was barely discernible through the open door. The shadow lurched into the room, slamming the heavy door behind him. He slid the bolt home and stood listening to the noise beyond.

"No. Please, please. Open the door," Lainie pleaded.

"Be quiet," the shadow commanded. Lainie felt she was drowning. She was locked in this room with the leering man she had seen in the corridor. Beyond the door, Lainie could hear Caloosa and the sound of flesh against

45

flesh. There were muttered curses, then footsteps hurrying away.

"They've gone now," the man said. He moved to the lantern and lit it. Lainie's panic died. It was the captain. For some reason, she now felt safe and protected.

"Unfortunately, they'll be back, unless I'm able to convince them otherwise."

Lainie was suddenly aware of how she must look, her eyes enormous with fright, hair tousled, shirt opened too low, the bed clothes in disarray around her. She had taken off the pants in order to sleep more comfortably and her long legs were once again exposed to his gaze. His eyes glittered in appreciation as he approached the bed, his steps a little unsteady.

"You've been drinking rum," she blurted out accusingly. The captain threw back his head and laughed, but his laugh was strangely without mirth, almost bitter.

"Yes, I've been drinking rum." He moved to the bed and sat down. "Pull off my boots," he commanded.

Lainie's mood swung from fear to anger. How dare the man? He was an insufferable barbarian.

"Pull off my boots," he roared, his eyes hard with anger. "Please," he said, and smiled, completely disarming her.

"Oh, all right," she muttered under her breath. Obviously he couldn't do it himself. She braced herself against his knee and tugged off first one boot, then the other. He leered down at the expanse of bosom exposed by her labors. Defiantly, Lainie glared back. She was sorry now she'd helped him. The pirate grasped her wrists and pulled her toward him.

"You're very beautiful," he said, his gray eyes black as they reflected the lamplight. Shadows and light carved the planes of his strong, handsome face, making him even more attractive and enigmatic. His gaze held Lainie's while he reached out one hand, slowly, carefully, as one would gentle a frightened foal. His finger caught in her hair, sliding downward through the silken tendrils.

For a moment, his gaze took in its rich color and texture, then moved back to the small, delicate face. Like a caress his glance touched on her wide brow, the incredible dark eyes, the softness of her cheeks, the perfection of her small straight nose and the inviting rosepetal sweetness of her lips.

Lainie remained silent before his scrutiny, her breath tight in her chest, her own gaze darting over his lean face, her body trembling slightly like a long-stemmed flower caught in a rush of wind.

"My men—" he began and paused, uncertain how to continue. To himself, he cursed the very men of whom he spoke, the rum he'd drunk, even the ship he sailed. All of it had brought him to this pass, standing before this slip of a girl, stuttering like a school boy about to sample his first conquest.

"On a pirate ship," he began again, "all spoils are divided equally among the men."

"No," Lainie cried, her eyes enormous. What did he mean? Surely he wouldn't give her back to his men.

"Unless one man has won a prize fairly, in a fight or through special bravery." She drew in a breath, anticipating his next words. "I fought for you, so you are my prize," he said. "However, if I don't want you, I have to give you back to my men."

"And do you want me?" she asked, her chin trembling.

"Of course, I do." Rikkar's voice was a whisper. He shook his head to clear his vision. The rum had gone to his head or the ship seemed to be swaying unnecessarily. The small figure before him wavered in the golden shimmer of light.

"And if I give myself to you, you won't turn me over to your men?" she asked softly. The pirate nodded.

"Why can't you just tell the crew I belong to you and be done with it?"

The pirate gave a short laugh. "That pack of rabble knows more of what goes on in here than I do. I must always be on guard with them," he muttered, then gave her a rakish grin. "For once I don't mind."

"Are you telling me I have little choice?" Lainie demanded.

"Neither of us has a choice in this matter," Rikkar said cheerfully. "We might as well not fight it. There are worse sacrifices we could have been called on to make."

"I'll never agree to this," she said, moving past him to put the heavy round table between herself and him.

"You're a fighter!" he said admiringly, approaching the table. Lainie grabbed a bottle of rum and held it menacingly.

"Don't come a step nearer," she grated.

"Careful with that," the pirate said, laughing mockingly.

"I'm warning you, don't come a step nearer, or I'll throw it."

"I'm trying to save you from the crew," the pirate went on. "Trust me, I'm just thinking of your own good."

"How noble of you," Lainie said sarcastically.

"It would be nicer if you were willing, it would save us all a lot of trouble," the captain said. "Why don't you put down that bottle and we'll have a drink and talk it over. I don't know why this should be such a difficult decision for you to make. Some women actually find me attractive."

Lainie didn't understand his attitude. She lowered the bottle slightly and looked at him with wide, puzzled eyes.

Interpreting her actions as acceptance, Rikkar moved closer. Startled, Lainie threw the bottle. Glass and rum splattered over Rikkar as it hit the wall.

"Why did you do that?" he roared.

"I told you not to come near me," Lainie cried, backing into a corner. She was sorry she'd thrown it; now she had no weapon. Hastily she looked about for something else but the pirate was there, pinning her arms behind her, bending her body into his.

"Don't fight," the pirate said softly.

"I detest you and men like you," Lainie cried out.

"That's a strange attitude for a woman of your profession," Rikkar growled. His hands locked in her hair, his lips settling firmly on her mouth. All too quickly he'd gained access to the sweet moistness beyond her soft lips. His tongue dueled with and subdued hers, rousing those frightening new sensations he'd awakened in her before.

"I think we'll come to find enjoyment in each other," he whispered hoarsely. He kissed away her protest, his touch sure as his hands brushed lightly over her body. An age-old ache rose within her, crying out for some release that was nameless and as yet unknown to her.

Expertly he played her and when she was soft and pliant in his arms, he released her, stepping backward toward the bed. Lainie stood by the wooden desk, her heavy-lidded gaze fixed on the dark pirate in puzzlement. He smiled, teasingly, his eyes glinting with fire.

"Come here," he commanded softly and she moved toward him as if in a trance.

"Do you understand why I've come to you tonight?" he asked, his voice a husky caress. Mutely Lainie nodded.

"And you submit yourself to me willingly?" Her dark eyes moved over his face. There was no other choice for either of them he'd said and she believed him. Again she nodded. Her pink lips parted slightly and a small sigh escaped her.

Rikkar looked at her passion drugged face. His need for rum had long sense vanished as a stronger need took possession of him.

"Take off your clothes," he whispered, his eyes boring into her very soul. She had no will left. Her fingers crept to the buttons that held the shirt front together. Slowly, she undid each one, until nothing held the shirt closed. Fire leapt behind Rikkar's gaze. Still he didn't touch her, and she wanted him to. She wanted his touch.

"Take it off," he said, his voice ragged and tight. Her eyes were unwavering, transfixed on his as her hands moved upward to obey. The soft shirt slithered across her satin skin, brushing against her swollen nipples as she pushed it over her shoulders and let it fall to the floor.

She watched Rikkar's expression as his gaze lowered to take in her naked beauty. She heard his sharp intake of breath and felt its release, hot against her cheek.

Rikkar's touch was silky and seductive, causing her to shiver slightly. His hands moved over her shoulders to the dips and hollows of her throat, slowly downward to brush against her breasts. His head dipped to claim her lips in a kiss that teased and tantalized, bringing a small groan of pleasure and anticipation from her.

He held her lightly, his body barely touching hers, the enlarged tips of her breasts brushing against the hard contours of his chest. She could feel the heat of his body and longed to feel his bare skin. Unbidden, her hands crept upward, searching for the buttons that held his shirt closed. They opened at her touch and she brushed aside the cloth. She felt the wiry tangle of hair swirling over his chest and flat stomach. She stepped forward, arching her body so her breasts were flattened against him. She gasped with pleasure, her slender arms going about his slim waist to hold him closer, curving backward in submission to the kisses he rained on her eyelids, cheeks and mouth.

Too long denied, Rikkar drank in her beauty and sweetness. Those long hours he'd sat beside her nursing her, tending her, he'd felt his desire for her grow, but he'd never dreamed of the sweet fires that burned within her. Now he drew that flame nearer.

Her hand moved to his waistband, then hesitated and drew back, too new to this role to overcome that final barrier between them.

With a smothered cry, Rikkar lifted her in his strong arms and settled her on the bed.

"Oh, no," she cried out feebly, but his mouth closed over hers and she was lost, spinning in a kaleidescope of color and motion and sensation such as she'd never experienced before.

I have no choice, she thought, no choice. The refrain beat through her head, salving her conscience as without any further struggle she gave up her innocence forever.

Chapter 4

Lainie woke slowly, drifting back through dreamy layers of sensuous feelings and hot responses. Rikkar was making love to her and she responded without reservation. His kisses burned her mouth, his touch seared her skin. Her body arched beneath his, warm and pulsing, yearning toward that release only he could give her.

What a wonderful dream she was having. Slowly she drifted upward. Rudely, reality intruded and she opened her eyes. It wasn't a dream! Memories of the night before flooded her and she gasped. Clutching the sheets to her bosom, she looked frantically about the room.

But she was alone and was heartily grateful for that. She couldn't have faced Rikkar this morning, not after she'd given herself so shamelessly.

She lay back against the pillows, flinching at the strange, new soreness of her body. Images and sensations swept over her, bringing a blush to her creamy cheeks. Even now, in spite of its soreness, her body tingled in remembrance of the passion it had come to know during the long night.

Why, oh why, had she responded to him as she had? She'd meant to submit herself coldly, making it clear to him that she did it only to save herself from a worse fate.

Then he had kissed her, and touched a core of passion that she'd lost herself in. He was a ruthless criminal and she was his captive. Yet, why this trembling within her when she thought of him? Why this desire to see his face once more, to feel his kiss? Surely she was bewitched.

Her body stiffened in anger. He was experienced at this sort of thing and he'd known just how to make her respond. She'd been innocent and he'd taken advantage of her.

Not wanting to stay in bed with its hateful reminders of the night before, Lainie rose and pulled the covers into place, shutting away the sight of blood that soiled the sheets.

Caloosa had left fresh water and towels. As she washed, she thought of the morning before when she'd struggled to remember. Now she wanted only to forget.

She'd given herself to a pirate, an outlaw. But she had done it in order to survive. That was the only reason she'd given herself to him! She must keep that thought always in mind. She'd had no choice. And she really hadn't enjoyed it all that much. She'd simply not hated it. It was all in the way one looked at it.

Lainie's new found rationale restored her to a much better humor. She put on the shirt and pants of the day before, tying the rope tightly about the waist and knotting the shirt beneath her bosom. Using her fingers to comb her hair, she braided it into one fat, golden rope that hung down her back.

Finished, she opened the porthole to air out the smell of rum. Picking up the shattered glass, she threw it out the porthole. She had never mopped a floor in her life, but the puddle of rum brought her to a swift decision.

When she finished, she picked up the wash bowl and rose to her feet to find Rikkar standing in the doorway, smiling down at her. The expression on his face made her seethe with anger. How dare he stand there smiling after what he had done to her!

Without another thought she flung the contents of the wash bowl at him. The water drenched him and the rag with which she had mopped the floor hit him squarely in the chest. In the corridor behind him, Lainie heard a smothered guffaw of laughter and steps double-timing up the stairs. Meanwhile the captain stood silent, his arrogant head held high, dirty water dripping from his brows and chin. His fury mounted as he stepped into the cabin and kicked the door shut behind him. Regretting her impulsive act, Lainie retreated behind the table.

"What was the purpose of this?" he asked, indicating his drenched clothing.

"I—" Lainie stammered, then anger took over. "How dare you stand there laughing after last night?"

He shrugged out of the wet shirt and stood before her barechested. "I'm sorry I disappointed you," he mocked. "I'd a bit too much rum."

"Disappointed me?" Pinpoints of anger shown from Lainie's eyes. "You great oaf. Did you actually think I would derive enjoyment from such an act?"

"Some women do." He studied her a moment, then moved to the table and picked up her discarded bath towel.

"I never shall. I'll always hate it and I'll always hate you for what you did to—" Lainie paused. He had stopped dabbing at his chest and was frowning down at the towel. The pirate crossed to the bed and jerked away the coverlet. Lainie shrank, folding her arms across her breasts, unaccountably ashamed at what he would find there.

"You were virginal," he stated in a flat voice. "I'm sorry."

"No sorrier than I," said Lainie bitterly.

"I didn't know. If I had I would—"

"You would have what?" Lainie interrupted him with a

bitter laugh. "Men set great store by a woman's maiden-head and for that reason so does a woman. It is the one thing of ourselves we have to give to our husbands. You have taken mine, too drunk even to recognize the taking."

"You're right," he said. "Carelessly I took something from you of irreplaceable value and I gave you nothing in return."

"Nothing in return?" Lainie repeated aghast. "Do you think I want money?"

"Don't you?" he asked, his mouth grim. "Otherwise what were you doing on the other boat?"

"What do you mean?" Lainie searched his face in puzzlement.

"The captain of the *Southern Moon* took on no passengers," Rikkar raised his voice accusingly. "You had to have been brought on by one of the crew members. No woman would come aboard a ship under those conditions without a clear idea of what was expected of her." Anger flared within Lainie and hot denial sprang to her lips.

"But I was a virgin," she cried.

"Every woman is for some time in her life," the pirate said dismissively. Could it be? Lainie wondered. Was she a woman of the streets? Lainie felt shaken at the idea, helpless in her inability to remember and defend herself against his accusations. Tears ran unheeded down her cheeks.

"I'm not a whore, I'm not," she sobbed, shaking her head.

Acting on impulse, Rikkar pulled the sobbing girl to him. She didn't object as he massaged the soft skin at the back of her neck. His other arm went about her waist and he gently stroked the smooth skin along her spine. His warmth and gentleness comforted Lainie. Slowly her sobs ceased. She became aware of the crisp curl of his chest hair against her wet cheek and quickly pushed herself away.

Rikkar was impressed by her spirit and resolved to mend the rift between them. She could make the voyage far more interesting for him. First he had to overcome their bad beginning.

"I'll have Caloosa bring you some clean clothes," he said, then abruptly left the cabin. Lainie sat on the edge of the bunk. For all her show of bravery she was still shaken by the encounter and the ideas about her identity. Who was she? Why was she on this ship? If only the dark shadows could be pushed away.

Caloosa was touched by her sad, tear-stained face when he brought her lunch. "You safe now," he reassured her, "you Rikkar's woman now. You safe."

"Safe from whom?" Lainie asked.

"From other bad men," Calossa said, puzzled by her question.

"Who will save me from your bad captain?" she asked. The Indian's normally friendly face turned cold and disapproving.

"Captain not bad," he said. "Captain save you many times. He fight for you with bad Monty. He jumped into the sea to save you and nursed you back to health. There were many nights we thought we would lose you. You talked and cried out many times during your illness. You had swallowed much sea water, so the fever and chills were upon you. Rikkar nursed you and he told the crew you are his woman. The crew could have mutinied and taken you for theirs, but the captain wouldn't let them. He took you for his woman. You are under his protection."

Lainie stared at the Indian. Slowly his words penetrated her mind and she sighed.

"I know what you say is true," she admitted. "I just feel so helpless and—and angry because I'm a prisoner."

"You are safer as Rikkar's prisoner," Caloosa said. "Rikkar will guard you very carefully."

"Yes, I know, and I am grateful, truly I am," Lainie said. She paused. She couldn't tell Caloosa her real unhappiness came because of her own feelings about the captain. Caloosa knew about last night and approved. He excused his captain's behavior. Lainie's frown deepened as she thought of something else.

Were the crew's threats the only reason Rikkar had seduced her? Would he have found some other way if she'd been old and ugly? Caloosa withdrew and left her with her thoughts.

Why should it matter to her what Rikkar's reasons were for saving her? He'd done it, that was all that mattered. Yet she found herself wondering how he felt toward her. Did he find her a worrisome responsibility? Had last night simply been a necessary duty? She remembered his love-making. He had been very smooth and sure of himself, even though intoxicated. Obviously he'd had much practice. How many women had he made love to? she wondered. Had he found her inexperience boring?

And what of her own feelings for the pirate captain? Try as she might, she couldn't hate him. She remembered his gentleness when she'd been ill. She felt drawn to him, to his strength and yes, admit it if she must, to his fiery passion.

Stop this, she scolded herself and restlessly moved to stare out the porthole. Oh, to be free, she thought, free to skim over the water as the ship was doing. She longed to leave this room and go to the deck, to feel the wind against her face.

Late in the afternoon, there was a light tap on the door and at her summons, Caloosa entered. He carried a small trunk in his hands.

"Capter Rikkar asks if you will join him for dinner," the Indian said with a formal bow.

"Dinner?" Lainie asked in surprise. Rikkar was asking

57

her company for dinner? She felt pleased at his gesture. A quick, playful smile lit her face and she curtsied gracefully.

"Tell the captain I shall be delighted to sup with him this evening," she said.

"He will be pleased," Caloosa said with a nod of his head. "The captain has also sent this trunk for you." He placed the trunk on the table and with another nod of his head, withdrew.

Eagerly Lainie opened the trunk and moved aside the protective muslin placed over the top of the contents. It was packed with pretty gowns and accessories. Something tugged at the back of her mind as she took out each garment and shook its folds free. She dug deeper and found petticoats and delicate nightgowns and best of all a comb and mirror. She held up the mirror and stared at the reflection in it. The sight of her own reflection brought no return of memory.

She spent the rest of the afternoon dressing her hair, combing the tangles from the long locks and fastening the golden curls high on her head. For dinner she chose a gown of rich blue velvet with simple lines. White lace edged its modestly cut bodice and large full sleeves. Another search in the trunk produced slippers, bedroom slippers, but no less welcome. When her toiletry was complete, Lainie strained to see the effect in the small hand mirror. The blue lent an ivory glow to her pale golden skin and blonde hair. Satisfied with the results, Lainie put away the mirror just as the door opened.

The Captain looked more handsome than before. Now that she was no longer so afraid of him, she took time to truly study his appearance. His broad shoulders filled the beautifully cut jacket he wore. Likewise his trousers were cut to such perfection they showed every ripple of his strong, well muscled legs. His dark, unruly hair had been combed smooth, yet an errant curl fell over his forehead.

Lainie thought she had never seen such a vibrantly handsome man before in her life.

"You look very beautiful," Rikkar said as he entered the cabin and closed the door softly behind him. He had brought a bottle of wine. Their fingers brushed as he handed her a glass. Not sure of how the wine might affect her, Lainie sipped lightly at first, then noticed the amused look on Rikkar's face. It rankled that he might think her childish, so she tipped her glass and drank down the contents quickly. When he offered more wine, she held her glass out unhesitatingly, then once again drank deeply. His amused look had turned into a smile and Lainie found herself lost in the dancing lights of his gray eyes. There were warm depths there that she hadn't noticed before.

"Caloosa told me about the crew," she said, "and about your rescuing me from the sea and nursing me back to health. Thank you."

"It was my pleasure." He bowed slightly from the waist, his teeth flashed in a mocking smile.

"I mean about rescuing me, not about . . . last—" Lainie paused and looked down at her glass. She was surprised to find it empty. The room had become stuffy and her head reeled a little. She was glad to see Caloosa arrive with the food.

Rikkar helped her with her chair before seating himself across from her. "I'm afraid our fare is rather limited this far out to sea," he said, "but one of the sailors caught some fish and Caloosa has prepared it for us."

"Where did you find someone like Caloosa and where did he learn to speak such impeccable English?" Lainie asked.

"Caloosa is a childhood friend. My father found him and his sister when he was exploring the islets at the tip of the territory. He brought them to our plantation. Unfortunately, the Calusa tribe is dying out, due to its exposure to the white man's diseases. The Indians have no natural immunity against them.''

"I see," said Lainie. "How bad for them."

Rikkar filled Lainie's glass, then his own. "When my father sent me to England to school, Caloosa went with me. Naturally, he created quite a sensation there with his height and his keen intelligence. He became our talisman."

"But why does he pretend to be uneducated?" Lainie asked.

Rikkar frowned. "Unfortunately, there are some people who are offended by an Indian who is better educated than they. Caloosa speaks that way to save himself a lot of trouble. He would be considered too uppity by his betters." Rikkar's voice was filled with bitter sarcasm.

"I know what you mean," Lainie said unexpectedly. "I had a friend once too. His name was Thomas." She stopped, startled, straining to remember more, but nothing else came to her.

"Yes, go on," Rikkar prompted.

"I'm sorry, I don't remember anything more. Just his name and that he was treated unfairly because he was different. But I don't even remember what was different about him."

"You can't remember anything more?" Rikkar's eyes showed his disbelief. "What about your name?"

"No," Lainie shook her head. "Nothing more."

"What a convenient memory."

"Do you think I want to forget my name?" Lainie asked hotly.

"Yes, I think you want to forget your name and you'll remember it again when it's convenient for you."

"That's not true, I really can't remember," she protested.

"Were you wanted by the police? Is that why you were on the boat? Did you stow away aboard the *Southern Moon* trying to evade the authorities?"

Lainie lowered her head. She didn't know. She could be someone's maid who had stolen from her mistress and had stowed away on the ship to avoid arrest. Hot waves of shame washed over her, then pride made her meet the stare of those penetrating eyes.

"I am not a thief. Inside of myself I know I am not."

"Perhaps not," Rikkar agreed probing her eyes with his own. He tossed his napkin on the table and reached for the wine bottle.

"No more for me," Lainie said, quickly covering her glass with her hand. Rikkar emptied the last of the wine into his glass, raising it to his lips.

"So, in the absence of a name, what are we to call you?" he asked before drinking. His gaze held hers.

"I don't know," she murmured, her breath caught in her throat.

"We'll have to think of something. Something suitable for a woman of fire and passion." Lainie tore her eyes away.

"You said earlier I had taken something from you," he continued.

"Please," Lainie said coloring. "It's done. Let's not speak of it again."

"But I gave you nothing in return."

"I told you I don't want money," Lainie said. "It won't change anything. If you truly want to make amends, free me."

"That's impossible, I'm afraid."

"Why?" Lainie demanded.

"For one very obvious reason. We are too far out to sea. I hardly think you'd be happy set adrift on a raft."

"Poke fun at me if you will, but I would gladly take the raft to staying here on your ship and submitting myself to you."

61

"You can't be that angry simply because I made love to you last night."

"There was no love between us, Captain Rikkar only lust."

"Whatever name you put to it, I'm glad you enjoyed it as much as I," he answered, his face expressing his amusement and arrogant assurance.

"This will no doubt be a blow to your ego, Sir, but I hasten to assure you there was no such enjoyment on my part, only the will to endure my trials here on your ship."

His laughter rang out, his eyes dancing with humor. He leaned forward, his warm breath grazing her cheek. "Even in my state of intoxication, I remember the events of the evening very clearly," he said softly. "I remember enjoyment on both our parts." His voice was a husky whisper and one finger stroked her cheek. "When something is so enjoyed by two people it should be repeated, don't you agree?" Lainie trembled beneath his touch.

"I do not agree," she said, hating the breathlessness that had crept into her voice. "I have no intention of submitting myself to your attentions again."

"Never?" His lips brushed along the flushed curve of her cheek, moving downward toward her mouth.

"Never!" she cried, tensing, ready for flight.

But there was no place to flee. He had effectively blocked any move she might make. His strong, sinewy leg pressed against her knees. She felt suffocated by the contact. A weak tremor started in her knees. She tried to turn away from the contact, but his hand on her shoulder stayed her. Then Lainie felt herself being lifted to her feet. She could feel the long, hard leanness of his body pressing against hers from shoulders to knees. He captured her chin gently in his hand and raised her face to his.

She had avoided looking into his bold eyes, but now she did so and was startled by the flame of desire she saw there. She stared, captive to his glance, not closing her eyes against it until she felt his lips touch hers.

"Fight back," an inner voice cried out and for a moment she struggled against him, but his strong arms only held her tighter and she could feel her nipples swell against his chest. His tongue parted her unresisting lips and when at last his kiss ended, Lainie felt drained. She stood within the circle of his arms, eyes closed, mouth moist and slightly parted. She floated through layers of newly aroused sensations before she could at last open her eyes. The first thing she saw was Rikkar's triumphant face.

"Teaching you the ways of love will be far more pleasurable than I had anticipated," he said, laughing.

Before she could protest Rikkar again pulled her to him. He trailed little kisses along her cheek and onto her neck. In spite of herself, shivers of delight raced along Lainie's nerves. His hands were swift and sure at the back of her gown and before Lainie could voice an objection the bodice fell to her waist, leaving her breasts bare to his demanding mouth. Lost in the hot waves that washed through her, she dimly perceived his hands, warm and possessive, as he pushed her gown over her hips. She stood trembling and naked before him.

"Don't be frightened," he whispered. "I won't hurt you. I promise."

Rikkar picked her up and crossed to the bed. He lay her gently upon it, then shed his own clothes and stood before her. Involuntarily her eyes were drawn to his magnificent body. In all her girlhood perceptions of men, Lainie had never realized how beautiful a man's body could be. His handsome head and strong neck were in perfect proportion to his muscular shoulders and slim tapering hips. Dark brown hair covered his chest and flat belly mingling with the darker hair at his loin. She couldn't avoid seeing his aroused state and found herself confused, feeling desire and fear.

He stretched out on the bed, and began to explore her body in every private place. She felt his fingers stroking her inner flesh, at first slowly, then with increasing tempo until she moaned and arched her back, every nerve in her body given up to pleasure.

She felt the probe of his manhood as it invaded her moist flesh. This time there was no pain, only a greater ecstasy than she had ever known. His body pushed against hers, withdrew, then plunged against hers again until Lainie felt she would dissolve in waves of pleasure.

She looked into Rikkar's eyes and found them glazed with passion as he moved rhythmically against her. Instinctively Lainie followed his rhythm. Faster, ever faster until she felt herself swell and tighten against him. She gave herself to the breathless velvet darkness where a million sensations exploded.

They lay sleeping as they had fallen, still connected by their passion. During the dark velvet night they awakened and again made love. This time, Lainie was a willing participant. Rikkar guided her and she delighted in the sensations she gave and received. She pushed aside the nagging inner voice that tried to intrude upon her new found world of pleasure. Tomorrow. Tomorrow she would face the realities of her actions. Tomorrow!

She wrapped her arms around Rikkar's warm, strong body and nestled close. Her eyes closed and soon she slept more deeply than she had for several nights.

Chapter 5

She awoke alone and lay looking at the sunlight pouring through the porthole. For a moment she was in another room where sunlight had poured through sheer curtains and the air smelled of flowered sachets and morning hot chocolate.

Reality intruded with the gentle roll of the ship. Lainie hid her face in the pillow as memories of the night swept over her. Once again she had been shameless, wanton. She had succumbed to the passion of the night, and had been a willing participant in all that had transpired. Indeed, she had followed her instincts and sought to give pleasure as well as receive it. She remembered her triumphant feeling when Rikkar had folded her into his arms and whispered his delight with her.

"The pupil surpasses the master," he had murmured. She had never felt so completely one with another person before.

A knock at the door interrupted Lainie's reverie.

"Who's there?" she called, pulling the coverlet about her.

"It's Caloosa with your bathwater."

"Come in." Caloosa entered with the bucket of water and fresh towels. "Where is the Captain?" Lainie asked.

"He's on deck, Miss."

"Caloosa, thank you for not pretending with me about your language."

"I think you are not one with whom one must pretend. You are a kind and beautiful lady who is surviving in a difficult situation. I have admiration for you." He bowed slightly.

"Thank you," she said softly.

After Caloosa left, she flung aside the coverlet and set about her bathing. She was just drying one beautifully shaped calf when a male whistle of appreciation made her whirl about. Rikkar was standing in the doorway, his gray eyes devouring her. Lainie quickly wrapped the large towel around her.

"What is this?" Rikkar asked, entering. "Is the blushing maiden back?" His eyes were filled with mocking laughter. He pulled her close and covered her mouth with his.

"Where is the fiery, passionate woman I found last night?" he whispered.

"You shall find her no more, sir," Lainie said sternly, pulling away.

Rikkar looked deeply into her angry eyes. She raised her chin defiantly. Once again the glint of mocking laughter returned to Rikkar's eyes and he reached for the towel. With a flip of his hand the towel was pulled free, leaving Lainie bare.

"Sir, I protest—," Lainie began angrily, her hands covering her breasts.

"So do I," said Rikkar pulling her close. "After last night such modesty is pretentious."

"No," she cried out angrily and tried to twist away.

"Must I subdue you each time?" he asked catching her wrists in a hard grip and holding them behind her back, crushing her against his chest. His lips came down on hers in a hot, demanding kiss that left Lainie breathless. Once again, she was caught up in a vortex of passion. Rikkar drew back and looked into her eyes.

"The blushing maiden is gone," he teased gently, "and the lady shows her true nature." Anger and shame washed over Lainie. Once again she had given in to the baser feelings this man aroused in her and now he stood mocking her for it.

"You beast," she spat at him furiously.

"And you are my beauty," he replied. "Beauty was a captive of the beast, I believe."

"Yes, she was," Lainie replied. "But Beauty was never used by the Beast as I have been by you." Tears welled in her eyes.

"No, she wasn't," Rikkar agreed lightly. "But Beauty was a lady of innocence and purity."

Lainie was outraged. She swung her arm with all her might and caught him on the cheek. Her hand stung with the impact and she hoped it hurt him as much as it had her. She swung her other arm to repeat the act, but Rikkar caught it and swung her about, flinging her across the bed. Lainie fell, golden hair flying, but quickly raised herself to a sitting position.

"How dare you speak to me like that?" she cried out angrily, brushing her hair from her eyes. "I was pure and innocent also before you took advantage of that innocence and seduced me."

Rikkar leaned over her, still gripping one wrist, his gray eyes cold as steel.

"You were indeed virginal the first night I took you, but I have never seduced a woman who did not want to be seduced and such was the case here. You, Madame," he emphasized the title derisively, "were a willing participant. As for your innocence, no woman who responds as

67

you did last night is an innocent about the act of love. You've been well-trained.''

"No," Lainie shook her head in denial of the implication of what he was saying. Tears flowed down her flushed cheeks.

"Someone saw the potential of your beauty," Rikkar continued in his cruel voice. "You've been trained in the ways of the most experienced courtesan. Why or how you came to be on that ship is a mystery I've yet to solve," Rikkar continued. "But one day you will tell me as you will tell me your name.''

"I don't know my name," Lainie raised her tear-streaked face to his beseechingly. "I don't remember. Please believe me.''

For a moment Rikkar was moved by her pleas and by her beauty, but he pushed the feeling away. He couldn't afford to be taken in by a woman, especially one of such magnetism. Her look of innocence was only a decoy, for he knew that underneath was an experienced woman of fiery passion. Her response to him last night made him wonder if her evidence of virginal purity hadn't been planted for his benefit.

"You look so untouched," he said, cupping her chin gently in his hand, then his fingers tightened, bruising her flesh. "But then I remember you in the night and I realize your looks are a sham. How many other secrets do you hide behind those innocent eyes?''

"Why can't you believe me?" Lainie asked, her eyes searching his.

"I can't believe you because you were on that ship," he roared.

"But why is that so important to you?" Lainie was trying to understand his anger. "Can't you trust me? How do you know the Captain didn't take me as a passenger?''

"I know," Rikkar said drawing away.

"Perhaps he made an exception for me. Perhaps he knew my father. Maybe he let me sail with him knowing I had family in Savannah." The words came in a rush. "When the *Southern Moon* docks in Savannah and I'm not on it, they'll be searching for me." She stopped speaking, dumbstruck at the rage mirrored on the pirate captain's face.

"How are you able to remember the *Southern Moon's* shipping schedule when you cannot even remember your own name?" he demanded. "Explain it to me!"

"I—I don't know," she stammered. "Sometimes, things—disjointed things come to me. They're like pieces of a puzzle, except they don't fit together. Perhaps when I've remembered more."

"And when will that be, Madame? Can you give me a day, a time when all your memory will return and you can coveniently tell me your name?"

"You must believe me. If I knew who I was, I would tell you. There's—there's probably a reward for my safe return."

"I truly doubt that, Madame," he scoffed.

"Why?" she challenged.

"My conclusions about you are correct," he said coldly. "You are a well-trained, no doubt, well-paid whore sent on the ship to spy and to aid your associates in any way you can. I hope the pay was high enough for the sacrifices you've been called upon to make." Rikkar moved to the door then turned back to her. "I should have given you to the crew," he said and left, slamming the door behind him. Lainie could hear the bolt slide home and Rikkar bellow. "Caloosa, stay by this door. No one is to go near her." His angry footsteps echoed on the stairs as he climbed to the deck, the sea and the open sky.

Lainie fell into a troubled sleep in which she called out for Rikkar and his face swam before her. At some point he kissed her. For a moment the passion flared between them, but then he turned cold and angry, and his mouth twisted bitterly as he called her vile names.

"No, no!" She was thrashing about when her arm knocked against something solid. She awoke to find Rikkar standing over her, his face as cold as in her dreams, his eyes veiled and unreadable.

"Your supper is here," he said indicating the dishes on the table, then he turned toward the door.

"Wait," Lainie called out. "Aren't you going to eat with me?"

Rikkar paused, his hand on the door, his eyes unresponding. Without answering he left, closing the door firmly behind him. The bolt rasped home and Lainie was once again alone. The day had waned and dark shadows crept into the corners of the cabin. She bit back her tears and rising from the bed, wrapped the coverlet around herself. Crossing to the lantern hanging on its peg, she struck a flint and lit it. The light cast a warm glow and made the room appear more cheerful.

She lifted the lid of the pot. Stew! It smelled wonderful and she was ravenous. Ladling a bowl full, she settled down to eat, but found after a bite or two she wasn't hungry after all. Depression settled heavily upon her again. She forced a few more spoonfuls down, then returned to the bed. Last night she had slept wrapped in Rikkar's arms, her body satiated by his love-making. Tonight she lay huddled under the covers weeping bitterly.

The next morning Lainie awoke oddly refreshed and newly determined. She would show Captain Rikkar he was wrong about her—all she had to do was wait for him.

She put on a drab, high-necked dress, and wound her heavy golden hair about her head severely, keeping it in place with a comb. She frowned at the bedroom slippers for their air of frivolity, but donned them anyway, for they were all she had. She was ready. Let Rikkar come to her cabin now. He would see that she was indeed a woman of modesty and character, and when he tried to apologize or treat her in a familiar manner, she would rebuff him as he had done to her. She would refuse to eat with him, and if he ever dared touch her again, he would find a woman of ice.

She sat in a chair by the table, her head held high, but the hours passed and Rikkar did not come. Caloosa brought her supper tray, then cleared it, and when Lainie asked for Rikkar, Caloosa only nodded his head upward to the deck and left the room. Brooding Lainie readied herself for bed and lay in the dark, listening to the lonely creaks and groans of the ship.

Again, as several nights before, she was awakened by the crash of the door, and through sleep-filled eyes she saw the same dark shadow. It moved forward and the door closed, leaving the room in darkness, save for a stream of moonlight.

"Rikkar?" Lainie whispered tentatively. She heard quick footsteps cross the room and he was standing above her. She could smell the rum on his breath.

"You little witch," he snarled. "You knew I would come." He lifted her to him, his mouth devouring hers.

"Rikkar, Rikkar," she whispered, wrapping her arms about him, all determined intentions to be dignified and cold lost in the heat of his touch. His kisses fired her. She pressed against him, reveling in the feel of his hands as they brushed along her body in swift caresses.

"You may be a prostitute sent to trap me, but I will enjoy what's here for the taking," he said hoarsely. "Some-one has already paid the price for you."

Lainie went cold at his words. She drew back from his kiss, but he didn't seem to notice. He freed her only long enough to strip off his clothing. His body was urgent with

71

desire as he joined her in the bed, his kisses painfully demanding.

She fought for control, but his hands were exploring her body everywhere, followed close behind by his mouth. His teeth closed on her nipples gently, and Lainie felt fire race along her nerves.

"Please don't," she cried out, striving not to give in to her body's responses.

"Why not?" he taunted tracing a line of fire with his mouth down to her flat stomach. Then she felt his tongue in her most secret place and her nerves screamed in response. Dizzy and breathless, she arched her body upward to meet the hot, rasping tongue. Just when she was sure she couldn't bear anymore, she felt his hardened shaft sear her. She was lost. She moved rhythmically with him, demanding he go faster, deeper, carrying them to the same rapturous heights. Afterwards they lay exhausted, arms and legs entwined.

Rikkar's kiss on her shoulder roused her.

"Where are you going?" she asked sleepily.

"On deck, I still have a ship to see to," he replied cheerfully. He looked at her, his gray eyes warm.

The next day, Lainie dressed once again in the drab dress she had worn the day before, making sure it was fastened high up on her neck.

Refusing to think about the night before, she concentrated on arranging her hair in the same severe style she had affected the day before. She had just finished when Rikkar entered. Head high, Lainie turned to meet his gaze. For a moment he stood staring at her then threw his head back and laughed in a way that was becoming all too familiar to her.

"I fail to see the cause for such mirth," she said primly. Rikkar stopped laughing and looked at her appreciatively.

"You are the reason for my mirth, my Beauty." Crossing to her he removed the comb that held her hair. The golden tresses spilled down over his hands and about Lainie's shoulders. "Don't try to be something you are not."

"But how can you be so sure I am not as I am dressed?" she protested as he began to unbutton the high bodice of her gown.

"Because you have told me so," he replied, his hands moving seductively.

"I?" Lainie asked incredulously.

"Yes, your body has told me much about you." He pulled her bodice apart, once more baring her breasts. "You're very beautiful," he said, tracing a finger from the pulse in her throat to one nipple.

"Just because I respond to you as I do, doesn't mean I am without moral character," she said weakly, trying not to show her pleasure at his caress.

"What does moral character mean to you?" Rikkar asked, pulling her against him and kissing the corner of her mouth.

"It means—it means—," Lainie struggled to stifle the passion that flooded her at his kisses. "I can't think when you're doing that," she protested.

"Doing what?" Rikkar kissed her, gently biting her full lower lip.

"Kissing me like that," Lainie said breathlessly.

"I won't kiss you." Lainie caught her breath, closing her eyes as he nibbled at her ear lobe. "You were going to tell me about moral character," he reminded her.

"Moral character is the strength to resist temptation and do the upright deed," she quoted properly from some forgotten childhood lesson.

"M-m-," Rikkar murmured against her cheek. "But have you resisted temptation?" His hands cupped her breasts, his thumbs brushing across her sensitive nipples.

"I—no," she moaned in a low voice.

"No, you haven't." Rikkar folded her in his arms for a kiss that left her longing for more.

"Your responses were not learned in a drawing room at your mother's knee," he whispered softly, then captured her mouth once more. Lainie's arms went around his neck and she returned his kisses feverishly. Every part of her body longed for intimate contact with his. Rikkar ended the kiss and drew back from her, a strange light in his eyes, a smile on his lips.

"This is what you are, Beauty," his gaze flicked across her bared breasts, her tumbling locks and back to her face, flushed with passion and desire. "Don't try to be something you're not," he said, his gray eyes suddenly cold. Turning sharply he left the cabin.

Caloosa found her in a pensive mood when he brought her supper. Lainie ate alone that night as she had the night before, but Rikkar joined her after for a glass of wine. He said nothing upon finding her dressed as before with her hair bound up, but one eyebrow was raised and a quirk of amusement appeared at the corners of his mouth as he poured the wine.

"Madame?" he said, offering her a glass.

"No, thank you," Lainie responded graciously, ignoring his mockery.

He stayed for only a short while, sipping his wine and eyeing Lainie speculatively while voicing mundane opinions on the weather. Lainie remained passive, mentally girding herself for the battle of wills that would ensue should he attempt to touch her.

Finally, without having made any references to that morning, Rikkar left. Lainie felt deflated. There was no feeling of triumph at rejecting Rikkar's advances for he had made no move toward her. Drat the man, he always seemed to keep her off stride. Yet she was glad not to have had her new resolve tested. Her resolutions had been broken all too quickly in the past with this man.

Lainie prepared for bed early and soon fell into a light sleep. She was awakaned by Rikkar's mouth on hers. His touch was soft and caressing; his kisses insistent and persuasive.

Lainie could not fight back as she had vowed. Instead she responded to the passion which flared within her, allowing his lips and body to draw her hopelessly into that special place of exploding sensations and breathless delights she had come to know so well with him. Afterwards she turned away and cried bitterly, a helpless captive of this man. Rikkar tried to hold her in his arms, but she refused his comfort. She lay against the wall of the cabin as far away from Rikkar as she could get and sobbed herself to sleep.

She spent the next day in a state of melancholia made worse by the boredom of nothing to do. Rikkar joined her for supper and again their conversation came around to why she was on the *Southern Moon*.

"I told you, I can't remember. I can't remember anything before I woke up in this room," she protested.

"It must be very difficult not to know who you are and what has occurred." Rikkar said softly.

"Yes, it is," Lainie said, wary for his understanding.

"Yet you remain remarkably calm about it," he pounced.

"I'm not as calm as I seem. I'm quite frightened about it," she said truthfully. "No one knows what's become of me."

"I don't suppose there are a great many people concerned about you," Rikkar goaded.

"No, I suppose not," Lainie said bitterly. "I'm only a whore, a prostitute, a woman of pleasure. We have no feelings and certainly no one to care about us." She rose from the table and flung herself across the bed, sobs tearing their way from her throat. Rikkar stood above her.

"I'm sorry," he said, but when she did not cease her weeping, he turned on his heels and left the cabin. He did not return that night or the next day.

Lainie passed the long, lonely hours watching the sea through the porthole. Other times she spent huddled on the bed racking her brain for any clue to her identity, until her head ached. She spent a second night alone and awoke feeling lethargic at the prospect of another long day by herself. Caloosa brought her the usual pitchers of water and trays of food, but Lainie longed to see Rikkar. Even if he said hateful, mocking things to her, he made her feel less alone in the world.

After a second long day by herself she was ready to scream. She couldn't bear another moment in that cabin alone. She paced about the small room feeling caged.

As she passed the door, she idly tried the handle and was startled when it sprang open at her touch. Slowly, carefully, she opened the door a few inches and looked into the corridor. No one was there. She opened the door further and stepped into the corridor.

Tentatively, she placed one hand on the ladder rail, then, as if a spring had been released, she vaulted up the stairs. Pausing for moment on the top step, she looked about. The sun was shining and its golden rays blinded her for a moment. She could see the dancing waves of the sea beyond the guard rail and it drew her like a beacon. She glanced around at the men who were busy on deck. Rikkar and Caloosa were nowhere in sight. As Lainie stood looking about one of the pirates spied her. His exclamation of surprise alerted his shipmates. Their attention made Lainie grateful that she wore the dull, high-necked dress and had wrapped her hair tightly about her head. She couldn't know that as she gathered her courage and walked with

queenly dignity toward the railing the sun caught her cap
of hair and turned it to a crown of gold.

Having reached the railing, she wrapped her fingers
tightly around the polished wood, grateful for its support.
Her knees trembled so she feared she would collapse.
Then a sea breeze caught the tendrils of her hair and blew
them against her cheeks, and Lainie forgot all else in the
delight of the moment.

"So there you be!" a rough voice growled and Lainie's
shoulder was caught in a painful grip as she was spun
around. She shrank back in terror. Before her was the man
from the corridor, the one who had frightened her so.
Stunned, Lainie could not run, but merely stood looking at
him. The evil man pressed her body to his. Terror over-
came Lainie as she screamed and struck out blindly. With
a howl of pain the pirate released Lainie and sprang back.
Before them stood Rikkar, a whip dangling from one
hand.

"I should have killed you the first time," he growled.
Rikkar flung a knife to the pirate who caught it and backed
against the railing. His eyes shifted about uneasily. He
didn't want to fight Rikkar, but fear lent him false courage
and he charged, his long knife held out straight in deadly
purpose.

"Rikkar," Lainie screamed. The momentum of the pirate's lunge carried him past Rikkar and before he could
turn and attack, Rikkar sank his knife deeply into the
pirate's soft belly.

Lainie turned away and retched. Rikkar stood by the
dead man, knife at the ready as his eyes challenged any of
the other men to take up the fight. No one did. He crossed
to Lainie and grasping her shoulder, pushed her unceremoniously toward the hatch.

"Caloosa," he called, "take care of the body." Without another word, Rikkar pushed Lainie down the steps.

Once in the cabin he flung her across the bed, slamming and bolting the door behind them. He tossed the still bloody knife into a corner and crossing to the chest poured some water into Lainie's bathing bowl. He dipped his hands into the water, and Lainie saw it turn pink.

"You're hurt," she cried, scrambling off the bed to help him, but the look on Rikkar's face stopped her as he reached for a towel.

"No, I'm not hurt." His voice was steel.

"I'm glad," Lainie said.

"Are you?" Rikkar threw the towel back on the chest and approached her, his eyes locked into hers.

"Yes, of course. If you hadn't come I don't know what would have happened."

"What did happen?" Rikkar asked.

"Why—I—" Lainie stammered under his gaze. "You saw what happened. I went on deck and he attacked me."

"What I saw was a man and a woman standing quietly at the rail talking. Then he supposedly attacked you. What did you do, spy me watching you and put on that little act to allay any suspicions?"

"I don't know what you mean," Lainie said bewildered. "I went on deck and that man came at me. You heard me scream."

"Yes, well done. Among your many talents, you are also a consummate actress," Rikkar said bitterly.

Lainie shook her head in denial. A knot of hurt settled in her throat and she couldn't speak. Rikkar stared at her, his eyes hard with anger and contempt.

"Because of you a man died today. He may not have been worth much, but his life was taken by me. "I don't like killing a man, but I do what I have to. I like killing a woman even less, but I will if I have to." Lainie shrank before the violence of his words.

78

"Do you understand?" Once more Rikkar gripped her arm. "Do you?" he thundered, shaking her.

"Yes, yes," Lainie sobbed, tears streaming down her cheeks.

"You are never to leave this cabin again, until I tell you to do so, is that clear?" Dumbly Lainie nodded agreement. "You are not to speak to any member of the crew, ever. If you do you will bring about that man's death as well as your own."

Abruptly he released her and Lainie sank to the edge of the bed. Rikkar stood before her for a moment, fists clenched, then one hand shot out as he grabbed her hair and forced her head up. His hard eyes searched her tear-filled ones for a moment, then he released her and turned away. Lainie stared at the door as it slammed behind him. For a moment she had seen a flicker of something in his eyes but she wasn't sure what it was. She lay back on the bed and stared miserably at the ceiling of her prison.

Chapter 6

Loneliness seeped into Lainie's very soul in the days that followed. Even Caloosa was uncommunicative as he tended to her needs. Rikkar never came to her cabin during the day. When he came at night, he came as if driven by need. There was a desperate urgency in his lovemaking and he never wooed her as he had done those first nights together. Her need for human contact made her welcome him to her bed.

"Please don't go," she would cry out and cling to him as he made to leave her, but he would tear her arms away and stalk from the cabin.

"Rikkar," she would cry out gladly the next time he came to her, holding out her arms for him. He would kiss her brutally and she would ignore the pain and concentrate on making each moment he was there last as long as she could. On those nights when he stayed away, Lainie lay in her bunk listening for the sound of his footsteps and his hand on the latch. When late in the night she would resign herself that he wasn't coming, she would roll into a ball and let the rocking of the ship lull her to sleep. She seldom cried for she felt too numb to show such an emotion.

"Rikkar says you are to dress in this today," Calossa

said one morning, laying the dull travel dress across a chair.

"Why?" she asked.

"We are nearing land and today we will go ashore."

"We're going ashore?" she asked incredulously. "Where?" She ran to look out the porthole, but she could only see water for miles. She turned back to the Indian. "Where are we landing?" she asked. "In Savannah?" Caloosa looked at her strangely.

"No," he said and left the room without further elaboration. Lainie couldn't contain her excitement. The depression of the last week was gone and in its place was a feeling of bubbling anticipation. She donned the travel dress and a pair of sturdy boots Caloosa had found for her, then dressed her hair loosely with combs, letting it stream down her back. Her eyes sparkled and her cheeks were flushed. A while later Rikkar came to the cabin. Lainie hadn't seen him in daylight for a while, and she was surprised by how drawn he looked. His eyes were flat and bleak, and deep grooves creased his cheeks.

"Caloosa said we land today," Lainie said to break the awkward moment. "Are we landing in Savannah?"

"Why would you think that?" he asked.

"Because that's where the *Southern Moon* was supposed to land." Lainie paused as twin points of anger flamed in Rikkar's eyes. How could she explain when she didn't understand herself the source of her knowledge about the *Southern Moon*. "I don't know how I know that—," she stammered.

"Spare me your lies," Rikkar snapped, his lips thinned in anger. "I haven't the time nor the inclination to hear them."

"I'm not—,"

"Listen to me very carefully," Rikkar said, brushing aside her defense, "and mind that you follow my instructions exactly or you will be killed." His eyes bored into hers and Lainie was aware once again that this was a dangerous, violent man and she was at his mercy.

"I will do as you say," she said with quiet dignity.

"I cannot leave you on the ship, you would be unprotected. So you must come with me," Rikkar explained. "Caloosa will bring you a hooded cloak. You are to cover yourself with it and keep yourself hidden from view as much as possible. You are to speak to no one.

"Don't try to escape," he went on. "It will be worse for you if you do. If you try to escape here, you'll have no place to go. We are docking on an island, a cayo. It is held by men who follow no laws but their own."

"Like you?" Lainie asked.

"Like me," Rikkar said smoothly. "In fact, you might find the men on this island worse than me," he warned as he turned to leave.

"But then again I might not," Lainie rejoined.

"It's your choice, Mademoiselle," Rikkar said coldly and closed the door behind him.

Later, when the ship gave a shudder then sat still in the water, Lainie knew the great billowing sails had been furled. Now the ship sat lifeless in the brilliant afternoon sun. She ran to the porthole and looked out. Other ships stood in the calm waters, their sails furled, their masts reaching empty arms to the sky.

A sound at the door made her turn and hasten to don the cloak Caloosa had left. Rikkar was waiting for her.

"I'm ready," she said eagerly.

"Do you have everything you want?"

"There's nothing here that I want," she said. Rikkar stood aside for her, and she stepped through the door and mounted the stairs toward the sky and freedom. But Rikkar's strong hand on her elbow reminded her that she was not free. They crossed to the railing and Lainie was surprised to see they were still some distance from land. She was disappointed. There were no towns, no wharves, only a small island in the distance and an expanse of colored water between.

"What makes the water that color?" she asked.

"There are coral reefs underneath," said Rikkar. "That's why we anchor so far out. We'll have to row to the island." Below them a long boat had already been filled with part of the pirate crew and was pulling away from the ship. Lainie looked over the railing at the rope ladder hanging from the side of the ship. Surely she wasn't expected to climb down that, but Rikkar's hand guided her to the ladder.

"Don't look down," he advised her as he helped her over the railing. In doubt, Lainie paused on the top step and looked back at him. For a moment the memory of a girl perched on a railing gazing back in terror at this tall, dark pirate before plunging into the sea flashed before her. Dizziness assailed her and she felt her grip on the ladder slacken.

"Don't look down." Rikkar's voice was like the crack of a whip. His hands on her shoulders hurt, but they brought her to and she quickly tightened her grip.

"I'm all right," she said and determinedly started down the ladder. Caloosa caught her at the bottom, steadied her and guided her to a seat. Swiftly, Rikkar descended and seated himself.

Almost immediately two sailors took up the oars, sending the boat skimming toward the island. Lainie looked back at the ship that had been the only haven of which she had any memory. Its name was carried on the sleek, dark hull just behind a great jutting bird of wood.

"The *Sea Hawk*," she said softly. Shifting about on the seat, she looked at the long boat in which she rode. It was a shallow vessel, but wide, really quite large for a boat of its kind, but every space was filled with trunks and sacks and barrels.

Plunder, she thought and turned to look at Rikkar. She could see the dark grip of a pistol shoved into the waistband of his breeches. Her eyes flew to his face only to find his inscrutable eyes upon her. Quickly, she turned away and looked toward the island they were approaching.

Here and there stretched along the shore line were small white, flat-roofed structures of stone, around which Lainie could discern a few brown-skinned people walking. She began to feel some dread. This was worse than she had imagined. There were no towns, no houses, and the island was inhabited by people strange to her.

"Why are we going here?" she blurted out.

"I want to find a man," Rikkar said grimly.

When they neared the shore, Rikkar carried Lainie to land in his arms, his strong legs and feet churning surely through the water over the uneven coral bed. Then the plunder was stored on the beach, well away from the high tide line, and Rikkar ordered the men to stand guard.

"Pull your hood up and follow me," he ordered Lainie and started toward the largest of the buildings. He opened a door recessed in the wall and entered. "Stay close to me," he instructed Lainie who was only too happy to comply. They stepped into a tavern crowded with men from the ships.

Rikkar stood taut and alert, his hawk-like eyes scanning the room. His gaze settled on a man in the far corner. Lainie looked at the large, dark-skinned man who was holding court at his table. His booming laughter echoed across the room. Lainie could sense tension in those men seated around him.

"Who is that man?" she whispered to Rikkar.

"Keep quiet and keep your face covered," he told her.

"I should have left you with Caloosa, but I'm not sure you would be safe there either," he muttered under his breath.

"Ree-kar," the huge man across the room called and with one large, dirty hand waved them nearer. Rikkar strolled across the room feigning a casualness Lainie knew he did not feel.

"Tortugas." Rikkar stood before the table and greeted the man. Lainie contrived to stay slightly behind Rikkar, head lowered, but she could still see the fat man's face. His small, piggish eyes were nearly lost between strands of black, greasy hair which fell across his forehead and a dirty tangle of beard covered his chin. Lainie caught a whiff of his body and she shrank even further behind Rikkar.

"So, Ree-kar, I hear good things about you from your crew," Tortugas made a grand sweep of the room. "You are a brave and fierce fighter."

"I have some goods to sell you," Rikkar said.

"Ahh, that is good. Much rich theengs, eh?" Tortugas rolled his eyes and smiled.

"There is rum and silk, some fine teas and spices," Rikkar said. "And there are jewels."

"Very good," Tortugas laughed. "Come, my friend, I will buy your goods. First you have a drink with me, eh?" Tortugas picked up an empty glass and sloshed rum into it. "Come, sit," he said pointing to a chair where a man was already seated. Quickly the man scrambled to vacate the chair.

Rikkar sat down and Lainie stood behind him, her hands gripping the back of the chair, her head, hidden within the confines of the hood, bowed. Tortugas looked at her and Lainie felt as if his little eyes penetrated the heavy wool of her cloak. She shrank back and pulled her hood forward still more. Tortugas laughed, his eyes glittering as he looked at her fine, white hands.

"You have a shy little bird," he said to Rikkar.

"She is nothing," Rikkar dismissed her. Lainie's heart lurched painfully, then anger made her raise her chin. The light from the window fell across her soft rounded chin and the corner of her mouth.

"Mon Dieu," Tortugas exclaimed. "Take off the hood," he roared, "and let us see this little, gray sparrow."

"No," Lainie cried out involuntarily and only Rikkar's grip on her hand kept her from fleeing. Tortugas laughed again.

"We are here to talk business," Rikkar said coldly.

"Ah, Ree-kar, always the business first. But you are new at this, my friend. You must learn, a little joke, a little laughter smooth the way. Come, tell me, how much do you have and I will tell you what price I will pay."

The two discussed their business at length, until it became obvious even to Lainie that Tortugas was delaying the trade.

Then the door opened and a man entered and paused at the door. He looked as if he had been battered about the face. Rikkar's back was to the door, but his eyes closely watched Tortugas's expression. The fat pirate looked up at the man in the doorway and upon receiving an affirmative nod, broke into a triumphant smile.

"So, Ree-kar, we talk too much, eh? I'll buy your goods if they are as you say and if you throw in your unimportant little sparrow."

"No," Rikkar said. "She is not for sale." Lainie released her breath in a sigh of relief.

"But you said she is not important," Tortugas persisted. "She is not the daughter of some famous man who would pay a beeg ransom to get her back?"

"She isn't," Rikkar said, "but I haven't finished with her."

"Ah, you will ransom her?" Tortugas stated.

"No," said Rikkar. "She is a woman of the street, a woman who follows men aboard ships. She is worth nothing, but she is the only woman I have at the moment, so she will have to do." A flip of his hand dismissed her. "I sell only the cargo," he went on. "It is of far greater value." Tortugas shrugged his acceptance.

"We go and look at the cargo now," he said and rising from the table indicated for Rikkar to lead the way. As Lainie hurried to keep up with Rikkar she couldn't resist giving vent to her anger.

"I am of no value, huh? Worth nothing am I?" she muttered at him under her breath. "I will have to do, huh?"

"Did you want me to sell you to him?" Rikkar whispered back. "I will be only too happy to comply with your wishes."

Angrily Lainie clamped her mouth shut and followed along behind him. She could hear the fat man wheezing and puffing along behind. When they neared the spot where Rikkar's men had stored the cargo, Rikkar paused and let out a curse.

"What is it?" Tortugas asked.

"My cargo is not here," Rikkar said.

"What?" Tortugas asked feigning great surprise. "Are you sure this is the spot where you left it?"

"Yes," said Rikkar. "There is the *Sea Hawk* at anchor. My men and I brought the cargo to shore here."

"Ah, but I do not see your men." Tortugas held out his arms and looked around in an exaggerated manner. "Perhaps," he said as if the idea had just come to him, "it has been stolen or," his eyes grew hard, "perhaps you had no cargo. Perhaps you play a trick on Tortugas, eh? You do the joke also, heh?" Tortugas laughed, his voice booming from his fat belly, but his eyes never left Rikkar.

"And perhaps you stole it from me," Rikkar said.

Tortugas's laughter ended abruptly and he raised his hand. A pistol was pointed squarely at Rikkar's chest.

"You call me a thief, my friend. I am very insulted."

"I didn't mean to insult you." Rikkar began to back away much to Lainie's surprise.

"But you did, my friend, and now you must make recompense." Tortugas moved like a cat toward Lainie. "I think you must give me your little sparrow for the insult you give me," he said as he grabbed the girl.

"No, no," Lainie cried out, struggling, but the man's grip was too powerful.

"Let her go, Tortugas," Rikkar shouted, launching himself at the pirate. Rikkar's attack bore all three of them to the ground, but Lainie fell clear of them, Tortugas's hold on her broken.

"Get down to the boat," Rikkar commanded. As Lainie scrambled to her feet she saw Rikkar's fist land with a thud on the fat man's chin. The sound of more blows followed as she raced toward the beach. Lainie threw herself against the prow of a boat, and tried to push it into the water, but it was too heavy for her to do alone. The sounds of fighting ceased and suddenly Rikkar was beside her.

"Push when I tell you," Rikkar said. Together they leaned their weight against the boat and it moved, stuck, then moved again, finally sliding smoothly into the water. Rikkar helped her into the boat, and by the time he had pulled himself in, she was seated with an oar in her hand.

The pirates ran into the water to grab hold of the boat. Rikkar took up his oar and cracked one of the men across his head and shoulders. Lainie followed suit. The pirates withdrew, and the tide carried Rikkar and Lainie further from shore.

"I've never rowed before," Lainie warned Rikkar as he fitted her oar into the wooden lock.

"Just pull when I tell you to," Rikkar said. The pirates had their own boats in the water. Lainie pulled hard to match Rikkar's stroke and their boat began to move in a straight line, but not fast enough. Lainie could see the pirates gaining.

When the first boat pulled beside them, two pirates jumped at them, long knives at the ready. Rikkar rose to meet them, an oar raised in defense. He feinted a sweep then swung back to hit a glancing blow to the other man. With a cry he fell overboard.

"Rikkar," screamed Lainie and wrenched at her own oar, but it was stuck in its lock. Rikkar swung around and his oar caught the pirate in the chest, sending him overboard to join his partner. But now the other boats were upon them. Rikkar stood in the center of the boat, head thrown back fearlessly, the oar his only weapon.

"Get behind me and keep low," he instructed Lainie.

Rikkar fought valiantly, but there were too many. Lainie saw him overcome by the pirates, the paddle torn from his grasp, the arc of a knife and then his limp, bleeding body was thrown overboard. She screamed.

"Let the sharks finish him," one pirate said.

"No," Lainie sobbed and pulled herself to the side of the boat. Rikkar's body was floating face down.

"Rikkar," she cried and quickly jumped into the water.

"The girl," one pirate yelled, making a grab for her, but Lainie flailed her arms and moved away.

"Go in and get her," one of the pirates shouted to his mate.

"Not me. The sharks'll be here any minute with all that blood. They're done for."

"Rikkar," Lainie whispered as she turned him about so

he floated on his back and his mouth and nose were clear of the water. He was losing a lot of blood.

"Rikkar," Lainie said again, and faintly, she heard him groan. He was alive!

"Oh thank God," she whispered fervently. She looked about seeking help. The pirates were bearing down on them, their oars clearing the boat she and Rikkar had been in. Lainie cast a look of despair over her shoulder at the ship they had tried so hard to reach. The *Sea Hawk* rode aloof and proud. Despair turned to hope, for a long boat had been launched from the ship and was even now closing the gap between them. Lainie could see Caloosa in the prow urging his men on.

Lainie reached under water and pulled her skirts up about her waist and tucked them into her bodice to secure them. Grabbing hold of Rikkar's shirt, she paddled clumsily toward Caloosa.

The pirates were closer and reached her first. One held an oar out to her. "Grab hold of this, girlie," he cried. "The sharks are goin' ter git yer." Lainie shoved at the oar and paddled herself and Rikkar away from them. She was tiring fast.

"Get in and get her," one of the pirates said, pushing another into the water. The man sank for a moment then bobbed to the surface and swam purposefully toward Lainie and the unconscious Rikkar. Lainie's arms were leaden, but she tugged at Rikkar's shirt and struggled through the water away from the pirate.

"Caloosa," she screamed and was thankful to see the boat veer toward them. Lainie placed herself between the pirate and Rikkar's inert form. She lashed out at the man when he reached for her. His hand caught in her hair and bore her down in the water. Lainie thought her lungs would burst and she felt a darkness creeping into the edges of her consciousness. The pirate and she rose to the sur-

face gasping for air. Once again he reached for her, but
Lainie gulped some air and sank out of his grasp quickly
swimming away from him. Rising to the top again she
found herself near Rikkar. Caloosa was only a few feet
away but the pirate was closer and once again reached for
Lainie. Suddenly the man stiffened in the water, his mouth
open wide in a terror-filled scream.

"Sharks," Lainie heard Caloosa say. "Get them into
the boat, quickly." Strong arms plucked them out of the
water, but not before Lainie saw the pirate jerk again and
fall forward. Both legs were nothing more than bloody
stumps.

Now the water roiled with violent movement and the
white foam turned pink as human blood stained it. The
pirate's inert body disappeared beneath the churning foam.
With a shudder, Lainie turned away.

"Back to the ship," Caloosa called and the men, four of
them, pulled against the oars. The boat skimmed over the
water toward the *Sea Hawk*, leaving behind the pirates
who sat stunned by the spectacle before them.

Quickly they reached the ship. Lainie climbed the ladder
and scrambled over the rail. The men quickly followed.
With her feet on the deck, Lainie pulled her skirts into
place and peered anxiously over the rail. She watched as
Caloosa bent and without effort picked up Rikkar and
gently placed him across his own shoulders. Then he
began his climb up the swaying ladder. The boat was left
to drift away. The pirates drew near and with bellows of
rage hurled knives at the two men on the ladder. The
knives thudded against the hull of the ship, some burying
deep into the wood, others falling harmlessly into the sea.

"Raise anchor," Caloosa called even before he was
over the railing. Hands raced to bring up the great weight
which held the ship in place.

"Be careful," Lainie said, springing to Rikkar's side as

the men lowered him to the deck. Cries of grief sprang from her lips as she saw his pale gray face. The white line about his mouth and the stillness of his body told her that Rikkar was dangerously near death, if he were not dead already.

Above them the great white sails billowed and the ship lurched and came alive as they caught the wind, but for Lainie the world was a black void in which she was aware only of Rikkar's too still body.

Chapter 7

When Caloosa saw the ship was underway, he kneeled beside Rikkar and felt for a thread of pulse.

"We must get him warm," he grunted.

"He's not dead?" Lainie raised a hopeful, tear-stained face to him.

"Not yet," the Indian said and again lifted his captain in his arms. Lainie followed him back to the cabin she had so gladly left a few short hours before. It seemed like a haven after the inhospitable island they had escaped.

Caloosa placed Rikkar on the bed and examined the wound which had gone deep between the ribs. He listened to the injured man's labored breathing, then rose with a satisfied grunt.

"I'll get some medication," he said and left. Lainie knelt to take off Rikkar's boots. Her mouth trembled at the thought of his amusement if he were to wake and see how willingly she did it now. She would happily removed his boots anytime, she vowed, if he would only live so she could once again see the mocking lift of his eyebrow, the flash of his smile. Caloosa returned with some leaves and a pan of water and removed Rikkar's breeches and shirt. Gently, they bathed the wound and Caloosa placed the dried leaves over it and bound them in place. Then he held a cup of dark liquid to Rikkar's lips and Lainie could see him swallow although his eyes remained closed. When all was done, Caloosa smiled at Lainie.

"He will live," he said. "The knife didn't reach his lungs. Now you must rest." The Indian looked at the girl's tear-streaked face, pale now with fatigue.

"I will bring you food," Caloosa said. "You must get dry."

"No," Lainie protested, "don't leave Rikkar, he may need you."

"He will sleep now," Caloosa said, then, as if to comfort her, added, "God turned away the knife." Once again he disappeared. Lainie slipped out of her wet dress and wrapped herself in a coverlet. She was perched on the edge of a chair, her eyes glued to Rikkar's pale face, when Caloosa returned bearing a tray of food. He broke open a coconut and drained the clear liquid into a cup.

"It is coconut milk," he said offering it to Lainie. "Drink it." Hesitantly, Lainie took a sip. The liquid was sweet and surprisingly good. Gratefully, she drained the cup, but was unable to eat. Silently Caloosa picked up the tray and her wet dress and left the room, closing the door behind him. She listened for the sound of a bolt sliding home, but no such sound came.

Shoulders hunched with fatigue, she looked down at Rikkar. He seemed to be sleeping easily. A wave of tenderness washed over her as she watched his still form. She was used to his vibrancy, his vitality, his mastery. Now he lay sleeping like a child, hurt and defenseless. Lainie lay beside him on the bed and cradled his dark head against her chest. How could she possibly grieve so for the man who was her captor? He was a ruthless pirate, a criminal, but in her heart she knew he was not an evil man. Tortugas was evil. Comforted by the warmth of Rikkar's body, she fell into a deep sleep.

Sunshine flooded the cabin when a movement at her side awakened her the next morning. Turning her head, she looked into Rikkar's fever-bright eyes.

"I am trying to decide," he whispered through cracked, dried lips, "if I have died and gone to heaven. The last thing I remember is fighting Tortugas's men but I awaken to find myself in bed, my pain greatly diminished and a beautiful angel sleeping beside me."

"Oh, Rikkar," Lainie cried, moving to carefully wrap her arms about him and lay her head against the uninjured side of his chest. "I thought you were dead."

"Ah, Beauty," he murmured. His tone made her heart leap, and tears rolled unchecked down her cheeks.

"Are those tears for me, Beauty?" Rikkar whispered, his eyes serious as they searched her face.

"I'm so glad you're alive," Lainie said fervently. Leaning closer she gently kissed his forehead. One hand stroked his brow and temple. The motion soothed him and once again the lids lowered over the gray eyes and she was sure he had fallen asleep.

Careful not to disturb him, Lainie rose and crossed to the sea chest, hoping to find another of Rikkar's shirts to cover herself. She was unaware of the picture she presented as she knelt to open the lid of the trunk. Her back curved gracefully as her slender arm raised to hold the heavy lid open while she searched the contents.

She's like a golden swan, all grace and fine beauty, the injured man thought as he watched her through half-closed eyes. Her hair caught the sunlight and reflected it in shimmery, golden strands. Her pale, beautiful skin seemed translucent in the light.

He sensed the melancholia in her. She had been through a lot and no matter what her past had been, it could not have prepared her for all she had endured. She had been brave and resourceful and he liked her spirit.

Lainie felt his eyes upon her and turned to face him.

"There is nothing for me to put on," she said simply, her chin trembling like a child's.

"Then you must come back to bed." Weakly, Rikkar patted the bed beside him with a leering smile.

"Sir, I think I would not be safe." She tossed her head saucily, her lips curved in a teasing, provocative smile. She picked up one of the coverlets and wrapped it about her.

"You are so beautiful," he whispered and would have said more, but pain engulfed him.

"Caloosa," Lainie screamed. Scrambling from the bed, she flew to the door of the cabin. "Come quickly, he needs you." Dipping a cloth into cool water, Lainie gently wiped Rikkar's fevered brow and cheeks.

Caloosa entered the room bearing a cup of dark liquid and raising Rikkar's shoulders held it to the injured man's lips, urging him to drink. With great difficulty Rikkar swallowed down the contents of the cup then lay back weakly. Anxiously, Lainie and Caloosa stood watching him, waiting for the drug to take effect. Finally, Rikkar opened his eyes and smiled wryly up at his Indian friend.

"We failed this time, eh?" he asked, and his voice grated with the pain he still felt.

"They were waiting for us," Caloosa said. "As soon as you left the beach, Tortugas's men attacked us." Rikkar nodded his head. "We were outnumbered, so I fought my way back to the ship to get help to come back for you. We were just leaving the ship when Tortugas and his men set upon you.

"You were right to send those men from the ship," Caloosa continued. "They were Tortugas's men as you suspected. They would have taken over the *Sea Hawk*. As it was, they tried to reboard her. We barely escaped. It was not a good time to stay and spring our trap."

"No, you're right," Rikkar said. "Thank you for saving me, old friend."

"I did not do it all. You owe your thanks to the golden-haired one," Caloosa said and Rikkar's eyes swung to Lainie. She was confused at the things they were saying. Why did they wish to trap Tortugas?

"Did you save my life, Beauty?" Rikkar asked softly. "I thought you hated me."

"No, I don't hate you," she half-whispered.

"What a dilemma we've made for ourselves, Beauty," Rikkar mocked gently and Lainie was surprised. Was he as confused as she about the feelings between them?

"We will try again," Rikkar muttered to Caloosa. "I won't let Tortugas get away."

"We have lost our bait," Caloosa reminded him.

"We'll get more—," Rikkar said and his voice dwindled away as he gave in to the healing sleep that engulfed him.

"We must move him off the ship while he sleeps," Caloosa said. "It will be less painful for him. Metoo will make him well again."

"Metoo?" Lainie asked.

"Metoo is my sister," Caloosa explained.

"Where will we go?" Lainie asked, thinking nothing could induce her to return to Tortugas's island.

"We are anchored at Rikkar's island," Caloosa told her. "Metoo is here. She will know what to do to make him well again."

"An island?" Lainie was surprised at the turn of events. "What if Tortugas comes and tries to kill him again?"

"We have left Tortugas far away at one of the other keys," Caloosa reassured her, "and no one can land on this one unless they know the channel into the bay. Otherwise, their ships will be wrecked on the coral reefs. We are safe."

Caloosa brought her dried clothes and left the room while she quickly dressed. When he returned he carried Rikkar's limp form to the deck. Bright sunshine spilled its golden light over everything, not a cloud marring the blue expanse of sky.

Lainie looked about and saw they were indeed in a small deep bay, surrounded by lush, green trees and thick, jungle foliage. They were well hidden from any passing ships. Even the masts of the *Sea Hawk*, free of all the flags and markings, blended with the tall trunks of the Royal Palms that circled the sparkling bay.

She turned her attention back to Caloosa and Rikkar. A sling had been improvised and Lainie watched mutely as Rikkar was lowered to the waiting boat. Caloosa helped Lainie down the rope ladder. As soon as she was seated in the boat, Rikkar's head pillowed on her knees, Caloosa and another sailor took up the oars and the small boat skimmed across the water toward a wooden pier. As they neared shore a beautiful, lithe Indian woman ran out onto the pier and waved.

"Rikkar, Caloosa," she called excitedly, her voice filled with laughter, then she caught sight of Rikkar in the bottom of the boat and her smile faded. "He is hurt," she cried anxiously as the boat scraped against the pilings of the pier. Deftly she caught the rope flung to her and tied off the bow of the boat.

So, this gorgeous creature was Metoo, Lainie thought, watching her supple, graceful movements. Rikkar's description of her as Caloosa's tag-along sister had given Lainie an entirely different image of the Indian girl. She was, in fact, not a girl, Lainie saw. She was a woman, a year or two older than Lainie herself and seen up close, stunningly beautiful.

Her long, dark hair was parted in the middle, pulled to each side and secured beneath each ear with a rawhide tie.

Dark eyes flashed as the Indian woman looked at Lainie for a brief moment. Her features were strong and chiseled in perfect proportion as was her slender figure. She was tall, with a regal bearing that was evident in spite of the simple cotton shift she wore.

"What has happened to Rikkar?" Metoo asked Caloosa.

"He was attacked by pirates and stabbed," Caloosa said as he bent down to hoist Rikkar's weight onto his shoulder.

"Bring him to the house," Metoo commanded, helping her brother climb from the boat with his burden. Scrambling from the boat Lainie hurried after them.

A narrow path bordered by a thick tangle of lush, jungle growth, wound through the semi-tropical forest. Brightly colored birds flitted among the tree tops. Lainie was breathless when at last they arrived at a clearing.

In the middle of the sun-washed space sat a beautiful two story structure with low spacious verandahs running across the front and along each wing. It was made of the same white pebbly substance as the houses on Tortugas's island, but this building delighted the eye with its spaciousness and beauty.

A red tiled roof and red shutters added gay color to the stark whiteness of the stone. Majestic royal palms stood like sentinels on either side of the building, dwarfing it by their very height. Metoo and Caloosa moved across the flagstone path toward the house.

The entrance hall was cool and inviting with a spaciousness she had seldom seen before, but Lainie had little time to admire the hall or the elegant rooms beyond. A quick impression of gleaming, dark wood floors and crystal chandeliers followed her up the stairs.

Rikkar was moaning with pain by the time Caloosa reached the landing and turned into a bedroom. Lainie followed them to the door. Suddenly Metoo whirled about, blocking Lainie's entrance.

"You go away now," the Indian girl hissed at her. "We do not want you here."

"I'm going to see to Rikkar," Lainie said stubbornly. "Let me through."

"No," the Indian raised her chin defiantly, her dark eyes flashing fire.

"Move out of my way this instant," Lainie demanded in a sharp, clear voice, putting as much authority behind her expression as she knew how. Rikkar's weak voice broke through their impasse.

"Where's Beauty?" he asked Caloosa who was tucking the covers about him.

"I'm here," Lainie called. "I'm coming." She cast a triumphant look at Metoo.

"How do you like my island?" he asked with a weak smile.

"It's very beautiful," Lainie said softly, "but I haven't seen very much of it yet."

"I will show it to you as soon as I'm feeling better, perhaps tomorrow," he said. Lainie didn't argue, although she knew it would take several days before he would be well enough to get out of bed, much less walk around the island. Caloosa brought Rikkar a cup of dark liquid and supported his head while he drank.

"Metoo," Rikkar said, "Beauty is tired and needs to rest. Take her to the green room." He turned back to Lainie. "It is a very beautiful room, you should be comfortable—" his voice trailed off as his teeth clenched in a grimace of pain.

"Oh, Rikkar," Lainie cried, tears sliding down her cheeks. Rikkar watched their slow progress against the soft flesh of her rounded cheek. Catching one perfect tear drop on the tip of his finger he carried it to his lips. Lainie's heart lurched at the tender intimacy of his gesture and the soft light in his eyes.

"I have made you shed many tears," he whispered.

"It doesn't matter," she answered softly, her warm gaze flying across each beloved feature of his face.

"It matters to me," Rikkar said gently and looked up at Metoo. "Go with Metoo, and rest."

"I will see that the room is prepared for her," Metoo said stiffly and left the room. Lainie watched her leave and turned back to Rikkar.

"Why are you giving me a separate bedroom?" she asked. "I prefer to stay here with you, so if you need anything, I can get it for you."

"I have Caloosa," Rikkar said, glancing at his Indian friend.

"Yes, but—,"

"You would not rest well here with me while I am so—indisposed," his mouth twisted in a wry smile as he glanced down the length of his injured body.

"If you put me in another room," she said, trying one more tact, "I may run away."

Again a smile. "Go to the window, Beauty, and tell me what you see," Rikkar instructed her, and after a puzzled moment she did as she was told. She looked through the opened multipaned, glass doors of the balcony. Her breath caught in her throat as she took in the beauty of the scene spreading away before her.

The sweeping vista of sky and ocean and the lush greenness of the jungle brought a swelling joy to her heart. It reminded her of some other place, a place she couldn't name, where she had once been very happy. "Oh, Rikkar," she cried, turning back to him with shining eyes, "it's so lovely."

"Yes, it is," he agreed, his eyes taking in the glow of her face, "but behind the beauty can be some harsh realities. Beyond the trees and the jungle is nothing but water. There is no place for you to go. You are still my prisoner,

Beauty. Do you mind?" he asked softly. His gray eyes held hers.

"No, I don't mind," she murmured, unable to tear her gaze away from his. Rikkar laughed softly as he relaxed back against the pillows and the rich, mellow sound was like a teasing caress on her skin.

The moment was broken by Metoo returning to the room. Lainie could sense the other girl's anger and disapproval toward her.

"Take Beauty to her room now," Rikkar ordered and with a bow of her head Metoo turned stiffly to Lainie. Reluctantly she trailed after the Indian girl.

Metoo took her to a room just down the hall from Rikkar's. The walls were a lovely pale shade of green as were the rugs scattered about on the polished dark, wood floor. Plants, some bearing magnificent flowers, hung about the room.

"Oh, how beautiful," Lainie said, lightly touching one of the delicate, pastel blossoms.

"They are orchids," Metoo said. "They grow everywhere on the island."

"They're lovely," Lainie said and turned her attention to the rest of the room. The linen of the large four poster bed was crisp and white as were the lacy gauze curtains hanging from the ceiling above the bed.

"You may wish to pull the curtains about you when you sleep," Metoo was saying. "The insects are not as bad as on the mainland, because of the ocean breezes, but sometimes we still have them."

"The mainland?" Lainie said, moving to the doors of the balcony. A soft breeze stirred the curtains. "How far away is the mainland?" she asked.

"Too far for you to swim or row in a boat," Metoo said stiffly. "And the water is filled with sharks," she continued, a nasty smile curving her lips.

"You need have no fear," Lainie told Metoo. "I have no intention of trying to escape." The Indian girl's expression showed her skepticism at this statement.

"I will show you the rest of your rooms," Metoo said, opening the door to a bathroom. A large, porcelain tub sat in the middle of the floor, with fluffy towels folded neatly on a bench nearby.

"A bathtub," Lainie cried delightedly.

"I will have hot water brought up for you," Metoo said, leading the way back into the bedroom. "There are trunks coming from the ship with clothes for you. Do you wish a fire?"

Hostility sparkled in the dark depths of her eyes. For a moment Lainie met her hard gaze, wondering if it would be worth the effort to make friends with the Indian girl. Deciding not, she moved to the fireplace and ran her hands along the smooth surface of the white marble mantel.

"It is warm enough without a fire," she said in a low voice, then anger and pride made her whirl and face the Indian with a haughty expression. "That is all I require for the moment. You may go now." The Indian girl flushed angrily as she turned to leave the room.

"I will return to Rikkar, he needs me," Metoo said. Lainie felt a stab of jealousy. The Indian girl was beautiful in a sultry way, and she wondered what her relationship was to Rikkar.

A knock at the door interrupted her speculations as two servants brought in hot water for her bath. Lainie had to concede that although hostile, Metoo was an efficient hostess. She spent the next hour luxuriating in the warm, fragrant bathwater.

Incredibly refreshed, she returned to her bedroom, where she found empty trunks at the foot of her bed and the armoire filled with beautiful dresses. A young, dark-skinned maid stood silently by, awaiting her instructions.

Lainie chose a light, cream-colored dress with a tiny, blue flowered pattern and blue satin ribbons. Cream-colored handmade lace adorned its square cut bodice and short puffy sleeves. Beneath her gown she wore a fine, lacy chemise and pantaloons, as well as stays. She pulled on sheer, white silk stockings and dainty slippers with matching ribbons that tied high up on her ankles. As she dressed she pondered the clothes. They fit so well, obviously they had belonged to someone about her size. Moving to the trunks, Lainie looked at the label on the trunk. They had belonged to a woman named Eugenia de Marcel. The name didn't mean anything to Lainie, and she wondered briefly if she could have been Eugenia de Marcel. It would explain the clothes, but shouldn't the name spark some glimmer of recognition? She would ask Rikkar about it when he was better.

Lainie was both surprised and pleased at the maid's dexterity as she brushed her hair into a mass of curls and entertwined it with blue satin ribbons. Lainie looked into her mirror with satisfaction. She knew she looked beautiful and she was eager for Rikkar to see her this way.

Happily she left her room and walked down the corridor to his door. She paused for a moment, smoothing her skirts and checking that no wayward curls had fallen loose. Her hand was on the knob when she was halted by a harsh voice.

"What are you doing?" Metoo demanded. She came up the stairs carrying a pot of coffee and a bowl of broth.

"I'm going to see Rikkar," Lainie stated, involuntarily stepping back from the door.

"He does not wish to see you," Metoo said, her eyes sweeping derisively over Lainie's finery. "He is sleeping now."

"If he is sleeping, why are you bringing him food?"

she asked, noticing Metoo's face flush with anger at being caught in her lie.

"He does not wish to see you," the Indian girl said angrily. "Why do you bother him?"

"I don't think I'm a bother to him," Lainie said. "Shall we ask him?" Spinning about she opened the door and strolled into the room.

"Lainie," Rikkar's voice was warm with welcome. His nap had given him renewed strength and he smiled when he saw her. Lainie cast a triumphant look at the scowling Indian woman before turning back to Rikkar.

"I was afraid I might bother you if I came in," she said softly.

"It would have bothered me if you hadn't come. You look very beautiful."

"Thank you."

"Breathtaking," he said, "like a beautiful tropical bird." His words were punctuated by the clatter of the dishes as Metoo set the tray on a nearby table. Rikkar turned a questioning face to her.

"I will come back later and feed you," she said stiffly, her brows pulled low in a fierce scowl.

"Nonsense," Lainie said, giving the girl a sweet smile. "We don't want his broth to get cold, so I will feed him. You may go, Metoo." Her tone imperiously dismissed the Indian girl who stamped out of the room. Lainie looked after her with a glint of humor. Metoo was hardly more than a savage, she thought smugly, settling herself beside Rikkar. As she lifted a spoonful of the liquid to his lips, she was startled at the dark frown on his face.

"What's wrong?" she asked.

"Metoo is a sister to me, not a servant," he reprimanded. "I had hoped the two of you would be friends."

"Perhaps we will sometime," she said vaguely. "Is she really just a sister to you?"

"Of course," Rikkar replied. "I told you once how we all grew up together." Old familiar lights of mocking amusement lit his eyes. "Are you jealous of Metoo?" he drawled.

"Of course not," Lainie scoffed and quickly spooned some of the broth into his mouth. "I had a wonderful bath," she said, attempting to change the subject, "and I feel like a new woman."

"Everything was satisfactory?"

"In France, we have nothing more elegant."

"What else did you have in France?" Rikkar asked, regarding her with now stormy eyes.

"I—I—" Lainie looked at his set face and the image of something remembered which hovered at the edge of her mind, slipped away.

"What were you about to say?" Rikkar asked harshly. "Perhaps you were going to tell me your name," he prompted when she remained silent.

"I can't remember. Only a brief flash of a steamy room and a bath tub."

"Your memory is again quite convenient, isn't it?" Rikkar said, his lips tight with anger.

"Perhaps these moments of memory wouldn't go so quickly if they weren't greeted by anger and disbelief each time," Lainie said hotly. "If you would not pounce on everything I say as if it were further proof that I have lied, I might not be so distracted when these moments come upon me. Perhaps if you were a little more trusting toward me, if you gave me a little more time to explore these flashes of memory—" Lainie left the sentence unfinished.

"Mademoiselle, you may have all the time you wish," Rikkar snapped. "Metoo," he called.

"Rikkar, wait," Lainie cried, but his face was closed

against her. Nothing had changed, she thought as tears clogged her throat.

"Metoo will help me," he said stonily. "You are free to go and explore your memory."

"Rikkar," Lainie said, wanting to try again but Metoo had entered the room and stood nearby, openly listening to their conversation.

"Well, what is it?" Rikkar asked impatiently. Lainie looked from Metoo's triumphant face back to Rikkar's angry one.

"Nothing," she said quietly and head held high left the room, closing the door behind her.

She wandered downstairs, not sure what to do with herself. Now that she had time to study the house, she moved from room to room with growing interest.

In one room stood a lovely old curio cabinet which held a shell collection. Another room was graced with gilded cages of various shapes and sizes where plumed birds cawed and chattered, turning their heads from side to side to catch a better glimpse of the visitor in their midst.

Tall bookshelves that reached the ceiling in another room signalled she was in the library. Comfortable, slightly worn looking chairs gave testimony to its frequent use. At the door a path beckoned her past kitchen gardens to a grove of trees, through which she could glimpse a lagoon.

She strolled along the path, marvelling at the plants and bright flowers. Now and then she paused to watch the flash of color as tropical birds flitted among the trees.

As she continued along, Lainie had an eerie feeling of being followed. Several times she paused to look back but the path was empty. As she neared the lagoon she impulsively ducked behind some bushes. Before long, Metoo came quietly down the path. Lainie rose to her feet and confronted her.

"Are you looking for me?" she asked. Metoo gasped in surprise then regained her composure.

"No, I'm not," she snapped.

"Then why are you following me?"

"You are very clever," Metoo spat out, caught off guard by Lainie's direct approach. "But not clever enough to fool Rikkar."

"What do you mean?"

"Rikkar knows you are pretending to have lost your memory. You lie to him about this and many other things."

"How do you know all this?"

"I listen at the door," Metoo said smugly. "Rikkar knows he cannot trust you. He told me to follow you and guard you."

"That is absurd," Lainie said. "I can't get off the island. Rikkar himself pointed out there is no way to escape."

"Perhaps you will try to signal to your friends."

"There is no one to signal," she said to the Indian girl. "Besides there is no way to signal, is there?"

Metoo's face took on a look of slyness. "Rikkar said you are very clever with your lies and innocent looks and that I must not be fooled by them. I will not tell you any information about secret things."

"What secret things?" Lainie asked, bewildered by the girl's ravings.

"Nothing," Metoo shouted at her. "I will tell you only this. Rikkar is not for you. You are like a fork-tongued lizard whose color is gone." Metoo snatched a handful of Lainie's hair. "There is no color there, you are like the old women who sit in the front of the hut with no love of life anymore. You are ugly and it is only this bleached out ugliness that made Rikkar interested in you at all, but now he no longer wants you."

"If I am so ugly, then why does Rikkar keep me with

him?'' Lainie taunted the Indian woman. ''Do you want Rikkar for yourself?''

''Rikkar is a brother to me, nothing more,'' Metoo said with such flat finality that Lainie knew it was true. ''You are not a good enough woman for Rikkar.'' Metoo cried, her eyes sweeping over Lainie's clothes and hair. Her lips curled contemptuously. ''He needs a woman who is as strong as he is, a woman he can trust. He does not want a woman like you.''

''If that is true, Metoo, then why are you so afraid of me?'' Lainie demanded and saw the rage flare in Metoo's eyes. One hand shot out to yank at Lainie's golden tresses, while the other swung across Lainie's face, landing a smart slap on her cheek.

Lainie would not be restrained. She launched herself at Metoo, and the attack caught the Indian girl off guard. The two of them fell to the ground rolling about, each landing blows where and when she could. Their rolling carried them over a small embankment, causing them to land hard and break apart. Lainie staggered to her feet. She stared at Metoo a moment, then extended her hand. Hesitantly Metoo reached forward and allowed herself to be pulled up. The two girls stared hard at each other.

With sudden insight, Lainie realized that Metoo loved Rikkar, not as a brother, but as a man, but she knew that Rikkar would never return that love. For a moment, Lainie felt sadness for the other girl's pain.

''If you must guard me, do so at my side rather than skulking along behind me,'' Lainie finally said to her. The Indian girl nodded affirmatively, the glow of anger gone from her dark eyes.

The bonds of friendship had not been fused, but this was a beginning. Time and the isolation of the island would aid in the growth of that friendship in the days ahead.

Chapter 8

Caloosa called to Lainie as she returned to her room. "Rikkar wishes to see you. Please will you come?" he said.

"Tell him I will be there soon," Lainie said. "I must change." She looked down at her dishevelment but offered no explanation.

"He has been waiting for your return," Caloosa urged her. "He cannot rest until he talks to you."

"Then I'll come at once," Lainie said and moved toward Rikkar's bedroom door.

"I will come too," Metoo said, stepping forward. For a moment their eyes met. Lainie read distrust and anger in Metoo's eyes. Metoo believed she would tell Rikkar of their fight.

"Of course," Lainie said and moved on through the door.

The look of welcome on Rikkar's face turned to surprise when he saw Lainie. As Metoo stepped into the room, his lips tightened in anger.

"What happened to you," he asked harshly. Lainie stood for a moment contemplating what to say, how to begin.

"Metoo and I went for a walk together," she said,

perching on the side of his bed, "and I fell down a steep incline. In trying to help me, Metoo lost her balance and fell as well. Fortunately, we are not badly hurt." She smiled into his fever bright eyes before turning her gaze to Metoo. The Indian girl's face registered her surprise at Lainie's words.

"Is that true?" Rikkar asked her, his eyes probing. "I thought you knew the island better than that," Rikkar berated her, his dark brows drawn down in a scowl. "I thought you would protect Beauty better than that."

"Oh, it wasn't her fault," Lainie was quick to say. "I saw a beautiful flower and went off the path to try to pick it." She didn't like the lies she was telling him, but it was best for him, she reasoned. To lighten the atmosphere in the room, she laughed and held up the skirt of her gown. "I'm afraid Beauty is not an appropriate name at the moment," she said, by way of changing the subject.

"You will always be Beauty to me," Rikkar said fervently as his hand closed around hers. Lainie's heart gave a leap as she looked into his eyes. The warm lights dancing there set her cheeks aglow. Suddenly shy, she lowered her lashes and drew a deep, quivering breath.

"I wanted to see you to tell you I'm sorry for my suspicions this afternoon," Rikkar said. "You were right, I must give you the chance to remember. I won't do that to you again," he vowed, and the sincerity and gentleness of his tone brought tears to her eyes. She blinked them back and getting to her feet, busied herself with straightening his covers.

"You were very brave when you helped me fight off the pirates," Rikkar was saying, his eyes watching her face closely.

"It was nothing," she said softly.

"But I haven't thanked you for doing it." He paused

and looked at her bowed head. The lamplight was making a halo around it.

"I'd better go so you can rest," Lainie said softly, but he caught her hand.

"Thank you, Beauty," he said and she raised her eyes to meet his, their dark depths expressing more feelings than any man could hope to see. He brought her hand to his mouth, his lips brushing across the leaping pulse of her wrist.

With a sigh of regret he released her and watched her glide from the room. He was far too ill and weak from his wound to begin the exciting explorations of this child-woman, but there was time. She was still his prisoner, but as sleep claimed him the thought drifted through his mind that he was the prisoner, the captive of an innocent faced girl with golden hair and eyes that were dark wells in which a man could drown himself.

The first night in her bedroom was a restless one for Lainie. She was too used to Rikkar's strong body lying next to her. The next morning she was awakened from her fitful sleep by the trill and call of birds outside her window. She scrambled from bed, eager to dress and be out in the glorious sunshine. Beyond the trees she glimpsed a narrow ribbon of water cutting through the jungle, and remembered the lagoon she had never reached the day before. She resolved to explore it today.

The air was already warm with a promise of even greater heat as the day progressed, so she chose a light-weight dimity. She found Metoo in the kitchen with the servants and was ushered to a morning room, where large shutters had been pushed back to allow a breeze to sweep through the room. A small boy stood waving a palmetto frond slowly. A light breakfast was brought of melon slices and other fruits.

As she was finishing her cup of strong black coffee, Metoo joined her. The Indian girl's face was expressionless as she sat across from Lainie.

"Is it true, you went into the water with the sharks to help Rikkar?" she asked abruptly.

"Yes," Lainie answered simply, "but I didn't know about the sharks."

"Would you have gone into the water, if you had known?"

Lainie's thoughts turned back to that moment when Rikkar fell into the water. She hadn't known how to swim, only that Rikkar would drown if she didn't help him.

"Yes, I would have," she answered quietly. Metoo nodded her head in satisfaction, then extended her hand to Lainie. Surprised and pleased, Lainie accepted the outstretched hand and smiled warmly at Metoo.

"I will show you the island, the best place to swim and where to find crabs," Metoo then said.

Soon, Metoo was showing Lainie around, taking her to where the sailors lived in coquina huts with their families, pointing out the coral reefs and the marine life living in them. Lainie watched as Metoo netted the crabs they would have for supper that night.

At last they stopped to cool themselves in the little lagoon. Metoo was amused that Lainie would swim in her dress. She drew off her own simple cotton garment and stepped into the water, showing no timidity over her nudity. Lainie stood uncertainly on the shore, thinking Metoo looked like a classic sculpture. Finally, she stripped down to her camisole and pantaloons and waded out into the clear water, forgetting her own self-consciousness in the delicious coolness.

Metoo paddled about the lagoon with strong strokes and by imitating her, Lainie was able to move through the water the same way, though not nearly as swiftly. When

they were tired, they swam back to the sandy shore, where
Metoo lay against a large flat rock and let the hot sun dry
her. Lainie came up beside her and wrung the water from
her pantaloons.

"Metoo, tell me about Rikkar," she asked idly.

"What is there to tell you?" Metoo replied. "Rikkar is
Rikkar."

"What made him become a pirate?"

"A pirate?" Metoo yelped, opening her eyes and looking at Lainie. "Rikkar is not a pirate." Her eyes flashed
angrily at the implied insult. Lainie was puzzled by Metoo's
attitude. Was it possible she did not know what Rikkar
did?

"He told me he was, Metoo," Lainie said reluctantly.
"I am his prisoner."

"I know you are his prisoner," Metoo said scoffingly,
"but—" she paused. "Perhaps it is best if you ask Rikkar
the questions you have," she said rising from the boulder
to put on her dress. Subdued and puzzled, Lainie followed, struggling to pull the petticoats and dress on over
her wet undergarments.

"You wear too many clothes," Metoo said abruptly.

"I suppose that's true," Lainie said. "There is no one
to see what I wear anyway except Rikkar and you and
Caloosa."

"Caloosa will not look upon the woman who belongs to
Rikkar," Metoo said, "and I do not matter. I think Rikkar
would not mind if you wore less and were more comfortable. Come, I will help you."

Her strong, nimble fingers worked at the fasteners and
in no time at all, the wet camisole and pantaloons, petticoats and stays had been shed and the lightweight cotton
dress was slipped back over Lainie's head. At first, she felt
wrong not wearing the layers of clothing though she soon

grew used to the freedom and comfort she felt without them.

Returning to the main house for lunch, Lainie took a bouquet of flowers to Rikkar. His gray eyes were clear of the fever and pain, and he leered at her in her light dress, reaching out a hand to catch at her playfully. Lainie stayed just out of his reach, her eyes sparkling with laughter.

Metoo brought broth and left it for Lainie to feed Rikkar. A quietness had settled over them, although each time their eyes met, their gaze held for a long moment before glancing away only to dart back again. When at last Rikkar waved away the broth, Lainie rose from the side of his bed and placed the bowl back on the tray.

"Beauty," Rikkar said, reaching out to hold her hand. Her dark eyes flew to meet his again, a flush staining her cheeks and her lips parted slightly as she caught her breath.

Slowly, he pulled her toward him, and she trembled as she sat on the edge of the bed again, her hip against the hard column of his thigh. She could feel the heat of his body through the light sheet that covered him. He brought her hand to his lips, lightly kissing each fingertip. Lainie swayed toward him slightly as his hands came up to catch her shoulders and pull her down to him. Their mouths locked as their glances once had and Rikkar's mouth plundered hers, his teeth catching at her soft lower lip, his tongue probing and demanding until she felt he was drawing her very soul from her. She whimpered with need.

"Oh, Beauty," he groaned in frustration, lips setting a fiery trail along the soft line of her throat. His hand cupped the smooth mound of one breast, his touch searing through the thin cotton material of her dress. His thumb rubbed across the hard peak of her nipple. Moaning low in her throat, she opened her mouth to receive his devastating kisses. She was lost in passion, unaware that anyone else was in the room, until Rikkar released her and gently raised her to a sitting position.

"You must be careful not to reopen your wound," Caloosa was saying as he crossed to the bed. Quickly, Lainie got to her feet and went to the foot of the bed, her back to the Indian and Rikkar as she sought to calm her rapid breathing and still the clamor of her body.

"I'll go now, so he can rest," she murmured. "If there is anything you need, just call me," she said, meeting Rikkar's eyes.

"I just did," he answered with a roguish grin.

In the afternoon, Metoo took Lainie about the parts of the island they hadn't visited yet. Tentatively the two girls began to talk about themselves, exchanging ideas and information. Lainie had little to share, but she listened with interest as Metoo told of her early years in the once fierce Calusa nation and how Rikkar's father had found the two children and had taken them back to his plantation.

"I do not belong to any world now," Metoo told her. "I have been raised in a white world and yet the white man rejects me. But here on this island, it does not matter what the white man thinks of me, I am happy."

"I can understand why," Lainie said. "It's so beautiful it seems like paradise to me."

"Paradise?"

"Paradise is the word for a beautiful, perfect place," Lainie explained.

"Yes, this is a paradise," Metoo agreed.

Lainie came to love the island and under Metoo's tutelage learned the names of the trees and flowers, differentiating between the graceful coconut palm trees and the majestic royal palms. She marveled at the beauty of the birds who lived there, the gorgeous roseate spoonbills and the pink curlews. She was awed by the great white herons and the snowy egrets. Metoo showed her where flamingos nested and the sight of the brilliantly plumed birds balanced on their long, skinny legs made Lainie want to laugh with joy.

She followed Metoo's example of shrugging out of her clothes to plunge into the sun-warmed waters and climb out onto a rock to dry. Soon, her golden locks took on a lighter hue and she acquired a golden tan. A dusting of freckles across her nose enchanted Rikkar when she went to his room to feed him or delight him with some tale of discovery about the island.

A new rapport had emerged between the two of them. There was no more evidence of anger or suspicion directed against Lainie and no more prodding her to tell him things about herself which she couldn't remember. Best of all, there were no more references to what Rikkar thought her earlier training had been.

As the days passed Rikkar grew stronger. Every day Caloosa brought him to sit on the wide, shaded verandah, and Lainie would sit beside, him telling him what she and Metoo had done that day.

When he was well enough to walk around, Rikkar took her to a section of the island more overgrown than the rest, where mangrove trees supported their canopy of green branches on stilt-like trunks and white pelicans nested among them.

These were the days of their courtship. Rikkar wooed her with the beauty of his island, bringing her a flower for her hair every day. His behavior toward her was almost courtly as he guided her about the island or sat on the verandah for afternoon tea. He never tried to make love to her, contenting himself instead with an occasional light kiss on her lips or more often on the back of her hand. A tension, like an overwound spring, grew within Lainie and the glint of Rikkar's eyes told her he felt it too.

One day when they were taking a walk, Lainie caught

sight of a tiny bird flying busily from one red hibiscus bloom to the next, its tiny wings a blur as they beat against the air. She could hardly believe what she saw. The bird was flying upside down!

"It's a hummingbird," Rikkar told her. "The natives call it a flower kisser."

"Because they go from flower to flower!" Lainie exclaimed.

"Because they sip the nectar from the flowers," Rikkar said, his lids lowered over his gray eyes as he studied her soft pink lips. The hunger in his eyes made her heart skip a beat.

"Now look," she cried, "he's flying backwards. He's a very mixed up little bird." She turned toward Rikkar. His gaze was hot and intense. "He can't seem to get enough necter," she whispered, her breath catching in her throat.

"Sometimes I feel like that hummingbird," he murmured. His hands settled on her shoulders and his lips met hers gently. A sweet passion ignited within her and she wrapped her arms about him, returning his kiss with ardor.

He guided her to the white sands of the lagoon and turned her to him, his hands coming up to cup her face, while he gently lowered his lips to hers, then slid his mouth along the curve of her jaw to the sensitive soft skin of her throat. She felt the rasp of his tongue and new fires were ignited, her breasts swelling against his chest.

Rikkar held her away from him as he rained kisses on her face and the hollows of her throat. His teeth nibbled softly, making her moan.

"Beauty, I want you," he whispered huskily.

"Oh, and I want you too," she murmured through lips swollen from his kisses, "but your wound—"

"It's healed enough," he said impatiently. "Tell me, Beauty, so I may be sure," he said softly against her ear. "Do you submit willingly to me or am I forcing you?"

Lainie laughed, the sound echoing in the still warm air. Winding her fingers through his dark locks, she brought his lips back to hers.

"Get on with it," she demanded hoarsely, "or I may force *you*." Any further attempt at words was cut off as Rikkar caught her in his arms, crushing her against him. All restraint was gone from his kisses, they seared her very soul. He released her mouth only long enough for them both to undress, then he lowered her gently to the warm, white sand.

She could feel him fighting to bring his raging desire under control, to slow down their lovemaking, and she wanted to cry out it wasn't necessary. She wanted him just as desperately as he wanted her, but she couldn't speak against the demanding urgency of his mouth. Her hands flew over his skin, smoothing and caressing the rippling muscles of his shoulders and hard, lean stomach. His hands caught in a tangle of her hair and held her mouth captive as he plunged his tongue against hers again and still again.

Now his hands moved to her body, running over the satiny skin with a light touch that made her writhe with desire. His fingers closed around her breasts and his mouth blazed a fiery trail over the slim column of her throat to her tender swollen nipples. Shivers of delight shook her as his mouth moved lower and lower, tormenting her with pleasure.

"No more, Rikkar," she whispered hoarsely. "No more, please. Take me now. Now!" she urged and he rose over her. His eyes were dark with passion as they looked at her, then he closed them and they both gave in to the tide of sensations washing over them.

Later, they lay resting beside each other in the sand, and Lainie closed her eyes. The tickle of sand falling against her skin roused her and she opened her eyes to find Rikkar smiling at her as he lightly let the sand fall through his fingers to her chest. She traced the line of his mouth gently with her finger, her heart singing with happiness. His hand closed around her breast then slid down to her flat stomach.

"Hasn't the hummingbird had enough?" she whispered.

"Hummingbirds never get enough, remember?" he growled and pulled her to him. Laughing, Lainie rolled away and leapt to her feet. Running to the water's edge she paused to pose provocatively before him, all shyness forgotten.

He quickly got to his feet, and she barely made it to the water ahead of him. She dove under water, swimming toward the middle of the lagoon until the lack of air drove her to the surface.

She looked about for Rikkar, but he was nowhere in sight. Puzzled she glanced back at shore. There was no sign of him on the beach. Where was he she thought, fighting back the panic. Suddenly Rikkar's arms closed about her from beneath the water. She barely had time to snatch a breath before he pulled her down with him.

They tumbled over and over in the clear, green lagoon. Rikkar grabbed her long hair and pulled her face to his. His lips closed over hers, hot and demanding. He drew her close to him as together they rose to the surface. He allowed her time for only a quick breath before claiming her lips again. He caressed her wet body, sliding his hands over her smooth skin, then swam toward shallow water, pulling her with him. They stood on a ledge in shoulder deep water, exploring each other in the cool weightlessness.

"You're so beautiful," Rikkar whispered. She felt the cold water against her hot flesh as he parted her thighs, and once again she melted against him as their bodies fused.

At last, Rikkar carried her gently to the sand. He lay beside her, his face buried in the warm curve of her shoulder. When the moisture had dried on their skin,

Rikkar helped Lainie dress and hand in hand they strolled back to the house.

During dinner that evening their eyes met often, but they spoke little. Smiles curved their lips as they studied each other, treasuring each intimate detail. Lainie mused on the shape of his lean, brown hands with their long fingers and remembered the pleasure they had brought her. She studied the curly dark hair on the side of his head and across his brow, remembering its texture when she wound her fingers in it. Rikkar's eyes went again and again to the flush of her round cheek and the sweep of her long, dark lashes. At last, dinner was over and they drew apart, each going to his own room, almost glad to be free for a moment of the overwhelming presence of the other, but later that night Rikkar came to her and Lainie welcomed him with open arms.

Their days were golden, their nights tender and passionate, and Lainie wanted it never to end. It no longer mattered to her that she had no past. She was starry-eyed, dreaming about her future. Although he never said he loved her, she knew he cared for her. She felt more secure than she could ever remember.

A few days later Rikkar and Caloosa left the island on the *Sea Hawk*, promising to be back within two days.

Lainie missed Rikkar more than she had thought possible and looked forward impatiently to his return. She thought she might have a surprise for him and wavered between telling him immediately upon his return or waiting until she was absolutely sure. Unconsciously, her hands went to her flat stomach.

"You will have news to tell Rikkar when he returns," Metoo said one afternoon, reading Lainie's thoughts. They were sunning themselves on a favorite boulder. Lanie smiled at her new friend.

"Oh, Metoo, do you think it might be true?" she asked, filled with happiness at the prospect.

"I have seen it in your face these past few days," the Indian girl replied.

"I hope this does not cause you pain, Metoo."

"I have put such feelings behind me," Metoo reassured her. "You are Rikkar's woman in every way and he is happy with you. Rikkar loves me as a sister. That is how it will always be. You have made him happy so I am happy too."

"Thank you," Lainie said, placing her hand over Metoo's. "I'm not sure I could have been that generous."

"There is an old custom among the people of these island keys," Metoo said. "The family of the sailors on the other side of the island practice it. When a family has a baby, they place a conch shell on a stick in front of their dwelling to announce the birth."

Lainie was so pleased with the custom that she immediately began to scour the beaches looking for a perfect Queen conch shell. When she found it, she washed the sand away, dried it and placed it on the mantel of the fireplace in her room. She envisioned Rikkar's face when she placed the conch shell before him. Would he be happy or angry? In her own joy in the event she could only imagine him feeling as happy as she did.

She dreamed of their future together. She would persuade Rikkar to give up his pirating and they would live here on the island forever. They would have many children; she wanted a large family. If her past was empty she would fill her future with people she could love and who would love her in return.

Far out in the waters of the mighty bay, at the last of the chain of islands, the *Sea Hawk* rode at anchor. Most of its crew and its captain had gone ashore, the crew to explore the possible pleasures of this newest outpost, and the captain and his Indian companion to a secret meeting.

They sat on make-shift chairs in the temporary office of their host, a man named Samuel J. Crawford. The air was already blue from the Cuban cigars he favored and pressed upon each and every guest. Rikkar covered a smile as Caloosa took a long puff of the foul-smelling cigar and slowly released his breath, his eyes rolled upward contemplatively as he savored the smoke. Caloosa had few vices, Rikkar knew, but smoking was listed among them. Surreptitiously, he snuffed out his own cigar to give to Caloosa for their trip back to the island.

"I'm glad to see you managed to escape from Tortugas's men," Crawford said, studying the young man before him. "Are you sure you want to try again? He's a pretty nasty character."

"Someone has to do it," Rikkar said. "I started this, I'd like to finish it."

"True, but maybe if someone else—"

"It would take time to set it up with someone else, time we don't have," Rikkar broke in.

"That's true, but we suspect your purpose has been discovered by Tortugas and his men."

"What makes you think that?"

"We have evidence that he did indeed have a spy planted aboard the *Southern Moon*."

"Do you know who it was?" Rikkar asked, his eyes and face without expression. Only Caloosa sensed the coiled tension in him.

"We can only speculate." Crawford rose from his chair and walked around to the front of his desk. "There have been rumors of a French woman, a Madame Davy and her daughter, Lise, who are part of the gang. It is said that Madame Davy and at times her daughter have been the mistress of Tortugas.'' Crawford paused, troubled by the look in Rikkar's eyes.

"Madame Davy and her daughter sailed a few months ago from New Orleans on a ship bound for France," Crawford went on. "They have contacts in France who keep them informed about valuable shipments and their dates of departure. Once their ship docked, the two women simply disappeared. No one saw them again, but the night the *Southern Moon* was to sail, our man saw a young cabin boy go aboard with an older man. The older man came off the ship, the cabin boy did not. The crew of the *Southern Moon* had already been hired and they were told not to let anyone on that ship who hadn't been authorized by Jean Gautier. I think that cabin boy was really Lise Davy."

Rikkar made no comment, but shook his head as if to rid it of the vestiges of a nightmare. The hand on his knee curled into a tight fist, his knuckles white. A vein in his temple throbbed.

Crawford returned to his seat and leaned forward, gazing earnestly at Rikkar. "If she was there, she would have recognized the trap and could have simply kept her disguise until the *Southern Moon* docked in Savannah. All she had to do was wait, sneak off the ship, and make her way back to Tortugas. She's had time to reach him by now and tell him what she's seen. If she has, he would know you aren't what you claim to be. Going back into that nest of vipers at Montecumbe Key would be suicidal.

"There's no danger of Tortugas knowing about me," Rikkar said, his voice grim and hard. "I *have* Lise Davy. Believe me, she's had no chance to get her message to Tortugas, but he knows I have her. He tried to take her from me when I was there the last time."

Rikkar got to his feet. "I'm going back to Montecumbe Key and this time we'll get Tortugas. This time I have the bait he really wants. Have a ship full of men just out of sight near the Lower Montecumbe tonight. My ship will signal when we've got Tortugas where we want him. We'll go in and clean out the whole nest of pirates this time.

"Are you sure about it, Rikkar?" Major Crawford asked doubtfully.

"Very sure," Rikkar snapped, then turned on his heel and left. Caloosa followed, a troubled look on his face. The prearranged signal was given and the crew was reassembled in record time.

All grumbling by the crew was quickly stifled when a glimpse was caught of the captain's face. Rikkar paced the foredeck, his mouth a grim line. Now and then he stopped long enough to pound his fist against the railing, speaking only to order more sail.

Rikkar's mind raced back over the past few weeks. It all made sense, he thought. All the pieces fit. How cleverly she had played her part. His fists clenched as he remembered the blood on the sheets that morning on the *Sea Hawk*. It was an old trick and he had fallen for it. He had actually thought her virginal when all the time she had already belonged to Tortugas! He should have suspected. Tortugas had been too eager to trade for her. He had even instructed his men not to harm the girl when they fought. They hadn't been trying to capture him as he had supposed; they had been trying to rescue the girl.

Caloosa had said she was in the water trying to help him, but perhaps not. If she had known he wasn't really a pirate, she would have suspected who he was. She would have wanted him for ransom. But Caloosa got there too soon and she had to pretend to want to be rescued. How cold-blooded she was.

The men looked at each other uneasily, holding their thoughts to themselves. The captain was like a man possessed by the devil. They had never seen him drive the little ship like this. Silently, they cheered when the island came into view, but their relief was shortlived, for Rikkar ordered only the smallest amount of sail lowered as they raced through the narrow hidden channel to the bay. Some men hung over the edge, their hearts in their mouths as the ship's sleek wooden hull slid dangerously close to the jagged coral beds, and then they were in the bay. The sails were loosened and flapping in the wind, and the crew looked at each other, not bothering to hide their relief.

Rikkar took little notice of them. He was over the side and being rowed to the pier. "Keep all men aboard ship, we sail again immediately," Rikkar ordered.

"Perhaps you should not act so quickly until you have thought this out," Caloosa said, speaking for the first time since leaving Key West."

"There is nothing to think about," Rikkar snapped. "We have a job to do and I am choosing the best way to do it."

"You are choosing out of anger," Caloosa said, but Rikkar was already stalking down the path.

Lainie was wading in the lagoon when she looked up and saw Rikkar striding toward her through the trees. With a welcoming cry she ran to him. Her bubbling emotions blinded her to the stoney look on his face. She threw her arms around his neck. Her happy laughter stilled only long enough to press kisses over his face and neck. Her arms circled his waist and she pressed herself against his warm lean body.

"I missed you so much," she sighed. She became aware of his lack of response. Instead of holding her tightly to him as she might have expected, his arms hung at his side. "What's wrong?" she asked, drawing back.

"I have to leave again," Rikkar said, pulling away and turning his back. "I stopped only long enough to take you with me."

"Go with you?" Lainie asked in happy disbelief. Although she loved their paradise, she had not enjoyed it as much without Rikkar and had determined never to be separated from him again.

"Come along," Rikkar said.

"Now?" Lainie was incredulous. "But I must go to the house and change clothes."

"The clothes you have on are fine," Rikkar said curtly. "Metoo," he called to the Indian girl who had followed him down to the lagoon. They walked a short way along the path, then stood whispering together. At one point, Metoo turned to look at Lainie, her face a mask, her eyes inscrutable. Lainie stared back, a sense of foreboding settling over her.

"Where are we going?" she called to Rikkar as she combed and braided her long hair.

"It's a surprise," Rikkar said. "Didn't you tell me once that you love surprises?"

"Yes, I do," Lainie said. "Don't you?"

"That depends on the surprise." She followed him to the boat that would take them out to the *Sea Hawk*. Caloosa rowed them out and boarded the ship with them. He barely responded to her greeting.

Once they were aboard the *Sea Hawk*, the sails were quickly raised and the ship set out to the open ocean. Rikkar ushered Lainie to a seat topside and took the helm, but she was too excited to sit still. Instead, she went to stand beside him. How wonderful to be sailing like this, with the wind whipping through her hair and Rikkar's strong, hard body to lean against. She felt invincible, as if nothing bad could touch her.

As the sun began its final descent they sailed into a cove at one of a string of small islands. As they drew near, Lainie recognized the island. Dread washed over her.

"Rikkar," she cried. "Tortugas is here. He tried to kill you the last time. He'll try again."

"No, I have something he wants," Rikkar said. "He won't kill me until he has that."

"What is it?" Lainie asked. "Couldn't you send it by Caloosa?" Rikkar's hard gaze raked her face.

"No, I want to deliver it myself," he said. They anchored in the bay as before and the boat was lowered. Rikkar placed a hand at Lainie's elbow.

"Am I to go too?" she asked.

"Yes, are you frightened?" Rikkar asked.

"Yes, I am," she admitted, but it was better to go with Rikkar than to stay on the boat worrying about his safety.

When Caloosa had rowed the boat close to shore, Rikkar stood up and shouted. "Ahoy, I'm coming ashore."

"Who's there?" a man shouted back.

"My name is Rikkar. I want to see Tortugas."

"He don't want to see you."

"Tell Tortugas I have something he wants and I'll make a trade."

The man ran along the path and disappeared into one of the stone buildings. In no time at all he reappeared. "Tortugas say, come ashore and bring the merchandise with you," the man called.

"Row out and wait for me," Rikkar ordered Caloosa. He picked up Lainie and carried her to shore. Together they climbed the bank and took the path as they had before.

Tortugas was seated at the same table at the back of the inn. As Lainie and Rikkar approached, the fat pirate's greedy eyes raked across her figure, stripping her of the thin dress she wore.

"Well, Ree-kar," the fat man laughed. "You wish to trade with me? You find your cargo from the *Southern*

Moon, maybe?'' His malevolent eyes studied Rikkar's face.

''I came to trade for the cargo you took from me the last time I was here,'' Rikkar said bluntly.

''Ah, Ree-kar,'' the man laughed. ''I tell you before, I do not steal your goods. I am sorry you think I am a thief.''

''I know you are a thief, but I am willing to trade you something for the return of my jewels. If you do not do so, I will bring in my men and we'll raid this village.'' Tortugas laughed at the threat.

''There are many men in this village, Ree-kar, but you may search it, if you wish. You will not find your jewels.'' He paused and regarded Rikkar for a moment. ''If I help you find your jewels, what have you got to trade?''

''That which you wanted most when I was last here.'' The pirates's eyes flew to Lainie.

''Rikkar!'' she gasped in disbelief.

''I will trade the girl for the jewels,'' Rikkar said stonily.

''No, Rikkar.'' Lainie's throat was so dry she could only whisper.

''Let me see a sample of the wares,'' Tortugas said, reaching out a hand. With a cry Lainie shrank away, but Rikkar moved her forward, ripping open the bodice of her dress to expose her breasts. Numb with shock, Lainie could only stand there. She made no attempt to shield herself from the leering men about her.

''Why are you doing this?'' she whispered to Rikkar.

''You shouldn't mind, Lise,'' he said, his eyes and voice hard. ''Isn't this what you were trained for?''

Rikkar's words whirled around in her confused mind. Lise, he had called her Lise, why? She raised pleading eyes to him. Perhaps if she told him of her love for him and of the baby she carried, his baby, he would put an end to this nightmare.

"Rikkar," she cried, reaching out to touch his sleeve. "Please don't do this. I love you. I thought you loved me too. I'm—"

"Love?" Rikkar interrupted contemptuously. "What would a woman like you know of love?" He pushed her away from him.

"You are getting a rare jewel here," Rikkar said to Tortugas, "but then you already know that. She is well versed in her trade. A trifle too eager at times, but an interesting diversion, nonetheless."

"No," Lainie whispered, listening to Rikkar's taunts.

"You liked her, huh? She's good, eh?" Tortugas breathed heavily as he leered at her.

"She's very imaginative," Rikkar went on, "both in bed and out. I wasn't bored with her until she'd run through all her tricks."

"Then why do you trade her?" Tortugas asked, a crafty smile distorting his fat face.

Rikkar looked at Lainie for a moment. "I know all her tricks now," he said evenly. "She's no longer of any interest to me." His gaze swung back to the pirate. "And now your part of the bargain," he said to the fat man.

"Ah, yes," Tortugas said. "My man will take you to your jewels." Without another look at Lainie, Rikkar stalked away.

"Rikkar," she called after him, but he did not turn his head. As he reached the door, Lainie saw one of Tortugas's men rise, a knife poised, ready to throw.

"Rikkar," she screamed, "he has a knife."

The door crashed against the outer wall as Rikkar spun to meet the attacker. Shimmery sunlight, blinding after the dimness of the room, spilled in and outlined the man in the doorway. Through painfully blinding shafts of light, Lainie saw Rikkar fire. The noise was deafening.

Suddenly, she was back aboard the *Southern Moon* with

the smell of gun powder in her nostrils and the groans of injured men filling her head. Before her stood the tall pirate, a pistol smoking in his hands, her father's crumbled body on the floor at his feet.

Disbelief swept over her. Her father was dead, killed by the hand of this man to whom she'd given herself. Revulsion and hatred swept over her. Now this same man contemptuously traded her away for jewels while she begged piteously, offering him her love. Her eyes opened wide. She even carried his baby beneath her breast. It couldn't be! Had fate played some cruel trick on her?

"No!" Her scream filled the room. Rikkar swung to look at her.

Her dark eyes were enormous in her small, pale face. There was shock and disbelief and horror such as he'd never seen written there. For the first time he realized the magnitude of what he might be doing, of the chance he was taking with her.

She took a step toward him, her movements wavering and unsteady. Her voice rang out.

"Murderer!" she screamed, then darkness closed about her and she fell to the floor.

Stunned, the men in the room stood looking at the slight still body. Rikkar could not move. Had her words been meant for him? Had he killed someone she cared about?

He would leave her for the moment and when he had captured Tortugas, he would shake every bit of the truth out of her lovely body. He would accept no more lies from her.

Before Tortugas and his men could react, he was away, a silent shadow fleeing painful confusion.

Chapter 9

She was lying in the bottom of a boat, and everything was dark. At first she thought she was still dreaming, but she could smell the sweaty odor of the fat man seated above her. Memory of Rikkar's betrayal, even more, the memory of his shooting of her father that day on board the *Southern Moon* swept through her, bringing despair. As she lay numbly trying to assimilate the black events of the day, the boat scraped over rocks and shale bringing a curse from the pirate. With a grunt he climbed over the side of the boat and hauled it to shore.

"Okay, girlie, I know you're awake. Come on out of there," Tortugas ordered. Roughly he pulled her from the boat and set her on her feet. The incoming tide drenched her thin shoes. Tortugas started off through a forest, dragging her along behind him. The trees and low bushes had encroached over whatever path had existed and Lainie's skirt caught and was ripped loose time and again. Finally they arrived at a shack well hidden among the dark trees.

Lainie stumbled up the rickety steps after the man who held her wrist so cruelly. They entered a dark, low room littered with all manner of booty. Gilded satin chairs and sofas, their delicate fabrics ripped, stuffing spilling out obscenely, sat side by side with wooden crates, up-ended to serve as seats. On the table, ornate silver forks and knives lay among dirty, chipped crockery. Tortugas threw the bags he carried into the corner.

"So your lover didn't want you anymore," he smirked at her, his eyes roving over her body. Lainie pulled her torn bodice around her and tried to will a numbness to her emotions.

"Maybe you weren't so good after all," Tortugas laughed. "That's all right. I'm not so particky as some," he laughed again, his foul breath forcing Lainie to turn her head. "Now don't be shy," Tortugas said, reaching out to grab a breast in a painful grip.

"Don't," Lainie cried, trying to back away, but Tortugas held her fast.

"I'm going to teach you, girlie, what it's like with a real man. You're goin' ta like it."

"Leave me alone," Lainie sobbed, struggling to fend him off. Tortugas planted a slobbering kiss on her lips. She recoiled in disgust and strained to break free of his grip.

"I like 'em with a little fire," he laughed. "It makes it more fun for me."

Lainie slashed out at him, raking furrows down his cheeks. The fat man let out a yelp, then seized Lainie by the hair and brought a fist down across the side of her face. Pain rocketed through her head, but anger and fear made her struggle on against the painful assault. More blows rained down on her, sending waves of pain through her body. Her struggles grew weaker until finally Tortugas was able to drag her to another room.

Breathing heavily with the exertion, Tortugas half-threw, half-pushed Lainie toward a bed in the middle of the room. She stumbled, falling heavily against the bedpost, its ornately carved post striking her sharply in the stomach. Lainie screamed against the searing pain, but Tortugas's hand grabbed her, spinning her onto the bed. He fell against her, laughingly ignoring her pleas. He jabbed at her pain-wracked body.

Flailing out, Lainie's fingers brushed against the cold hard edge of metal. It was a knife. It had fallen unheeded from the pirate's waist band during their struggle. Desperately, she grabbed it and gathering a last bit of strength plunged it into her assailant. It sank deep in the hollow between his shoulder and neck. With a roar of pain, Tortugas lurched backwards.

Blood gushed from the wound, staining the pirate's shirt and covering her. The sight of his own blood frightened and enraged Tortugas. Lainie saw the madness in his eyes as he prepared to launch himself at her again.

Wildly, she struck out again and the blade sank deep into the evil man's throat. She watched, horrified, as he opened his great, ugly mouth and blood poured from it. He fell forward half on and half off the bed, his grotesque head with its unseeing eyes landing near her feet.

Nausea welled in Lainie's throat, cutting off her scream. Whimpering, she pulled away from the menacing figure, but when he didn't move, she pushed against the matted, dirty hair with her foot, and the heavy body fell to the floor with a thud.

At last, the sobs came, hysterical sounds that filled the dim shack, wracking her body as she fought for control. She had to get away, but she was too weak. She tried to push herself off the bed, but the exertion of even that movement brought a fresh stab of pain. At last she stopped trying and lay still, her breathing growing shallow, her eyes glazed. The night sounds closed around her and the gruesome corpse that kept her company throughout the night.

She prayed for unconsciousness and release from the

agony she was suffering, but no such comfort awaited her. The horror filled night was etched irrevocably in her consciousness. Toward morning she slid into a half-conscious state and for a short while she escaped the shack and its bloody remains. She returned to a happier time in her life, riding across the fields of Belle Fleur with her father. She was on her favorite pony and the wind was streaming through her hair, but it was the wind of the sea and she was on a ship with great white sails above her and Rikkar at the helm. Rikkar, she moaned and cried out, and then she was back in the shack, Tortugas's blood-stained body on the floor at her feet.

"I curse you, Rikkar," she whispered through cracked and bloodied lips. "May the devil take your soul." She shuddered and drew her knees up, curling herself into a ball against the pain and welcoming the darkness that again came up to claim her.

The sound of bodies moving through underbrush woke her the next morning.

"Tortugas, come on out. We have you surrounded," a man shouted.

"He's not in here," a man yelled from another room.

"Search the island, we don't want to lose him now," ordered another man.

"Well, we've found it," said a man in the other room. "Tortugas's nest."

"Look at this loot," a third exclaimed. "He's got a fortune in stolen goods here."

"Several fortunes," his partner replied. "After the raid on that island cujo village and now this, the pirates are pretty much wiped out in these parts."

"Yeah, but we've still got a bunch of them north along the gulf coast," the other said pessimistically.

"We'll get 'em. We got Tortugas."

"Yeah, but we couldn't have done it without Captain Rikkar," the young man said. "He'll probably get another medal for this."

"Probably," his friend grunted. "He earned it. He's going out of the service in grand style."

"Sir, someone's in the next room." Lainie heard the men approaching, but she was unable to move.

"This one's dead," he said. "It looks like Tortugas." He stepped around to examine Lainie, looking into the wide dark eyes, which mutely begged for help.

"Quick, get the Captain," he ordered tersely. "She's the woman Captain Rikkar used as bait to catch Tortugas. Looks like she's been hurt bad. Didn't Rikkar say she was supposed to be one of them?" he asked of no one in particular. "Why would they hurt one of their own like that?"

"She's the spy they put on board the *Southern Moon*," his companion replied.

Confused thoughts bounced around inside Lainie's head. Rikkar had killed her father and had given her over into the hands of that horrible man who had inflicted such pain. A small core of hate had been slowly growing inside her, now it flamed higher as she thought of the things she'd overheard the men say. Rikkar had used her as bait in his plan to catch Tortugas, not caring what would happen to her. Beyond the room, boots shuffled on the porch. The two men hovering over Lainie turned quickly and hurried to the porch.

"Tortugas is dead in a room back there, Sir. The girl is there too. She's been hurt, but she's still alive. It looks like she killed him. Do you want to see her?" There was a pause, then Rikkar spoke.

"No, there's no reason to see her again. She's served her purpose. Let's start getting this cargo aboard ship."

Lainie heard the sound of boot steps moving away. When she opened her eyes, Caloosa was there. His gaze swept about the room, taking in the dead body of the pirate and the injured girl. He bent over Lainie, his brown eyes filled with sympathy.

"Caloosa," Lainie forced her swollen and blood stiffened lips to move, her voice a sigh. "Take me—Metoo."

Gently the big Indian gathered her in his arms and cradled her to his chest.

"Caloosa." Rikkar's voice was an angry bark.

"She is hurt," the Indian spoke. "She wants to go to Metoo."

There was a long pause and Lainie sensed Rikkar was near. She heard a smothered expletive then he was shouting at some of the men to make a path through the woods. Soon Caloosa was gently placing her in the bottom of a boat. He pushed away from shore, and Lainie sank willingly into the darkness that reclaimed her, leaving the pain behind on the island. She had no knowledge of the dark-haired man who stood on shore, his eyes bleak with his own special hell.

When she opened her eyes again, she was back in her bedroom on Rikkar's island.

"You are awake," Metoo said, one hand smoothing the hair from Lainie's brow.

"Metoo," she whispered. "I thought I would never see you again." Tears spilled over her cheeks and wet the pillow beneath her head.

"You are safe. You will be all right, the bleeding has stopped."

"Did I lose the baby?" Lainie asked.

"Yes, the baby is gone," Metoo said. "I am sorry."

"Oh Metoo," Lainie cried out.

"I have told Rikkar he has done you a great wrong," Metoo said. Lainie turned her head away from Metoo, not wanting to speak of him.

"Do not be too bitter against him," Metoo said. "He is a good man."

"He is an evil murderer, a liar, and he betrayed me!"

"I cannot speak of what has happened between you and Rikkar. Only the two of you know of it, but he is not a murderer."

"He murdered my father," Lainie flared at her, "and he gave me to that pig, Tortugas."

"He was wrong," Metoo said, "but his decision was made from anger and wrong information about you. Rikkar's anger has always been his worst enemy. Try to understand."

"I understand only too well," Lainie said. "He used me to catch Tortugas and he didn't care that I might be hurt. I shall always hate him and one day, I swear on the death of my baby, I will pay him back. One day, Rikkar will suffer as I have."

"Be careful you do not hurt yourself," Metoo cautioned.

"If it means repaying Rikkar, any price is worth it," Lainie declared. Metoo searched her face.

"You are not the same woman who came to this island," she observed.

"No, Metoo, I am not. That woman is dead forever."

"I do not think Rikkar will love this new woman," Metoo said, her dark eyes sad and troubled.

"This new woman does not love Rikkar."

Not answering, Metoo left the room. Lainie lay back against the pillow, tears trembling on her lashes. Angrily she brushed them away.

"I will not cry and be weak again," she resolved, "for the weak are destroyed. I will be strong and I will destroy Rikkar."

Lainie soon fell into a deep sleep, and gratefully she gave in to its healing oblivion. When she awoke, the sun was shining through the windows, but its light did nothing to brighten her mood. Metoo entered the room and silently tended to Lainie, bathing her and helping her into a fresh gown, even feeding her some hot broth.

Lainie was able to eat only a little before her stomach protested and she pushed aside the spoon. Without a word Metoo went away. Soon there was a knock at the door. At her acknowledgement, it swung open and Rikkar stood in the doorway. For a moment, surprise made her speechless as she took in his haggard face and bloodshot eyes.

"Get out," Lainie spat out. "Get out!"

"I came to talk to you," Rikkar said, moving into the room. "Metoo persuaded me there are things between us which we must clear up."

"There is no longer anything between us and never will be again. I don't wish to speak to you. Get out."

"Not until we've talked."

"What shall we talk about?" Lainie asked cynically. "Shall we talk about our time together on the *Sea Hawk* or here on the island or would you like me to tell you all about that night with Tortugas? Would you like to know how he attacked me and how I killed him?"

"I know it must have been a frightening experience and you're angry that I used you to catch him, but—"

"Angry? Angry?" Lainie's voice rose mockingly. "Your concern for me is a little late."

"I didn't think Tortugas would abuse you as he did."

"Didn't you? I remember the warning you gave me the first time we went to that island."

"That was only to frighten you so you would have second thoughts about joining them."

"Why would I have joined them?" Lainie asked.

"To give them information about me and about the shipping schedule from France to Savannah," Rikkar explained.

"Why? Why would I do that?"

"Beauty," Rikkar said, taking a step closer to the bed. "Let's not play this game anymore. Let's be truthful with each other. You have nothing to fear from me. You don't have to continue this life. Tortugas and his ring of pirates are broken up. They've been arrested. You saved my life in the tavern and I'll intervene in your behalf, so you won't be arrested until you're well, but don't continue with this lie. I know who you are."

"Why should I be arrested?" Lainie asked in amazement.

"Major Crawford told me that Lise Davy stowed away on the *Southern Moon* in France. I know it was you. I know it all now," he went on wearily. "You and your mother have been Tortugas's lovers for years and you've helped him pirate the ships that trade in these waters. Your lover has murdered hundreds of innocent people and burned and pillaged many ships, but now it's over, it's finished."

"And what do you propose to do with me, whore and murderess that I am? What fate awaits me?"

"You must be punished for your crimes," Rikkar said. "I can only ask for clemency for you."

"And what about you, Captain Rikkar?" her voice shook with rage. "What punishment will you receive for *your* crimes?" A slight smile touched the corners of Rikkar's mouth.

"And what crimes have I committed?" he asked. "Do you speak of my seducing you? Your reputation and subsequent actions make that accusation a farce." He smiled again, although his eyes remained cold and hard.

At the sight of his mocking smile, white heat exploded behind Lainie's eyes. "I shall report that you are a murderer,'' she rasped. ''I shall tell them you are a murderer twice over.''

''Whom am I supposed to have murdered?'' Rikkar asked, his eyes darkening at the accusation. ''If you mean Tortugas's men, that was self-defense.''

''Was it self-defense when you murdered the captain of the *Southern Moon*?'' she demanded.

''The captain of the *Southern Moon*—'' Rikkar gave a dismissive shrug and Lainie's rage boiled.

''Yes, the captain of the *Southern Moon*. I saw you shoot him without mercy after one of your men knocked him down. Was that in self-defense? No, Captain Rikkar, it was murder.''

''You don't understand—'' Rikkar began, his eyes amused.

''Oh, I understand all too well. You are a murderer. What were you going to do, claim one of Tortugas's men shot him? You won't get away with it. I'll see you're hanged for your vile deed.''

''It isn't what—'' Rikkar began in amazement, but Lainie rushed on with her tirade.

''Not only did you kill the captain of the *Southern Moon*, but you murdered someone else as well.'' She glared at him. ''You murdered our unborn child when you gave me to Tortugas,'' she spat out. At Rikkar's sharp intake of breath, a cold smile twisted her lips although tears flowed down her cheeks.

''My God, I didn't know,'' he whispered hoarsely.

''Would it have mattered to you if you had,'' she cried. ''Would I have had more value to you then? I think not. I was far more valuable to you as bait to catch that pig. Well, you got what you wanted. Your men said you'll get a medal. I hope it was worth the price paid. I'm glad I no longer carry your child.''

"Beauty," he said and his voice was ragged with grief. "I'm sorry." He crossed the room and gripped her shoulders.

"My name is not Beauty," Lainie cried, wrenching away from him. "Nor is my name Lise Davy. I am Elaine Marie Gautier, daughter of Captain Jean Gautier, the man you murdered."

Blackness settled over her but not before she saw the final shock on Rikkar's face or heard his anguished cry in the still air.

Chapter 10

Belle Fleur! Beautiful flower! It lived up to its name, standing on a slight incline in an otherwise flat part of the Florida landscape, the added height accenting the regal lines of the magnificent plantation house.

Eagerly Lainie raised her head from the pillows which had been placed around her to cushion her from the jolts of the carriage as it travelled over the dirt roads. She looked at the lines of her beloved home and a joyous smile lit her face. The carriage turned into the tree-lined lane that wound its way across the flatland to the main house still some distance away. Even from here, Lainie could make out the red tiled roof and the main house with its pillars and the spacious balconies running along the top story. Belle Fleur stood high and proud above the barely discernible circle of cabins, barns, stables and sheds which housed the slaves and the special work areas needed to maintain a large plantation. Huge oak trees, trailing wisps of silver Spanish moss, mingled with the ever present palm trees in shading the yards and gardens.

Lainie lay back against the pillows, exhausted by even that small exertion and turned an excited face to the man seated next to her.

"It's so good to be home again," she whispered. "I

can't believe I'm finally here and you're here with me.''
She gripped the man's hand and impulsively carried it to
her cheek, where he felt the moistness of her tears. "I
can't believe you're really alive,'' she said.

Jean Gautier tightened his hand on hers. Lainie knew he
was as thankful as she that they had found each other again
after all the misfortunes and misunderstandings. Her eyes
had hardly believed what they were seeing that day Jean
Gautier walked into the bedroom on Rikkar's island and
gathered her into his arms.

"Lainie, my child,'' he had cried in a voice rough with
emotion. "Thank God, you're alive. When I got Rikkar's
message, I could hardly believe it was true.''

He had been part of the scheme to establish Rikkar's
identity as an outlaw and so infiltrate the pirates, and
Lainie in her stubborn waywardness had gotten caught in
the middle. She had suffered for it, and although Jean
Gautier had no idea of all that had befallen his daughter,
he knew that she had undergone a terrifying experience.
No word of reprimand was uttered to her. He waited
patiently for her to gain enough strength to travel so they
could leave the island and head for Belle Fleur.

At first, Lainie had been fearful that Rikkar would try to
see her again, but he had not. After that final scene in her
bedroom, he had taken the *Sea Hawk* out to meet the
Southern Moon and guide it to the bay.

In the days that followed Jean Gautier's arrival and their
departure from the island, Lainie and her father had talked
of all that had happened and she discerned he had no
knowledge of her relationship with Rikkar, nor was he
aware that she had killed a man or that she had lost a baby.
And she decided not to tell him. It was best forgotten as if
it had never happened.

The trouble was that she couldn't forget. Even as her
body began its healing, her mind reeled under the horror of

144

her memories, and she awoke from her dreams screaming and trembling. Her recovery was slow and she knew her father was worried about her. For that reason she put on a cheery smile when he was in the room, pretending a vitality she did not feel. Only when she was alone again did she give in to the fatigue that plagued her. Slowly, however, her young body responded to Metoo's nursing and she grew better.

The day Metoo said she was well enough to travel, her father had two seamen come to her room with a stretcher between them. Lainie was carefully placed on it and covers were tucked about her before she was carried gently down the curving stairs, through the beautiful vestibule and out into the verandah were Metoo stood.

"Wait," Lainie called to her bearers. She turned her head and looked into Metoo's fierce, dark eyes.

"Thank you for your help and friendship," Lainie said softly, holding out her hand. The Indian woman took Lainie's slim hand in her own. "Good bye, my little sister," she said. "I wish for you that the pain goes away soon and you will smile again."

In her anticipation at finally seeing Belle Fleur again, Lainie put all her melancholia behind her and now, with the graceful silhouette of the plantation growing on the horizon, her eyes sparkled. For the first time since he had found his daughter, Jean Gautier observed a flush of color staining her cheeks. And for the first time, he began to feel some easing of his own anxiety. She would be all right. Suddenly, he, too, was glad to be home again.

His thoughts turned to the plantation. It had been too many months since he was last here and he was anxious to put his feet on Belle Fleur soil again. He had neglected much of his plantation business in helping to destroy the pirates, but it had been a necessary task. His own ships had been menaced by the hordes of pirates who plagued the shipping lanes. He and other influential land owners had appealed to their new government for help and they had quickly joined forces to put an end to the destruction of their ships and cargo.

Wearily Jean Gautier sighed. Too much time had been spent in defending his property, first from the Seminoles and now from the pirates. It was time to relax and enjoy the fruit of his labors and get to know his daughter. He'd missed too much in life. He was getting older and hadn't much time left. He wanted to make the most of it. He looked at the pale, beautiful young woman who rested beside him, her eyes feverishly bright as she gazed past the trees lining the drive, straining to keep Belle Fleur within her sights as if afraid it would disappear if she did not. He understood how she felt. It was good to be home.

The carriage swept around the last curve and came to a halt before the great steps and pillared portico of the plantation house. All the house servants stood on the steps, their brown faces beaming a welcome.

The stretcher was brought and Lainie was placed on it again as two husky slaves held each end. The servants strained to get a look at their young mistress.

"Lawzy, Miss Lainie's don' cum home," Bessie, the cook, exclaimed, "and she be a beauty." Her laughing comment triggered an excited welcome from the other servants as they rushed forward, bobbing their heads and smiling at the young mistress they hadn't seen in ten years.

Their happy voices and smiling faces followed her up the stairs as she was carried to her old room.

It had been changed of course. Gone was the little day bed in which she had slept as a child and in its place was a huge four-postered bed, delicately carved and painted a creamy white with gold trim. The rest of the furnishings in the room matched the bed; even the china bowl and pitcher on the delicate washstand were painted with pastel scenes of the French countryside. Lainie looked about the room as two slave women, one a girl about Lainie's age, hovered nearby, their smiling faces a little hesitant as they awaited her response.

"This is beautiful," Lainie murmured.

"I'm glad you like it," her father said. "Elizabeth helped me do it. We wanted you to feel at home here and not long too much for France."

Lainie turned to look at him with wide, dark eyes. He was afraid she would miss France. If he only knew how long she had wanted to be home.

One of the young slave girls moved forward to help her from the stretcher.

"I's May," the girl said in a shy, soft voice. "I gwine be yo'r maid."

"Hello, May," Lainie said, smiling warmly at her.

"Lainie, this is Elizabeth," her father said, indicating the other slave woman and something in his tone made her look up and study the slim, pale brown young woman who stood near her bed. A smile trembled on the woman's lips and her eyes were wide and wary. The woman was a mulatto, Lainie thought. One of her parents had been a black slave and one had not. The result of her parentage had produced a woman of incredible beauty. Her face was almost patrician in its regal lines, yet her eyes, dark and liquid, lent a quality of vulnerability that softened the haughty aloofness of her features.

"Hello, Elizabeth," Lainie said quietly.

Later, when everyone had left her room and May had helped her settle into bed for a nap, Lainie thought about the proud slave woman who was her father's housekeeper. There had been something about the way her father had introduced her that had proclaimed her special. Lainie pushed the nagging thoughts away and lay looking about the room. She sighed with contentment and her eyes drifted shut.

In the days and nights that followed, Lainie slept a great deal, trying to regain her strength. Many times she awakened screaming and crying, lashing out against some foe only she could see. Not all her dreams were nightmares. Sometimes her night visions were filled with Rikkar's face and the feel of his lips and hands on her body. The images were so devastatingly real that when she awakened her lips felt swollen from the dream kisses and her body clamored for release from the passion stirred within it. Then she would curl into a ball, drawing her knees up against her chest, and concentrate fiercely on something else. She did not want to desire a man ever again and certainly not Rikkar with his lies and betrayals. She reminded herself how much she hated him, whispering the words through stiff lips until her body stilled its clamor and she straightened herself on the bed and contrived to sleep once again. But then the tears would come, unbidden and uncontrollable.

He would never hurt her again, she vowed. She would never allow anyone to bring her such pain again.

At last the day came when the doctor took away all restrictions, and in the days that followed she delighted in poking her nose into places she hadn't seen since she was a child of ten.

One day, a steamy hot afternoon, Elizabeth invited her to cool off in the kitchen with an iced tea. Bessie and her assistants were busy dropping pieces of floured chicken into a pot of bubbling hot grease.

"Yo' shor' growed purty," Bessie said, turning to smile at her young mistress. "We nerber thought nobody grow purtier 'n yo'r mama, but yo' did."

"Thank you, Bessie," Lainie said. "I wish Mama was

here now. She was so unhappy in France. All she wanted was to come back to Belle Fleur once again.''

"Wha'z that?'' Bessie looked at her in amazement. "Chile, yo' wrong 'bout dat. Yo' mama don' neber like it here at Belle Fleur. She say we too po' and country fo' her. She go back to where people is civilized, dat what she say.''

"No, Bessie, she was very homesick for Belle Fleur. I was too. I couldn't understand why Papa had us leave.''

"Lawd, chile, he neber had yo' leave. He beg Miz Marie, don' go. Afta yo' go, he like a mad man. We 'fraid he goin' ta lose his min'. Then Miss Elizabeth co—''

"Bessie.'' Elizabeth's harsh voice cut across the cook's words. Lainie looked from Elizabeth to Bessie and back again.

For a moment the three women were frozen as in a tabloid. Bessie's face was flushed with guilt, Elizabeth's hard with anger and something more, while Lainie's showed her alarm. She felt afraid, as if she had come too near a bit of knowledge it was best not to pursue. Then Elizabeth smiled at her and crossing the room, set the chilled glass before her.

"Thank you, Elizabeth,'' Lainie said quietly, sipping the cool drink she no longer wanted. When the glass was half empty, she rose to her feet.

"I'm afraid that's all I want,'' she said apologetically. "I'm a little tired from my walk.''

"Perhaps you should lay down for a while and rest,'' Elizabeth said solicitously. "Do you need someone to help you to your room.''

"No, that won't be necessary,'' Lainie said walking to the door. "Thank you for the iced tea. Bessie, it was good to see you again.''

"I be here anytime you wan' me, Miss Lainie,'' the

cook called after her, her big face once again open and friendly.

Lainie hurried to her room. She tried not to think about the incident in the kitchen. Whatever was behind it, she didn't want to know, at least not yet.

With each day that passed now, Lainie was growing stronger physically, although her screams still rent the night as she fought her way out of old nightmares. She knew her father was worried about her and sometimes she thought of telling him of all that had befallen her while she had been Rikkar's captive, but something made her hold back. And just as she could not quite trust him enough to tell him of her ordeal, neither could she give her love as wholeheartedly as he wished. He sensed her reserve and she saw the hurt in his eyes.

He concentrated on helping to reacquaint Lainie with the workings of the plantation. Often some of his neighbors dropped by and most of the talk was about gaining statehood. The territory had just been admitted to the union the year before, but to some men that had been a mere stepping stone to their real objective.

In her childhood Lainie had dimly perceived that her father was an important figure, but she had been surprised in the weeks since her return to discover just how powerful and wealthy a man he was. She was proud of her aristocratic father and of the sway he held with other powerful men.

The things her mother had told her about the plantation were in conflict with what she saw about her. One day she asked her father about it, and he sat holding her hands tightly in his while he told of the efforts he had made over the past few years to enlarge the plantation and make it the most elegant in the territory in the hope he could persuade his wife to return.

"If only Marie had been a little more patient," he said sadly, "but when I married her in France, her family had lost all its money and she assumed she was marrying a much richer man than I was at the time. Marie was young, much younger than I and she was too lovely to want to pine away here in this half-settled territory waiting for me to make a fortune. Now I can give her the lovely, rich life she wanted, but it's too late." His voice was filled with grief and regret.

As he spoke Elizabeth silently entered the breakfast room and bent to whisper in Jean's ear. Resentment at the easy familiarity between the two made Lainie abruptly get out of her chair and leave the room.

"Lainie?" She didn't pause to answer her father.

One of Lainie's callers in the weeks that followed was Miles Wentworth, the man her father wished her to marry. As he stood before her during her father's introduction, she noticed that his eyes were on the same level as hers. His silvery blond hair and light brows were colorless against his pale skin. Even his cold blue eyes were too light to add any real warmth or color, and the detached expression in them only made him seem more aloof.

He had asked her questions about herself, those strange eyes regarding her unwaveringly as he listened to her answers. He made little or no response to her replies, not even to smile and since he spoke little of himself, it became increasingly hard to converse with him. Lainie was thankful her father was in the room to smooth over the awkward moments. As she sat back against her chair and listened to the two men discussing local business, she thought of Rikkar and his sun-darkened features alight with laughter. He seemed all the more alive and real next to the cool, aloof shadow of Miles Wentworth.

Angrily she pushed the image out of her mind and tried

to view Miles with a less critical eye. At one point, she asked him about his plantation, Wentworth Hall. Instantly his eyes grew warmer and a slight smile touched his thin lips as he spoke of his estate.

It was obvious he loved his home, and on this alone Lainie began to feel a kinship with him. His life was woven around Wentworth Hall just as hers was around Belle Fleur. As she listened to him speak of his plans for his plantation, she suddenly envisioned the two of them together, building the two plantations into a mighty empire which one day would pass on to their children. For the first time the idea of marriage to Miles Wentworth did not seem repugnant to her. It wouldn't matter that they did not love each other; there was enough love in each of them for their land and that would be the bond that would hold them together.

When Miles took his leave after that first visit, Lainie warmly bid him to come again. In the weeks that followed, he called several times. It was obvious to all that he was paying court. If there was no romance, Lainie was glad. It meant she didn't have to pretend to emotions she did not feel and never would again.

One morning as Lainie and her father sat in the bright morning room having breakfast together, as had become their custom, he surprised her with an announcement.

"We are going to have a ball," he said as if the idea had just come to him. "This old house hasn't seen any excitement in I don't know how many years, and we're going to end that now."

"Papa, how wonderful!" Lainie said, truly pleased.

"I want to introduce my beautiful daughter to the neighbors and having a ball will be a splendid way of doing that. You and Elizabeth can plan the details," he said.

Lainie did not want to work with Elizabeth on the ball. Ever since that day in the kitchen she'd had trouble warming up to the beautiful woman. She couldn't explain her feelings and felt a little guilty over them, the more so because Elizabeth went out of her way to befriend her. For some inexplicable reason, Lainie found herself avoiding the other woman as much as she could.

"What is it, my dear," you seem troubled. Lainie looked at her father's face, alive and happy as a child's and her protest died on her lips.

"Nothing," she said, smiling back at him. "Thank you for giving a ball for me."

"I'll tell Ben to tell the slaves. Our people need to have a party too. It's been a long time for all of us." He hurried from the room, humming a song under his breath.

Lainie sat at the table thinking of the ball and of the close contact she must have with Elizabeth as they prepared for it. Perhaps it would be a good thing, she decided. It would force her to face her feelings and deal with them.

Chapter 11

The next two weeks passed in a whirlwind of activity. Everyone was excited about the ball and went about their tasks happily.

The great ball room, which had been kept shut for all the years Lainie and her mother were gone, was reopened and aired. The windows were washed until they sparkled, the floors waxed and polished to such a shine they dazzled the eye. The twin crystal chandeliers were washed and the multi-faceted prisms radiated brilliant lights. When sparkled by candle light, they would be even more beautiful. Elizabeth and Lainie were pleased.

The work on the ball was helping Lainie to overcome her hostility to her father's housekeeper and she was finding that she was actually beginning to like her. Elizabeth was quick and intelligent as well as beautiful, and Lainie could see why her father had chosen her to run the house for him.

Her way with the other slaves was uncanny. None of them seemed to resent her authority over them and sprang eagerly to do her bidding. Elizabeth never seemed to set herself above the others, never asking them to do anything she was not willing to do herself. She could often be found immersed in some task another housekeeper would have assigned to one of the lesser ranking slaves. Lainie's respect for Elizabeth grew considerably.

This was to be a grand ball indeed, Lainie realized, as she stood one day watching Ben, her father's butler and personal servant, as he supervised the polishing of the huge silver platters and ornate candlestick holders. Piles of intricately wrought knives, forks and spoons lay nearby, awaiting their turn with the polishing cloth. Out in the kitchen, Bessie was producing a myriad of foods. Rich cakes, dark with molasses and loaded with fruits and pecans had been baked ahead and were aging. The best cured hams had been put aside to be baked the day of the ball.

The menu had been set and like most dinners of that time was elaborate and extensive as befit a man of Jean Gautier's means. Dinner would begin with turtle soup and would be followed with the tender meat of warm water lobsters served with melted butter. Then the succulent tender hams would be served with baked sweet potatoes. There would be baked wild turkey with a dressing of walnuts and cornmeal, as well as mounds of fried chicken. Asparagus, beans and corn would be followed by a last course of cold venison and cheese.

For dessert there would be Bessie's wonderful pastries of all kinds, pecan pies, sweet potatoe pies, fruit cakes and corn fritters smothered in syrup.

After dinner, they would all retire to the ball room and dance to an orchestra composed of several of the talented slaves on the plantation.

On the morning of the ball, Lainie had breakfast with her father.

"Is everything ready for tonight?" he asked.

"Almost everything," Lainie reassured him. "Elizabeth and I still have the bouquets to see to and things like that."

"Good," he said. "Guests will begin arriving early, you know. Do you have rooms ready for those who plan to stay overnight?"

"Yes, Papa, they're aired and ready."

"You've handled this ball with great skill, Lainie."

"Thank you, Papa," she replied, "but Elizabeth has been responsible for a good portion of the preparations."

"I know," he said, "I've already expressed my appreciation to her." He paused for a moment, looking at his lovely daughter with a measuring eye before continuing. "You and she seem to get along well." Lainie kept her eyes on her plate as she sought a careful reply.

"Yes," she said slowly. "She's an excellent slave woman." She dared not look up to meet her father's eyes for she sensed he wanted a different response from her. For a moment she felt his resistance to her answer, then he sighed and, picking up his fork, continued eating.

"Miles came by to see me this morning," he said after some time.

"Oh?" Lainie said. "Why didn't you invite him to join us for breakfast?"

"I wanted this time to speak with you alone. You do care for Miles, don't you, Lainie?" he asked, his dark eyes searching her face.

"Yes, he seems very nice," Lainie answered casually.

"I was hoping he'd made more of an impression on you than that," her father commented dryly. Lainie remained silent, her eyes once again on her plate.

"Miles has asked me for your hand in marriage."

"I see." Carefully Lainie laid down her fork and raised her eyes to meet his. Suddenly, she felt trapped. "And what did you tell him?"

"I told him it would depend on you. I don't want you to be rushed. I want you to have time to adjust to your new life here." A feeling of relief washed through her and she turned a brilliant smile upon her father.

"Do you still want me to marry Miles?" she asked.

"Yes, I do," her father replied. "Together our plantations could be the biggest in this territory. Soon we will be a state and our combined land holdings will give us a great deal of power in our new government. Miles is one of the most eligible bachelors in the territory. Your life with him will be secure and one day you will own not only Belle Fleur but Wentworth Hall as well."

She looked at her father's earnest face and noted the tired lines about his eyes and cheeks. While she had been growing stronger every day, her father seemed so tired. She thought of his words. One day she must marry and she had already made up her mind that a union with Miles would suffice. She was no longer a giddy school girl who expected love and romance in her marriage. It was better this way. And there was something more, she reminded herself. If the merging of the two estates gave Miles and her father more power, might not some of that power be hers as well?

"If you want me to marry Miles, I will," she said softly, meeting her father's eyes.

"Lainie, it would make me very happy," her father said, taking her hand in his. "Miles will ask you at the ball tonight and we can announce it then. It will be a perfect time."

"All right," Lainie agreed, "but Papa, I want it to be a long engagement. I want to have more time to be with you here at Belle Fleur."

"My dear girl," he said, his dark eyes warm with love, "I want that to. We'll announce your engagement tonight, but you can wait until you're ready to marry Miles. I still have some time left." Lainie looked at her father in puzzlement, but he had already risen from the table. Now that the question of her engagement had been settled his thoughts had turned to other things. Absently, he kissed her cheek and bade her good day.

She turned back to the breakfast table, and thought again of their conversation. If there would never be a spark of love with her new husband, neither would there be the hurt and disillusionment she had known with Rikkar.

She must forget Rikkar and the passion he had fired in her. She must block out the treacherous image of his lean saturnine features which forced its way into her mind. All that had gone before in her life was forever dead, as dead as her unborn child, and she must never forget who had brought about that death. One day perhaps, as mistress of Wentworth Hall, heir to the great Belle Fleur plantation, she would be powerful enough to repay Rikkar for his betrayal.

Shaking herself out of her reverie, Lainie set her mind to the list of things that had to be done this morning, resolving not to think about the past. The future must be her only concern.

The morning was spent on last minute preparations, and after a light lunch in her room, Lainie settled down for a nap, but her anticipation for the evening was too keen to give her any rest. Her mind ran over the preparations again, seeking to find any task left undone.

She'd finally given in to the lazy somnolence of the afternoon heat and was just starting to drowse when a thought came to her. They hadn't seen to the chilling of the wine.

She went downstairs and hurried toward the kitchen to tell Elizabeth, but she wasn't there. Lainie then went to Elizabeth's room. She paused, hearing a man's voice from within. She thought she had the wrong room and was about to turn away, when her arm brushed against the door. Silently it swung open.

Lainie stood stunned at the sight before her. Elizabeth sat on the edge of the bed, her dress about her waist, her gleaming breasts bare. Bending over her, his hands caressing, his lips moving hungrily over her face and neck was Lainie's father.

Even as Lainie watched he pulled Elizabeth up to him and kissed her deeply, his hands moving across her rich, honey brown skin to push at the dress so it fell to the floor in a heap. They were too absorbed in each other to notice Lainie in the doorway or hear her muffled gasp as she fled down the hall.

How could he? Lainie thought miserably once she was back in her room. How could he have turned away from the beauty and grace of his wife for the sordid favors of a mere slave? No wonder her mother had fled Belle Fleur those many years before.

He was like all men, Lainie thought cynically, giving free rein to his baser nature without regard for the pain and shame he brought to the women who loved him. Because of his desires for his slave, his daughter had been denied shelter in her own home! By his very action he had exiled his wife and daughter to another land and the careless charity of others. True, he had given his money freely to see to their material comforts but what of their emotional needs?

She sat on the edge of her bed, too numb to cry. No wonder Elizabeth always exhibited such serenity, such confidence in her position here. She knew just how secure she was.

And she, fool that she was, had begun to believe the loving smiles, the looks of concern her father had turned on her, when it was only to lull her into accepting his slave lover. Once again she had been misled by her need for love. Two men had won her love and each had failed her, had used her.

It was time she stopped being their victim and became a user herself, a user of men. She would begin with Miles Wentworth. Wasn't he trying to use her too? There was a difference with Miles, though. He didn't pretend to love her, and he didn't ask her to love him back. She would be like that from now on. She would ask nothing and she would give nothing. She would take everything she could and think first of herself and the rest be damned.

They would never hurt her again, she vowed, these men who swept through her life and turned her dreams into nightmares. She would never allow herself to be that vulnerable again. Now it was her turn and she would be as ruthless as they had been with her. Now they would learn the bitter lessons and she would be the teacher.

Chapter 12

Lainie spent the rest of the afternoon in her room, leaving her father and Elizabeth to greet the guests who had arrived early and would be staying overnight. She knew her father would have liked her to act as hostess to these early arrivals, and she had planned to do just that. Now, she sent word of a headache and a need for additional rest. Elizabeth was the true mistress of Belle Fleur, Lainie thought angrily, and she had no desire to supplant her in that role.

The afternoon wore on and Lainie could tell from the revived bustle of activity below that final preparations were under way. Hot water was brought for Lainie's bath and May was waiting to help her mistress with her dress. For Lainie, all the joy and anticipation had gone out of the day and she went about her toilet listlessly.

May brushed Lainie's hair into a pile of curls on top of her head, expertly weaving ribbons and pearls in and out of the ringlets. Wispy curls were left to hang down at her temples and to brush across the tender nape of her neck. Lainie added light color to her cheeks, eyes and lips. Then May helped her with her gown. It was a rich wheat color that matched her hair perfectly. The lines of the dress followed the Empire style, the low cut bodice leaving the tops of her breasts bare, barely covering the pinkness of her nipples. The sleeves were encrusted with lace, pearls and ribbons, and were draped off the shoulder leaving even more creamy skin exposed.

As if to make up for the more daringly cut bodices, the skirts were now a little fuller, but when worn with only one or two soft petticoats, still molded themselves against the figure when one moved. A shawl of matching silk was meant to be draped about the shoulders and over the bodice for those who wished it, although the ladies of Paris did not wear them. Tonight, Lainie lay aside the shawl. She chose to wear the dress as the Parisians did.

The gown was perfect for her, she decided, as she stood before the mirror smoothing on her long gloves. Lainie's graceful shoulders rose bare and beautiful above the softly gathered silk of the bodice, and the soft color cast a honey glow to her skin and hair. With her hair swept up as it was, her long graceful neck was even more apparent and she held her head high, as regal as a queen.

Lainie went slowly down the stairs, and a hush fell over the people who stood in the hall as they caught sight of her, but she was unaware of the breathtaking picture she made. The only thought in her mind was to not let her father guess how she truly felt this night.

"I'm sorry to be late, Papa," she said demurely, eyes lowered.

"It does not matter. You look very beautiful tonight, Lainie, worth the wait," Jean Gautier said.

"Thank you, Papa."

In a flurry of silken, swirling petticoats, and expensive cigar smoke mingling with equally expensive perfume, their guests swept through the doors of Belle Fleur to shake hands with its powerful, influential master and to be introduced to his daughter. Soon enough, Miles Wentworth arrived, dressed in a cutaway that only seemed to accent his short stature. A flame burned hotly behind the cold blue of his eyes as they swept over the soft silky skin of Lainie's shoulders and the curves of her breasts. Lainie shuddered against the raw lust she saw on his face. Then the mask was back in place and Miles smiled at her distantly as if barely aware of her presence.

The shock over her daring European-styled dress was apparent with each new arrival, yet Lainie felt sure tomorrow morning would dawn with many a lady in conference with her seamstress making alterations to her gowns.

Servants circulated with silver trays bearing long stemmed goblets of sherry and wine. In the background the soft strains of dinner music could be heard although dancing would not begin until later. Jean Gautier lifted two glasses of pale sherry from a tray and handed one to Lainie.

"Everything is going very well," he said, smiling at his daughter over the rim of the glass.

"Yes, it seems to be," Lainie answered without enthusiasm. She felt weary and unhappy, and the whole evening stretched ahead of her bleakly.

Another arrival at the door suddenly made her breath catch in her throat and for a moment she felt dizzy. As if in a dream, she stared at the handsome, dark-haired man who stood greeting her father. White teeth flashed against tanned skin in an all too familiar smile, and the air filled with his rich, warm laughter.

Then Rikkar turned and saw her. The smile that lit his face faded. A giant fist seemed to squeeze his heart as he stood drinking in her beauty and he had to school himself not to take her into his arms. He wanted to kiss away the bruised, hurt look in her eyes and capture her soft, full lips with his own. She'd haunted his dreams for all these weeks. Try as he would, he couldn't erase the memory of her beauty, her gentleness and her passion, especially her passion. In his arms she'd grown to be a woman of fire, and her flame ignited his soul in a way no other woman could. His nights had been long, lonely reflections of the love they'd shared and he'd cursed himself for all he'd lost.

He loved her! He had since that first moment he'd seen her lying helpless and terrified on the deck of the *Sea Hawk*, the lecherous pirates looming over her. He hadn't wanted the entanglements of loving a woman, but she'd stolen into his heart, his very being and he couldn't exorcise her.

He'd tried to believe the worst about her, to think of her as a well-trained prostitute, but his instincts had told him none of it was true. How could he have believed such innocence was calculated? How could he have thought her purity and gentleness a ruse? How could he have mistrusted the passion she gave rein to so innocently and turned it against her? How could he have betrayed both of them so badly?

He wanted to cry out all these things, yet her eyes told him she wouldn't listen, wouldn't believe anymore. She stood looking at him with the cold hostile eyes of a stranger, her face aloof and proud. She was so close, he could reach out and touch her, yet he knew she was unreachable.

He would bide his time and be patient. He would win her back. He had to. Somehow he would make her his again and he would spend a lifetime making it all up to her.

"Miss Gautier," he said softly. "You are more beautiful than I remember you." Although his tone was soft and caressing, his words acted as a catharsis, releasing her from the numbing surprise she'd felt at seeing him again.

"I have no doubt I am more beautiful now than the last time you saw me," she said scathingly. "If you'll remember, the last time you saw me, I had suffered much at the hands of Tortugas."

"Would it help any if I told you how sorry I am for your suffering? I've blamed myself time and again for all that befell you."

"And well you should," Lainie said unyieldingly. "And now, Mr. Rikkar, if you will please go. This is a private party for invited guests only."

"Lainie!" Jean Gautier was shocked. "Not only is David Rikkar the man who restored you to me, but he is an old friend as well. He's just returned from Washington, where he reported on the demise of those pirates. David has been a great force in opening the shipping lanes into the Gulf. Those islands are an important key to helping make Florida a rich and powerful state someday. Statehood is coming soon thanks to the efforts of men like David Rikkar. Please show some courtesy!"

"I'm sure I should be impressed," Lainie said, smiling sweetly, although her eyes met Rikkar's without wavering in their animosity.

"We all are," Jean Gautier said. "When I heard last week that David was stopping at St. Augustine on his voyage home, I extended my invitation to him. I'm glad you could make it, David."

David, his first name was David. She had never known him by any other name than Rikkar.

"Since you are my father's guest," she said, "I will leave you in his care and see to my other guests. If you'll excuse me."

"Lainie, I'd like to talk to you," Rikkar said quickly before she could leave. He held her elbow and she could feel the heat of his touch through her long gloves.

"I'm sorry, Mr. Rikkar, I can't think of anything you might have to say that would be of interest to me. Now if you'll excuse me."

Before her father could reprimand her again, Lainie

entered the parlor and began to circulate among the guests. After about twenty minutes, dinner was announced.

In the large, formal dining room, long tables that could seat twenty had been set up. The long sideboard and extra tables were laden with food. Gautier led his daughter to the head of one table and he sat at another while their guests found their seats. Miles was seated to Lainie's right and she smiled warmly at him, glad for his presence. Once again his blue eyes ran boldly over her low-cut gown, lingering at the shadow of cleavage. Lainie felt uncomfortable under his gaze but told herself, that he was doing no more than every other man had done this evening.

Absently she looked about the room, and her eyes were drawn unwillingly to the dark head and flashing white smile of Rikkar. He was seated halfway down her father's table, between two young women who were vying with each other for his attention.

The lamplight cast brilliant lights in Rikkar's dark hair and gave his lean, tanned face a devilish look as he smiled at one of the girls. Lainie felt a murderous urge to slap her face as she placed a hand on Rikkar's sleeve and leaned forward so he could have the full benefit of the charms displayed by her modestly cut gown. Angrily, Lainie turned back to Miles who had been saying something to her.

"I'm sorry, Miles, I'm afraid my attention wandered for a moment." She smiled at him with more warmth than she usually did, wishing that Rikkar were watching them.

"I was saying, Lainie, that I would like to have a moment alone with you sometime this evening."

"Of course, Miles, if you wish," she said demurely. "I'll meet you on the east verandah after dinner." Miles nodded his agreement.

Servants with bottles of pungent, sweet Madeira and delicate white wines imported from France moved about the table keeping glasses filled. Others started serving the sumptuous feast. Laughter rang out frequently and voices were light as the guests partook of her father's hospitality. Lainie only picked at her food, and sought to keep her eyes away from the handsome man at the other table. For the first time she felt keenly the fact that Miles was no conversationalist.

When at last everyone had had their fill, Jean Gautier gave a signal to his daughter and Lainie rose to lead the ladies from the dining room. The men would linger over their cigars and some fine old port. The ladies would go to refresh themselves and prepare for the dancing that would follow.

The giggling, relaxed ladies followed her up the stairs to the rooms that had been prepared for their use. Seeing that her guests' needs were well attended, she left the room and walked to one of the back stairs which led to the east verandah. She was halfway down the stairs before she realized someone stood in the shadows of the hall below.

"Miles?" she called softly and a tall, dark-haired figure stepped forward.

Lainie halted where she was, her hand gripping the railing.

"What are you doing here?" she demanded harshly.

"We have to talk," Rikkar said quietly.

"We have nothing to say to each other," she snapped.

"Quite the contrary." Rikkar mounted the stairs. "We have a great deal to say."

"No." Lainie started to back up the steps but a hand closed hard about her wrist. She tried to wrest her arm from his grasp, but his strong fingers held her firmly.

"Let go of me," she gasped.

"Not until we've talked."

"Mr. Rikkar, I am expecting my fiancé any moment," she grated through clenched teeth. "I advise you, sir, to let go of my arm."

"Your fiancé!" Rikkar repeated harshly.

"Yes, Miles Wentworth and I are going to be married. He has made his intentions known to my father and I have told my father that I will accept him. Now, let go of my arm." She drew herself up haughtily, a smug smile crossing her face.

"Have you told him about us, about our baby?" Rikkar asked and at her sudden silence continued. "Will he understand your pain, will he feel your sorrow?"

"I feel no pain or sorrow. I'm glad the baby is dead," Lainie flared, her eyes overly bright.

"I know that isn't true, Lainie," Rikkar said softly. "Would Miles know it? Would he be patient with you?"

"Miles is not like most men. He is not guided by fleshly concern."

"All men are," Rikkar replied, "and most women as well if the truth be known."

"I warn you, I am not a prisoner of your boat now, Mr. Rikkar. I have only to call for help and it will be forthcoming. I warn you not to press yourself upon me any further!"

A grim smile curved Rikkar's lips. Letting go of her wrist, he wound his fingers in her hair, and his lips captured hers. Lainie tried to stop the familiar flare of passion he ignited within her, but her lips turned soft and clinging beneath his.

Rikkar spoke, his voice ragged. "You're not going to marry Miles Wentworth, you belong to me."

"Never," Lainie spat out.

"Tell him about us." Once again Rikkar's fingers held her wrist in a firm grip. "Tell him about us and see how he reacts. See if he wants to marry you then."

"He will, he loves me," she cried, knowing it was untrue. "He'll protect me and take care of me and when I have his babies, he'll see that we are safe. He won't care what has happened to me in the past."

"When he turns you down, come back to me, Lainie. I'll marry you."

"Never!" she screamed at him. "I'll never marry you. I'll kill you instead, I swear I will." She glared up at him, her eyes bright with anger.

"We belong together, Lainie. I'm sorry for all your pain, but let's put it behind us and start again. We can still build a life together."

For a moment, she longed to rush into his arms, but a door opened into the hall below her and the sound of footsteps sounded across the wooden floor.

"What on earth is going on, Lainie, I heard you scream," her father said, reaching the bottom of the steps.

"Oh, Papa, I . . . I—" Lainie looked around. There was no sign of Rikkar.

"I lost my balance on the stairs," Lainie improvised. "I'm sorry if I worried you."

"I was looking for you," Jean Gautier smiled up at his beautiful daughter. "It's time to begin the ball, and that is one of the privileges of being the hostess."

The chandeliers cast their brilliant lights on the elegant company. Eyes sparkled as brightly as the jewels adorning the ladies. The excited laughter and talk stilled as Lainie and her father entered and moved to the middle of the dance floor. A hush fell over the crowd.

"Apollo," her father said, bowing slightly to the man who stood waiting expectantly. And then the light strains of dance music filled the air.

Jean Gautier danced well despite his limp but soon tired and signalled Miles to take his place. Lainie followed Miles's stiff lead, seeing that he was as uninspired a dancer as he was a conversationalist.

"I'm sorry I wasn't able to keep our rendezvous," she said when the set ended. "I was detained. Would you like to go for a walk on the verandah now?"

"By all means," Miles said and extended his arm. She placed a hand lightly on his sleeve and they moved through the milling couples.

"There you are, Miss Gautier," a man said, descending on them. "May I have this next dance?" he asked, bowing. Without waiting for an affirmative answer, he took her hand and led her away. A glance over her shoulder showed her a tight-lipped Miles being pressed into a dance with one of the girls who had been seated next to Rikkar during dinner. Lainie smiled and suddenly felt gayer than she had all evening.

As soon as one dance ended, another began, and Lainie was asked for every one. She moved gracefully, and a becoming flush settled on her cheeks; her eyes glistened with enjoyment.

A lively reel ended and Lainie smiled her thanks to her partner. Suddenly, a tall figure stood before her, and two mocking gray eyes were looking into hers.

"Mademoiselle, s'il vous plait?" he said, extending his arm to her for the next dance. She opened her mouth to refuse but the music began and Rikkar had hold of her hand and was leading her to the floor.

"I don't wish to dance with you," Lainie hissed angrily, even as she positioned herself for the first moves of the dance. "Why don't you go away and leave me alone?" she asked, looking up at him with glaring eyes. "Don't you know you're not welcome here?"

"Come now, mademoiselle," he mocked. "Is this the famous hospitality of Belle Fleur?"

"Perhaps, Monsieur," she retorted, "I am simply remembering your own hospitality and am reciprocating in kind."

"I have hurt you a great deal," Rikkar said to her in a low voice, "but you mustn't make irrational decisions about the rest of your life because of it."

"And what irrational decision, pray tell, am I about to make?"

"This marriage to Wentworth."

"I am very fortunate to be marrying Miles Wentworth," she said lightly. "There are any number of girls in this room tonight who would give anything to marry him."

"That's because it would be a real step up for most of them to become the Mistress of Wentworth Hall, but it's not to your advantage," Rikkar said firmly.

"Why not?" Lainie asked, her eyes widening at his statement.

"Belle Fleur is already unmatched in the territory, but someday when your father is no longer here and the property falls into Miles Wentworth's hands, it will be used to keep Wentworth Hall alive."

"What do you mean? Wentworth Hall is a prosperous plantation on its own."

Rikkar's gray eyes were unyielding as he looked at her. "Wentworth Hall is over-extended now, although the news is not generally known yet. It soon will be. Miles is fanatical about his family home. He'll do anything to keep it going, even—"

"Even marry the neighbor's ugly daughter?" Lainie snapped. "Perhaps Miles wants to marry me because he loves me. Is that too difficult for you to understand?"

"You don't really believe Miles loves you. He is incapable of such an emotion."

"Like you, Mr. Rikkar?" Lainie asked quickly.

"You taught me what that emotion is, Beauty," he said softly and Lainie drew in her breath, fighting the feelings washing over her. Her body remembered too many things her mind was trying so hard to forget.

"Don't let your hatred for me blind you to Miles and his real motives." Lainie said nothing and Rikkar went on, "If you are so misled by him in this, perhaps you misunderstand him in other ways as well. Like how he would react if you told him what has happened to you.''

Absently, Lainie moved through the steps of the dance, her mind in turmoil. She knew that if she were to marry Miles, she must tell him about her adventures aboard the pirate ship and on Rikkar's island. She would have to tell him about Tortugas and about the baby she had lost. It was the only fair thing to do.

The music stopped and all around her couples were smiling at each other. Laughter and talk filled the air, but Lainie stood staring up into Rikkar's eyes, the expression on her face troubled. Then Miles was at her side, his cold blue eyes even colder as they looked at Rikkar. Possessively he took Lainie's arm.

"If you'll excuse us," he said, "Lainie has promised me this next dance." His tone was meant to antagonize, but Rikkar refused to rise to the bait, his eyes riveted on the confused and hurt girl standing before him.

"Come with me, Lainie," Miles commanded and his hand tightened on her arm. Rikkar's lips were a grim line and the gray of his eyes, which had been soft and full of concern for Lainie, now flashed like steel. Lainie glanced at him. It was the same fierce look he had worn when he gave her to Tortugas. Blindly she turned to Miles.

Chapter 13

The night air was like a warm caress on Lainie's skin and the golden disc of the moon shed its bright light over everything, lending an air of mystery and beauty to the garden. Miles led her along the paths of the garden where roses, gardenias and bougainvillea filled the air with their exotic perfumes.

It was a night made for romance, Lainie thought. The man walking beside her was about to propose to her, and she should be caught up in the magic of the moment—but she felt nothing. The thought crossed her mind that it should have been Rikkar walking beside her.

"You seem very far away tonight," Miles said, breaking through her tumultuous thoughts. "Did David Rikkar give you cause for alarm?"

"No, no, it is nothing," Lainie said hastily, sitting on one of the white marble benches placed about the garden. In the distance she could see couples strolling about, but in this isolated corner, she and Miles were afforded some privacy.

Miles sat beside her, and she sensed a hesitancy in him. She smiled, wanting to put him at ease, unaware of the lovely picture she made in the moonlight. Her blonde hair was turned to finely spun gold and her small face seemed even more delicate with the shadows cast on it. Her bare shoulders and full breasts rose from the shimmery gold of her dress.

"I've spoken to your father," Miles began.

"Yes, he told me," Lainie said.

"Then you know that I wish to offer marriage to you." Lainie had steeled herself not to expect a passionate declaration of love, but surely there could be some feeling, not this cold blooded discussion.

"Yes, he told me that as well," she murmured.

"Your father indicated you were willing for this union between the two of us," Miles said, and Lainie wasn't certain if they were talking of a business merger or a coming marriage.

"I don't know what to say," she stalled, suddenly feeling trapped.

"Am I to take it that you do not agree to our marriage?" Miles asked stiffly.

"No, no, that isn't it," she hastened to assure him and he relaxed visibly. "It's just that you seem so sure you want to marry me when you've known me for such a short time. Do you wonder about the kind of person I am, whether I throw temper tantrums or get into a sulk over little things, or . . . or"—her babbling died away.

"No doubt we will adjust to each other," Miles said and as Lainie sat silent and unhappy, he felt the inadequacies of his words. She was, after all, a woman, he reminded himself, and they expected to be flattered and wooed. "I had spoken to your father about this union long before you came to the territory," he said slowly. "When you finally arrived and I saw how beautiful my future bride was, I was pleased. Beauty and wit are always appreciated. You'll be a fitting mistress for Wentworth Hall."

When she still remained silent, he rushed on. "I've tried

to be patient, to give you time to recover your health, but I thought the ball tonight would be a perfect time to announce our engagement. We can be very happy together. You will be the mistress of the most outstanding plantation in the South."

"I already am," she said spiritedly. She was annoyed with Miles and his stiff-necked arrogance. He need not know that her place had been usurped by her father's mulatto housekeeper. She would not go to Wentworth Hall as a beggar. Miles saw his error and hastened to soothe her.

"It's true that Belle Fleur is equal to Wentworth Hall, but someday Wentworth Hall will far surpass her. With Belle Fleur behind her, Wentworth Hall will be the most powerful plantation in the territory and you'll be *her* mistress."

Lainie listened to his words and Rikkar's warning came back to haunt her. Her thoughts were jumbled and confused, and pressing through them all was the knowledge that she had to tell Miles about herself.

"Miles," she said, "has my father told you anything about my illness?"

"Only that you had contracted a fever aboard ship and needed several weeks to recuperate."

"That is partly true," she said, "and if we are to begin a life together, I must tell you the rest, the part that my father does not know."

"I'm listening," Miles said, drawing back slightly.

Taking a deep breath, Lainie told him everything. When she finished, he said nothing for several minutes.

"Miles," Lainie said uncertainly when the silence began to make her nervous.

"You were very foolish to steal aboard your father's ship like that. Your own impulsive action placed you in that situation." Miles's voice was accusing.

"Yes, I suppose that's true, but I didn't know. I didn't think it would turn out as it did."

"You didn't know?" Miles's voice raised incredulously. "You've acted a fool in every way," he said scathingly.

"I know I have," Lainie said, "and I've learned a lesson from all this. Now I just want to put it all behind me and go on with my life. I want to pretend it never happened."

"But it did happen!" Miles exclaimed, turning on her. "You've killed a man and you've conceived a child. You've ruined everything with your foolishness."

"But we can go on with our plans to merge Belle Fleur and Wen—"

"Wentworth Hall has been graced by only the greatest of ladies. There has never been a breath of scandal about them," Miles said almost to himself.

"I see. And I don't qualify," Lainie said stiffly, rising from the bench and backing away from him.

"I don't know what to say to you, Lainie," Miles said, looking at her, and she noted the familiar use of her name. "I can't bring such dishonor on my mother's memory by bringing you to Wentworth Hall as its mistress."

Lainie stared hard at him. His idealized memories of his mother would have been an exacting measure for her to live up to. She shuddered to think what he would have been like if they had married first and then he had found out about Rikkar and the pirates. With a sudden clarity of vision she realized that he would have made her life a hell. Proudly raising her chin, she turned from him, but before she could walk away, he rose and blocked her way.

"There is another way," he said, grasping her arm tightly. "Although there will be no marriage, we can still see each other." His normally cold, aloof voice was almost comical in its attempt to sound seductive and persuasive, and his hand on her arm slid upward toward her bare shoulder, causing her to shiver with repugnancy.

"If you'll excuse me—" she began furiously, but Miles would not let her go.

"You are no longer an innocent and cannot expect to be treated as such," Miles continued in his oily voice. "What man would want to marry a woman with your history, but you needn't be lonely." His hand brushed the smooth skin of her shoulder and moved toward the curve of her breasts.

Lainie tried to jerk away, but he held her fast. Rage gave her the strength to push him over the bench where they had been sitting. He landed among the roses, thorns scratching his hands as he sought to catch himself and cushion his fall.

"You are a truly despicable man," Lainie snapped, glaring down at him. "Don't ever come near me again." She stalked away, leaving Miles sitting in the dirt of the flower bed.

"You'll be sorry for this," Miles called after her, his voice shaking with fury and injured dignity.

Lainie hurried up the steps to the verandah and into the ballroom. In her anger she did not notice the man in the shadows of the verandah who had observed all.

Lainie joined the gaiety of the ball with a vengeance, dancing every dance, flirting outrageously with her partners. Gradually she became aware of a change in the air. Her partners pressed her a little closer than they should and she glimpsed malicious eyes peering over fans spread wide to hide whispered comments.

Something was going around the room, and as she watched surreptitiously, she saw that wherever Miles stopped to talk with a group of people there were gasps of shock followed by avid questions and stifled giggles. Obviously he was taking malicious satisfaction in spreading tales of her misadventures.

Declining the offer of a persistent escort, Lainie excused herself and went outside, welcoming the cool breeze. She tried hard not to feel hurt or dismay over the vicious gossip that was circulating in the room behind her, but she knew she would be ostracized for the rest of her days. Tears of frustration welled in her eyes. Suddenly, a snow white handkerchief was thrust into her hands and she turned to see Rikkar standing beside her.

"Isn't it about time we had your father announce our engagement?" he asked quietly. Startled, Lainie raised her eyes to his shadowed face.

"Never!"

"That's all very admirable," Rikkar's voice held an amused tone, "but the people of this town are not concerned with how bravely one can hold up one's head in times of adversity. They are concerned with their concepts of the virtuous woman. You, my dear, have flaunted their fine ideals and they will make you pay."

"Yes, they will," Lainie said, "but marriage to you won't change any of it."

"It will help."

"I can't marry you. I hate you with all my heart and soul," Lainie cried.

"Hate me if you must," Rikkar said softly, "but don't deny my help. You will only hurt yourself and your father."

"My father!" Lainie's scorn was evident in her voice.

"He's very proud of you, Lainie. He is happy to have you back with him and he wants above all else for you to be accepted here. As my future wife much of the gossip and speculation about you will end, otherwise, you're in for a rough time."

"You must be very proud of your handiwork," Lainie hissed at him. "You've brought me to this impasse. May your soul rot in hell!"

"It probably will," Rikkar said cheerfully. "In the

meantime, we have now to think about. What is your answer? Shall we go tell your father that we wish our engagement announced? It will give the gossips something else to buzz about.''

"All right," Lainie said suddenly, "and after all this fuss has died down, I will break the engagement."

Rikkar smiled at her enigmatically, then led her back to the ballroom. Together, they sought out Lainie's father. No one spoke to them as they wove their way among the clusters of people.

"David!" Her father came forward when he spied them approaching. "Are you enjoying the ball? I see the two of you have made peace," he said looking at them fondly.

"Jean, my old friend," Rikkar said, placing a hand on Lainie's father's shoulder. "I have a great favor to ask of you and I hope you will meet my request with as much joy as I feel."

Gautier stared at him with puzzled eyes.

"I wish to ask for your daughter's hand in marriage," Rikkar said in a low, steady voice.

"I had no idea!" Gautier exclaimed, his face registering his shock at the turn of events.

"An attachment formed between us during Lainie's captivity," Rikkar said. "When we saw each other again this evening we realized that we loved each other. She's tried to ignore her feelings for me, even to deny they exist, but she can't." Outraged at his words Lainie sought to pull her hand free, but Rikkar held fast, hiding her movement by bringing her slim hand up to his mouth.

"She wants very much to please you by marrying Miles as you wish, but her heart is not in it. She loves me too much," Rikkar continued.

"Lainie, is this true?" Jean Gautier asked his daughter. "Is it David Rikkar you love?"

"Yes, Papa," Lainie said and lowered her lashes so he wouldn't see the flare of anger in her eyes.

"What of Miles?" Jean asked.

"Miles knows about Rikkar," Lainie said tersely and her father accepted the explanation without question.

"But this is wonderful," her father cried. Lainie raised astonished eyes to his beaming face. "Oh, I'll have to speak to Miles to express my sorrow that he has lost out, but I am most happy at this turn of events."

He shook hands with Rikkar, then hugged him and kissed him on each cheek in the French fashion. His eyes gleamed with pride and happiness as he looked at the young man, then he turned to his daughter.

"My darling child. I am so happy to know you are marrying someone you truly love." He hugged her briefly. Lainie was amazed that he seemed not to mind that Belle Fleur and Wentworth Hall would not be joined.

"Come, come, we'll announce it now," he insisted, not giving Lainie or Rikkar a chance to say a word. "I want to share my happiness with all my friends." He urged them toward the ballroom. Lainie and Rikkar followed behind as he walked to the center of the dance floor where he held up a hand to signal the orchestra to silence. At his instructions, servants moved quickly among the guests with glasses of champagne.

"My dear friends," Jean Gautier said. "I ask you now to share this moment of great joy in my life. My daughter, who has lived in France for many years and has only recently come home, has informed me that she wishes to leave again, this time to marry a man whom I have come to love as a son, David Rikkar." There were murmurs among the guests.

"David and Lainie met when the ship she had taken to America was captured by pirates," her father continued. "David rescued her and they fell in love. David has come from his plantation near Fort Brooks to ask for Lainie's hand in marriage and I have given my consent. I ask you all to drink a toast to the happy future of my daughter and her husband-to-be.''

Jean Gautier lifted his glass in a toast and all his guests did the same, masking their surprise. Lainie saw Miles leave the ballroom, his face ugly with anger. Other guests were noting his retreat as well, and their titters followed him.

Rikkar and Lainie smiled at their guests as exclamations of good wishes filled the air around them. With a teasing light in his eyes, Rikkar stepped forward and clasping Lainie about the waist, pulled her against his chest.

"Oh no you don't," Lainie hissed under her breath, but Rikkar only laughed.

"You mustn't struggle," he murmured against her mouth. "How will it look to others?" His lips settled on hers in a kiss that took her breath away. Lainie fought down the desire to push him away and slap his laughing, taunting face. She must endure this for the moment she told herself, but in a few weeks, she could end this farce. When at last Rikkar let her go, angry color stained her face.

"Very good," Rikkar observed dryly, "you already look like the innocent blushing bride." He stepped back so the others could observe her flushed, embarrassed face. As the men cheered and the women laughed, she lowered her eyes deliberately playing the part. When some of the tumult died down, Rikkar stepped forward.

"Ladies and gentlemen," he said, "I, too, wish to propose a toast to my bride-to-be, a woman of courage and exemplary virtue. I could not help but admire her bravery and ladylike demeanor at all times during her narrow escape with the pirates. If it had not been for Miss Gautier, we would not have been able to capture the most dangerous pirate of them all.'' Turning to Lainie he raised his glass.

"I raise my glass to Miss Gautier,'' he continued. "She is a shining example of the genteel and beautiful ladies who have made our Southern heritage so proud.'' His toast seemed to include every lady there and his words stirred their hearts. He knows just what to say, Lainie thought, as she listened to the men cheer before drinking a toast to their ladies. Again Rikkar signalled for their attention.

"As you all know, planting time draws near and I must leave soon for my own plantation. I have stayed away overlong as it is. Therefore, I ask Jean Gautier for his permission to have our wedding very soon, within two weeks, so that I may carry my new bride home with me.'' Ignoring Lainie's outraged gasp, Rikkar turned to her father questioningly.

"Permission given,'' her father declared grandly, caught up in the excitement of the moment. He seemed not to remember the conversation he'd had with Lainie just that morning at breakfast. Had he forgotten about the Wentworth land or had it not been as important to him as she'd imagined? Was Rikkar a more powerful man than Miles? Was that why her father wasn't objecting? Was she once again the pawn, being played by two ruthless men who cared more about their own gains than they did about her? Anger tightened the corner of Lainie's mouth at the thought.

"It is done,'' Rikkar declared. "In two weeks time, you are all invited back here for our wedding, and now I wish to dance with my beautiful bride-to-be.'' He signalled the orchestra and they picked up their instruments. As the lilting strains of music filled the air, Rikkar swept Lainie out across the floor.

Others joined the newly engaged couple on the floor and soon the ballroom was once again filled. Lainie's eyes spit fire as she glared at Rikkar.

"You tricked me," she ground out between bared teeth.

"Smile, sweetheart. You don't want people to think we're having out first quarrel."

"I don't care what people think," she snapped.

"Ah, but you do, Lainie," Rikkar reminded her mercilessly. "That is why you agreed to have our engagement announced this evening, or am I wrong? Perhaps there was some other reason you wanted to be engaged to me?" His lazy glance swept over her face and low-cut bodice suggestively.

"I find you totally despicable," Lainie hissed and Rikkar threw back his head and laughed, the rich sound carrying around the room, so that others turned their heads to look at them and smile.

"I find you totally adorable," he said and lowered his head to brush his lips across her cheeks and hair. Inside, Lainie seethed although she smiled shyly as if enjoying his attentions.

When the music ended, she fanned herself with the ivory fan hanging from her wrist and exclaimed, "my, it's hot in here for so early in the spring. Would you be so kind as to get me a glass of punch?" she smiled sweetly at Rikkar for the benefit of those near them.

"Certainly, my dear." Rikkar gave her a short bow and strode away. Lainie took advantage of his leavetaking to escape out onto the porch.

Wanting only to be alone and sort out her feelings, Lainie made her way to her father's study at the back of the house. She slipped inside the dimly lit room and stood revelling in the peace.

"So, he's going to marry you after all," a voice sounded from the deep recesses of one of the wing-back chairs and Lainie whirled to confront Miles Wentworth. "He's going to make an honest woman of you."

"I've always been an honest woman," she snapped, "which is more than I can say for you, you hypocrite."

"Don't call me names, you little slut." Miles rose to his feet. "Remember, I know you now for what you are."

"And I know you for what you are," Lainie said, "a little man who has no compassion for anyone. A man so filled with spite that he would spread gossip and rumor to deliberately injure someone. You disgust me."

"Be careful what you say, Madame, for someday you may need me. When Rikkar is tired of you and throws you out, my offer still stands. I'm influential in this territory, almost as influential as your father. I'll set you up in your own house and protect you."

"Oh, you will, will you?" Lainie advanced toward him, her eyes narrowed to cat-like slits. "And who will protect me from the likes of you? Tonight you tried to destroy me. Well, I'm going to destroy you. You'll rue the day you ever met me."

Miles looked at her lovely face, alive with anger and determination, and felt a great regret at the loss of her as his wife. It would have been interesting to see how long it took to break that spirit. He ran his tongue over pale, thin lips as he contemplated the spectacle of the proud young woman before him, nude and broken beneath his lash, but now it was not to be.

"My mother would have turned in her grave if she had known I even considered a whore such as you as mistress of Wentworth Hall," he said as a parting shot, then left the study, slamming the door behind him.

The hatred Lainie felt for him was like a living, breathing force. Here was one more betrayal, one more insult she must endure and all because of Rikkar and what he'd done to her. She took several deep breaths, forcing herself to relax, willing the stiffness to leave her features. Then she returned to the ball. Rikkar went to her immediately.

"Are you all right?" he asked, his eyes concerned.

"I'm just very tired, it's been a long evening," she said wearily.

"It will soon end," he comforted her. "Your father is looking for you to say good-bye to his guests. Come along and I'll stand with you."

When at last the hall was empty and the servants moved about cleaning up the debris left from the party, Rikkar took Lainie's hand and led her back into the empty ballroom. He held one of the empty chairs for her and brought her a glass of champagne.

"I think it's time we talk," he said as he seated himself beside her.

"You helped me out of a tight spot," Lainie said tiredly, "but then I wouldn't have been in that situation if you had acted like a gentleman in the first place."

"That's all behind us now. Please, let's put it out of our minds and begin anew," he implored her.

"That's easy for you to say," she retorted bitterly. "You haven't suffered as I have."

"I know, but if I could go back and endure it all for you, I would. Lainie, you've survived it, don't let it make you blind to the happiness we can still have. I'm a wealthy man, I have a profitable plantation south of here, it's a good place to raise children and make a good, rich life for ourselves. I offer all of it to you."

"It's not enough! You can't buy away what you've done to me."

"I know that, but I want to help undo some of the unhappiness I've caused you any way I can."

Lainie said nothing. He hadn't mentioned love, she thought, but she no longer wanted it, did she? Why not take all the material wealth he offered her? Then she would have enough power that no man would ever hold sway over her again. Why not make him pay for her pain? She had earned what he offered.

"I will marry you," Lainie finally said, "on two conditions. One is that you sign a paper giving me full access to all your material wealth."

"I will attend to it tomorrow," Rikkar said readily.

"And second is that our marriage will be in name only. We will not consummate it."

"In name only?" Rikkar stared into her eyes. "Isn't it a little late for that?"

"Those are my terms," she said stiffly.

"Is that what you really want?" he asked softly and she was forced to turn her gaze from his.

"That is the way it must be," she stated unequivocally.

"All right, Lainie, I will agree to this and only this," he said, his eyes dark with determination. "I will not make love to you unless you want me to."

"It is the same thing," Lainie said quickly, "for I shall never want you, ever."

"We are agreed, then," Rikkar said. "Tomorrow, I will see to the paper that will give you free access to my accounts and free rein at Greenwood."

"Greenwood?"

"That's my plantation, our plantation, our home and the home of our children."

"There will never be any children between us. We will be married for the rest of our lives, but you will never possess me. I have no love for you and no desire for you."

With a swirl of silken skirts, she hurried out of the room, across the now empty hall and up the stairs. At the curve of the stairs, she paused for a moment and looked down into the magnificent hall. Rikkar stood in the center of the rich, wooden floor, his head cocked thoughtfully as he looked up at her. For a moment, there was a special communication between them, reaching across space and time. A pact was made between them, a pact that offered no quarter, a pact of war between a man and a woman.

One of them would emerge the final victor from their struggle together. Slowly, Lainie turned and ascended the remaining stairs. He was a proud and ruthless man, she knew, but she would match his ruthlessness with the same brand of steel, for she planned to win and in the winning she would destroy her opponent. For Lainie, it would be a fight to the death.

Chapter 14

The days raced by, in a blur of preparation for the wedding, but Lainie remained indifferent through it all. She had seen Rikkar only twice since the night of the ball, when he had come to see her father. Once he had been persuaded to stay for supper and Lainie found him an upsetting presence seated across from her. As soon as the meal was finished, Lainie excused herself and rose to leave the room.

"Lainie, you can't just go upstairs like this and leave David down here with my staid company." Her father's protest halted her flight up the stairs.

"I'm sorry Papa. The days are so busy now and I am very tired. I'm sure David understands."

"Of course, I understand," he said smoothly, rising to follow her. "By all means get your rest, dearest. I want you to be well the day of our wedding."

His eyes held a double meaning as he lowered his head to brush a light kiss across her lips. Lainie's first impulse was to back away, but her father stood in the hall, watching them. She steeled herself and was rewarded by Rikkar's laughter as he pulled her closer.

"Well done," he whispered, "you're behaving just like

a skittish bride anticipating her wedding night. Only I know it's an act.''

"You're despicable," Lainie rasped back at him.

"Don't feel bad, my darling," Rikkar raised his voice. "I know you're counting the hours just as I am. Good night."

A few days before the wedding a note arrived for Lainie and was delivered to her as she sat in the breakfast room with her father.

"I've been invited to tea by that dreadful Mrs. Southfield," she said, referring to a large, very wealthy gossip. "I really can't spare the time. Do you suppose she would understand if I just sent my apologies?"

"I wouldn't, my dear," her father said. "I believe the ladies have a special tea for a bride-to-be, and they all bring a gift of some sort. You really ought to go."

"I suppose so," Lainie sighed, putting the invitation aside. "I'll send back my acceptance right after breakfast."

"There is something I want to talk to you about, Lainie," her father continued. "David and I have to make a quick trip to Savannah. I wouldn't go right now, but there are some questions about an old property law that's flared up. Belle Fleur isn't in any danger, but several plantations were when the law was first passed and they might be again. We're going to see a senator who may be able to help us. There is one problem, however. I have to sell off four of the slaves.

"But why, Papa?" she exclaimed.

"Sometimes circumstances dictate that we do things we wouldn't normally do. Please don't worry yourself about it. I need to reduce some of my holdings anyway. The thing I want to tell you is this. I have made out a letter which gives you the power to sell the slaves for me. The buyer is scheduled to come sometime in the next few days. I'm sorry to leave you such a task, but all that is really required is your signature on the bill of sale. Do you mind doing this for me?"

"Of course not, Papa," Lainie answered him dutifully.

"Thank you, my dear. And rest assured David and I will be back in plenty of time for the wedding." He turned toward the window as the sound of a galloping horse reached them.

"That must be David now," he said, and headed for the front drive, Lainie following close behind.

"Good morning," Rikkar said, his eyes unswerving as they gazed into Lainie's. "I'm sure your father has reassured you that we will be back in plenty of time for the wedding."

"Yes, he has," Lainie said.

"Good, I wouldn't want my bride to worry about being left at the alter."

"I assure you, that wouldn't be a worry to me." The flare of temper between them was broken by the whinny of her father's horse. The horse reared back his head, protesting against the pull of the reins in her father's hands. Even as they watched, the horse jerked backwards, bucking and kicking. Quickly Rikkar moved across the space and grabbed the bridle, pulling the horse's head down with a strong arm, while his other hand stroked its quivering neck. In a short time the horse was gentled, and Rikkar turned to Jean Gautier who had moved to one side of the drive.

Now that her attention was no longer focused on the lunging animal, Lainie noticed her father's pallor and his quick, shallow breathing. She felt some surprise, for she knew her father wasn't afraid of horses and the horse's wild rebellion hadn't been that menacing.

"Are you sure you're up to this trip, sir?" Rikkar asked.

"I have to be, David. Too many people are depending on me. We must have this issue settled once and for all."

"But not at the risk to your health. We need men like you too badly," Rikkar protested. Gautier shook his head.

"Help me to my horse, David. I'll be all right."

"Papa?" Lainie moved forward, her eyebrows drawn together in concern and puzzlement. Was her father ill? She longed to throw her arms about him and end the estrangement that had existed between them since the ball. But Elizabeth approached and pressed a bundle into his hands.

"Take care of yourself," she said. Gautier's eyes filled with such a light of joy and tenderness that Lainie was suffused with jealousy. He had never looked at her with such feeling, she thought.

She looked away and her stormy gaze met the cynical glance of Rikkar's knowing eyes. She raised her chin and with a whirl of skirts ran back to the porch. She would not stand out in the dust of the drive, competing with a slave for the attention of her father, she vowed angrily. But once she had attained the cool recesses of the porch, she lingered to watch the two figures on horseback ride away.

"Elizabeth," Lainie called impulsively as the slave was about to enter the house. With a questioning smile on her intelligent face, the woman waited for Lainie to go on.

"How long have you been a housekeeper here in my father's house?" she asked.

"Master Jean me brought into the house about ten years ago," Elizabeth replied. "I worked as a serving girl first and helped the cook. When he knew your Mama was never coming back to Belle Fleur, he made me his housekeeper."

"I see," Lainie said, "and that must have required you

to perform very special tasks.'' The smile on Elizabeth's face faded as she searched Lainie's face.

"Yes, it did," Elizabeth said, "and I always tried to do the best I could. Master Jean has been very kind to me.''

"I'm sure he has," Lainie answered. Elizabeth's eyes flickered with suppressed emotion.

"If you'll excuse me, I'll go back to my duties," she said and disappeared into the house.

Two days later, Lainie had a carriage hitched up and was driven to Millicent Southfield's plantation for the tea party. With a beaming face, Millicent Southfield ushered Lainie to a place of honor in the stately parlor. Lainie settled herself gracefully and turned a candid, friendly smile upon the ladies who tried not to be too obvious as they studied her.

After the tea, the ladies settled back comfortably in their chairs, while servants brought out many gaily wrapped presents. Lainie looked about the room, her smile conveying her delight and gratitude. She unwrapped her gifts while the ladies continued to talk.

"My dear, I can't tell you how surprised we were when your father announced your engagement to David Rikkar. We had heard rumors that Miles Wentworth had been courting you and your father had indicated even before he went to France to fetch you that he planned for you to marry Miles," one of the women said.

"Yes, that's true," Lainie replied with a deep sigh, "and I would have done so just to please my dear father, but then I met David Rikkar and I knew I could never love any other man.''

"That's understandable," one young woman said. "He's quite the most handsome man I've ever seen. Miles Wentworth is so staid and stuffy.''

"Staid and stuffy, nonsense," her mother scolded. "He's

one of the most eligible bachelors around and you'd do well to remember that young lady." Her daughter lowered her head meekly.

"He does seem to be desirable husband material at first glance," Lainie said meaningfully.

"Why, my dear, what is wrong with Mr. Wentworth?" Millicent Southfield pounced.

"It isn't so much what's wrong with Miles as with his—" Lainie paused and let her eyes sweep around the circle of attentive women. "I really shouldn't be so uncharitable as to say anything about the poor woman. She can't help what her ancestors were."

"Do you mean his mother?" Millicent asked. "She claimed to come from the Beaufords of Georgia. I remember how she used to tell me that her family was appalled that she had married beneath her when she married Matthew Wentworth. What was wrong with her?"

"I'm not quite sure what my father meant, but he said he heard that her family had been touched by a tar brush or something like that. I'm not sure if I have it right or what it means."

"Why, you would never have guessed," Millicent gasped.

"Well, I guessed as much," one woman sniffed. "You had only to look at all that black, curly hair and you knew she wasn't all she claimed to be."

A short while later, Lainie rose from her seat. "I want to thank you for your kindness. I'll treasure each gift and think of you all every time I use them."

The ladies stopped their buzzing long enough to bid Lainie good-bye and to reassure her that they would be at her wedding two days later. Alone in her carriage, Lainie collapsed against the cushions with a chuckle of satisfaction.

Chapter 15

There were strange horses tied to the post in the side yard when Lainie arrived home. "Well now, lookee who's here," a bearded man drawled. "The scenery sure is pretty in these here parts." He stepped in front of Lainie, leaning so close that she could smell the unpleasant odor of his whiskey-soured breath.

"We've come to see Mr. Gautier on a business transaction. Wilson's the name. Jackson's my partner."

"My father had to be away, but he asked me to represent him in this matter. Apparently all business has been concluded, I have only to collect the money and sign the bill of sale and you are to collect the slaves."

"So, you're here all by yourself?"

"There are the servants," Lainie said quickly. "If you'll excuse me, I'll get the bill of sale for you."

She hurried to her father's study, and crossed to the large walnut desk. As she opened the drawer, the door opened and the two men entered.

"We just thought we'd save you a few steps," Wilson said, his eyes roaming about the office.

"That was thoughtful of you," Lainie said stiffly, "but we'll go outside so you can view the slaves you want to buy."

"There's no hurry, is there?" Jackson said softly, his voice low in her ear as he moved forward and brushed a rough hand along her cheek.

"I beg your pardon," she said, glaring into his eyes. "I'm sure my father and the other gentlemen in this area will be interested to hear how you conduct your business in their absence," she snapped. "Please allow me to pass!"

Outside, four male field hands were brought forward.

"Well, this is a disappointment," Wilson said. "Your father promised me prime stock."

"If that is what my father promised you, then I am sure that is what you are getting," Lainie said.

"Why, no Ma'am," Jackson said. "You see, the whites in this here man's eyes, they's yellow. That means he's been real sick and like as not he ain't goin' to recover. Also, your daddy promised a female."

"Mr. Jenkins," Lainie said, turning to the overseer. "Has this man been sick?"

"No Ma'm. This here's Clay, Ma'm, he's one of our very best field hands."

"You can see, sir, my father has offered you his finest workers, but since you seem unhappy with this man, I'll will replace him with another. Clay, you may go back to work," Lainie dismissed the man as he bobbed his head in thanks and hurried away. Wilson sputtered his annoyance. They had just lost a prime field hand.

"Don't worry, we'll find a replacement for you," Lainie said. "Fetch another man," she ordered Jenkins.

"I don't know, Ma'm. Your daddy had those men picked out to sell and I'm not sure who else I should get without his say-so."

Lainie turned away in exasperation. She wasn't sure what to do. She would just have to sell the three slaves who remained and explain to her father.

As Lainie again faced the men, she caught a glimpse of Elizabeth. There was anger in the woman's eyes, an anger unfairly directed at Lainie. But she was only carrying out her father's orders. What right had this mulatto woman to judge her?

"Your daddy promised us a female," Jackson reminded her, and his eyes were focused on Elizabeth.

"I'll take this little lady right here," he said, grasping her arm, "and we'll call it an even swap for that buck."

"I wouldn't get rid of that slave, Ma'm," Jenkins shuffled forward uncertainly. "Your pa sets great store by her."

"I'm sure he sets great store by all his people, but the deal has been made," Lainie said, and her tone stopped any further opposition.

"I don't want no uppity female on my hands," Wilson whined, but Jackson was there, his eyes never once leaving the mulatto slave.

"She'll fetch a high price in New Orleans, Wilson," he said. "You know how them people are always looking for someone different."

"Yeah, but they like 'em younger."

"They'd take her, she's special," Jackson argued. "Just look at that light skin and them eyes." Jackson ran his hand up the mulatto's arm, laughing when she shivered against his touch. "And look at her respond." Jackson's laughter made Lainie sick at heart for what she was doing. She was about to tell them she had changed her mind, but Elizabeth cast her such a look of contempt that Lainie flushed angrily and held her tongue.

"All right, we'll take the woman in the man's place," Wilson said, "but we won't pay as much for her as we would have if she had been a man."

"We won't haggle about the price. As you pointed out earlier, my father had promised one female, the price was set and you agreed to it. We will make no more changes,'' Lainie snapped.

Wilson's cold, deadly eyes studied her for a moment, then he shrugged and counted out the coins.

"Thank you," Lainie said. "I believe that concludes our business. I'll sign the bill of sale and you can be on your way."

As Elizabeth approached the men's wagon, she turned and stared at Lainie. There was no pleading in her eyes, just a dull understanding and acceptance of what was happening to her. Her dark eyes looked into Lainie's and they held a deep sadness that Lainie had never seen before.

"Tell him that the name will be Jean, as he wishes," Elizabeth said to Lainie as she stepped up to the wagon. And then Wilson, Jackson and the slaves left.

The servants were quiet and sullen as they went about their evening chores. Lainie had difficulty eating any supper and retired early to her room. She lay in the darkness and thought of the day's events. Guilt swept over her. In one weak moment, she'd allowed Jackson to take Elizabeth. What could she do now to get her back? It was too late. How would she ever break the news to her father?

The nickering of a horse woke her from a fitful sleep. Rikkar and her father must be back. She might as well go down and tell him about Elizabeth, she decided as she threw aside the covers.

The dim light of her candle barely lit her way down the stairs, but her steps were firm and sure on the woven carpet. At her father's study door she paused for a moment, her hand raised to knock, but there was no murmur of voices beyond the panel.

Lainie pushed open the door. Frozen in the unexpected spill of light from her candle were the two slave buyers. Jackson was crouched next to her father's safe. Behind him stood Wilson, his gun drawn.

"What are you doing here?" Lainie demanded.

"Why, Miss Gautier, we forgot something and we thought we'd just come back and get it," Jackson said.

As he spoke Wilson grabbed Lainie, extinguishing her candle. He slammed the door just as Lainie opened her mouth to scream. Jackson clamped a dirty hand over her mouth.

"Now, little girl, you're going to make things easier for us. You're going to open that safe for Wilson and me, and we'll be on our way. Maybe if you're a good girl, I'll take time and give you a little reward for your help." His free hand slid insinuatingly over her breasts.

"Leave her alone," Wilson warned. "These planters will be after us fast enough as it is."

"She'd probably like it," Jackson breathed noisily in her ear. "Besides, we can't leave her here to identify us."

Lainie tried to shake her head but Jackson only laughed, and pulled her around to face him. Lainie struck out blindly and her hand brushed against a gun, tucked in his waistband. With one motion, she got it out and without hesitation, pulled the trigger. Jackson's hold on her loosened, and he began to slide to the floor, his hands still gripping Lainie for support.

"Jackson," Wilson yelled, raising his gun. Lainie freed herself of Jackson's hold and ran past Wilson out the verandah doors and into the orchard. A shot whined past her ear, but she didn't look back. Feet pounded on the hard dirt of the driveway, a horse whinnied its protest, then thundered away.

"Miss Lainie, Miss Lainie," Eli's urgent voice called to her from the darkness. Eli stood in the driveway, a lantern held high in one hand, a still-smoking gun in the other as he peered anxiously into the darkness.

"Eli, I'm here," Lainie answered faintly from behind a bush.

"Miss Lainie, thank the Lawd," Eli hurried toward her. "I shot one in the shoulder, but he got away."

"Eli, I'm so frightened," she cried. "But there's another man in father's study. We'd better go see if he's alive." Jackson lay as he had fallen. Eli set the lantern on the edge of the desk and bent to examine the still figure.

"He dead, Miss Lainie," Eli told her.

Lainie shrank back, then forced herself to take charge.

"Eli, drag him out of here into the yard," she ordered.

"He heavy, Miss Lainie, I don't think I can do it myself," Eli protested. "Let's wait for Mr. Jenkins and some help."

"No, I want him out of here now. I'll help you."

Jenkins came up as they rolled the body over the edge of the verandah. "Miss Lainie," he exclaimed. "My God, what's happened?"

"I caught this man trying to rob my father's safe. I want his body removed from this land at once."

"I'll take him into Ocala in the morning," Jenkins said.

"No, you are to take him now," Lainie insisted, her command tinged with hysteria. "I want you to hitch up the wagon and take him away now."

"But it's the middle of the night," Jenkin protested.

"Nevertheless, I want this man off our property. Now! Then tell the sheriff to call on me in the morning and I'll explain what happened."

She left them there and went to her room, and spent a night as anguish-filled as her day had been.

Stripping off her nightgown she scrubbed herself thoroughly.

Chapter 16

Jenkins returned late in the morning, bringing with him the sheriff. He accepted Lainie's explanation without question.

"Will you be going after him?" Lainie asked.

"We'll track him, but we may not get him. He's had a good head start on us. We ain't likely to see him in these parts again anyways."

Lainie drifted in a fog. Her numbed mind rejected the events of the day before, focusing instead on her wedding, now just one day away. She had heard nothing from her father or Rikkar as yet. Lainie wasn't sure she could handle any more.

The day stretched ahead of her endlessly. In the early afternoon, Lainie decided to take a ride. She guided her mount past towering oaks on the river bank and deep into the forest where the sunlight filtered through the leaves in a pale green glow. Suddenly, the peace was shattered as horses hoofs struck against stones, and a man's voice hailed her.

"Well, if it isn't the virtuous bride," Miles Wentworth sneered. He allowed his horse to cantor forward until his leg brushed against Lainie's. Quickly she pulled against the reins of her own horse, moving away.

"If you'll excuse me, I'll be on my way," she said coldly.

"Not yet." Miles caught the mare's halter and held her still. "I want to talk to you."

"We have nothing to say to each other, Mister Wentworth," Lainie snapped. "I advise you to let go of my horse or—"

"Or what?"

"Or this," Lainie cried and brought her riding whip down across his cheek. Instantly, a red line appeared and he released her horse. He emitted a string of curses as he glared at her, but Lainie paid little heed. She had already turned her horse in the small space and quickly spurred it back along the trail they had followed. She kept the mare moving at a gallop, only slowing down when the outbuildings of the plantation came into view.

Her ride had been cut short, she reflected, by still another man who wanted only to use her and dominate her. She remembered the tea party and her good humor returned. She was not a victim anymore. She could show them all that she must be approached carefully or else *they* would pay the consequences, not she. Now, even the killing of the man the night before seemed less tragic to her. She would do what she must in order to protect herself, she vowed.

After turning the horse over to the stable hands, she strolled back to the main house. All about her the people were busily preparing for the wedding. There was gaiety in the air, for these occasions occurred rarely in their life and to have the wedding follow so quickly on the heels of the ball was an extra treat they hadn't expected. They put aside the events of the day before. The selling of slaves had seldom happened in their lives, maybe it never would again.

In big pits by the slave quarters, a huge pig was being readied for roasting over an open fire. It would hang on

a spit, tended by willing volunteers throughout the night.
Tomorrow, after the wedding, which would be attended by
field hands and invited guests alike, the slaves would retire
to the great square in front of their cabins, and have their
own feast. A barrel of beer was out, waiting to be distri-
buted to the slaves after the wedding.

The reception for the invited guests would take place in
the ballroom, the parlor, the verandahs and the front lawn
of the house. Their menu would be varied and elegant.
Even as Lainie approached the kitchen entrance, she caught
whiffs of mouth-watering delicacies being prepared. The
tables in the storage room were already groaning under the
weight of their load, as room was made for yet another
ham or another flaky pie.

Lainie entered the steamy kitchen. All eyes swung briefly
toward Lainie then returned to watch as Bessie, the cook,
placed another delicate, iced rose around the multi-tiered
wedding cake. Everyone held their breath as the fat cook's
nimble fingers placed the flower just so. At the other end of
the table on which she worked were cakes, dark with
molasses and filled with fruit and nuts. No one should go
away from her wedding with an unsatisfied appetite, Lainie
reflected and a fleeting thought of the cost of feeding all
these people for a second time within the past few weeks
crossed her mind.

Lainie passed on through the kitchen and went thoughtfully to her room. She still hadn't heard anything from her
father and Rikkar, and wondered if there had been a delay.
Surely, they would have sent word to her if they couldn't
make it in time. In just a few more hours, overnight guests
would be arriving.

In a shroud of unreality Lainie welcomed her first guests,
and the afternoon was spent settling them. As each guest
arrived, they inquired about Jean Gautier and her bride-

groom, and hearing of their continued absence, would playfully tease her about being left at the alter.

During supper a man rode up and explained that her father and Rikkar had requested him to ride ahead and reassure Lainie and her guests that they would arrive the next morning in plenty of time for the wedding. They had been detained for a day longer in Savannah.

"Well, Lainie, looks like you're going to have a bridegroom after all," one man called laughingly and the others joined in with their cheery comments. Lainie laughed along with them.

Finally the long day ended and Lainie gratefully bathed and got into bed. Her eyes closed and she slept, drifting on moon-spangled night winds that swirled around her. Rikkar was there, holding her in his arms, kissing her and she held him to her breast and wept tears of joy. When he raised his head Lainie saw the face of Tortugas. She screamed and ran through the night mist, Tortugas's laughter following her. She fell and he was upon her, but it was Jackson and his face contorted dreadfully as he fell to the ground at her feet, his blood staining the billowing skirts of her gown. She raised her hand to her mouth and saw that it, too, was covered with blood. The man at her feet became Elizabeth, whose dark eyes looked up sadly at Lainie. "Tell your father, the name will be Jean as he wishes," she whispered, then disappeared.

Rikkar and Jean Gautier finally returned home late the next morning. Lainie found her father in his room, with Rikkar. An exhausted Jean sat slumped in a chair.

"Papa, are you all right?" Lainie asked, kneeling in front of him. "Papa?"

"I'm fine, Lainie," her father reassured her. "I'm just tired. Eli has my bath ready and I will be revived in no time. The question is will the bridegroom be ready on time?'' He cast an eye at the dust covered man standing next to him.

''I wouldn't care if he wasn't,'' Lainie said coldly to Rikkar.

''Lainie, don't be angry with Rikkar for being so long detained. Blame me if you must blame anyone. We tried so desperately hard to save a good man's land for him. I fear we have failed.''

''You mustn't think of that now,'' Rikkar calmed him. ''We'll think of something yet.''

''You're getting an excellent man for a husband, Lainie,'' her father continued. ''I don't know what I would have done without him.''

''So you see, my absence was unavoidable. Now come give me a kiss and I'll forgive you for pouting.'' Rikkar raised her to her feet, and his lips settled on hers. It was a long kiss and Lainie could hear her father chuckle from his chair, then Rikkar released her. Before she could sputter her anger at his high-handed tactics, he was hustling her to the door.

''We'll see you downstairs, sir,'' he called over his shoulder. She allowed Rikkar to walk her to her own room before turning on him.

''That was despicable of you to take advantage of my father's presence to kiss me,'' she muttered savagely.

''I wanted to take his mind off his disappointment and depression,'' Rikkar replied. ''The trip was very hard on him, harder than I had anticipated.'' His worry gave way to a soft smile as he looked at her, his glance travelling over her features, reacquainting himself with each one.

''I missed you.''

''Well, I didn't miss you,'' she hissed, turning away from him, ''and you are never to kiss me again, ever.''

''Won't that seem a bit strange to our wedding guests? I

believe there's a portion of the ceremony where the preacher says 'you may kiss the bride'."

"Well, that's the only time," Lainie conceded furiously, pushing open the door of her bedroom. Without looking to see if he still stood there, she slammed the door as hard as she could.

Lainie dressed in a white silk wedding gown with thin, satin ribbons adorning the front. The skirt and bodice of the gown were encrusted with the very finest lace and tiny seed pearls. The collar buttoned high, accenting her slender, lovely throat. May set a crown of silk flowers on her golden curls and straightened the yards and yards of sheer veil that floated out behind Lainie, then handed her a bouquet of rose buds, picked fresh that morning and twined together with lace and ribbon.

"It is time to go down, Lainie," her father said, entering the room. "You are so lovely," he whispered, pressing a kiss against her brow. "I want to give you something that came from your grandmother," he said, taking out a flat, velvet box. "Your mother left these behind when she went back to France. She said pearls didn't suit her and perhaps she was right, but I think they would be perfect for you." He fastened a long strand of exquisitely matched pearls about her neck.

"Pearls take on a warmth and hue from the human skin. They are much like people, shaped and colored by the events that touch them. Don't let the bad things that touch you harden or embitter you, Lainie. Let your life take on the warmth and glow of those who love you and try to protect you, and you will always be as beautiful as you are this day."

"Thank you, Papa," Lainie whispered.

"My dear girl, I love you so much and there is so much of your life that I have missed," her father continued. "It is a loss which I will forever regret. But now, our guests wait with the man who will take you from me." He held out his arm.

Blindly she walked forward to meet the man who had betrayed her. Numbly, she felt her father give her hand into Rikkar's and then they were standing side by side while the preacher read the marriage vows. Like an automaton, she answered at the appropriate places, her voice barely above a whisper, while Rikkar's rang clear and firm.

Then it was done, the ring was heavy upon her finger and Rikkar was turning her toward him, his mouth lowering to gently kiss her. The music swelled around them and well-wishers pushed about them.

Tables of food had been set up on the verandah and the guests moved outdoors to partake of the food and drink and to stroll about the gardens. Lainie and Rikkar moved among their guests, thanking each one for coming and for the gifts they had brought.

Eventually the ladies all gathered together to pass along the lastest gossip, while the men stood in groups, smoking and discussing the latest problem threatening their foothold here in the new territory.

"Gentlemen, I assure you we will not lose our lands," her father's voice rang out strong and sure, and Lainie felt a thrill of pride. She glanced around and saw Rikkar leaning against the verandah railing. His eyes studied her as she moved toward him.

"Rikkar, what are they talking about?" she asked softly.

"There's a clause in the Adams-Onis treaty which was signed in 1819 when the Spaniards left the territory, and that clause states that all land grants signed before January 22, 1818 are ratified, all land grants purchased after that date null and void. That affects a lot of Americans who have bought land down here after that date."

"I can understand the reason for their anger," Lainie said.

"If they won't be hot heads and stir up trouble, I'm sure we can save all the land grants, but we've just gotten out from under Jackson's military rule. I sure don't want to have him back down here again. The Congress has declared us a territory now, Lainie, that means we can stop fighting and go forward building this territory up into one of the richest and best on the continent."

Lainie looked at his animated face and realized she was seeing a rare side of Rikkar. This was a man dedicated to a cause, to a vision far and above his personal gains.

"Just think, Lainie," he said, gripping her shoulders, "one day this territory will be a state and we, you and I, and our children will be a part of that beginning."

His eyes, so full of vitality and enthusiasm stared into hers, willing her to share his dream. For a moment, Lainie was caught up in his visions, then she pulled free of his grip.

"Lainie," his voice held an urgent persuasion, but whatever he had been about to say was delayed by the opening strains of a waltz filtering through the verandah doors.

"May I have the first dance, Madame?" Rikkar asked bowing to her. Before she could protest, he took hold of her hand and pulled her into the ballroom. Rikkar swung Lainie out onto the floor and into his arms. He hesitated for a breathless moment, his eyes looking deeply into hers, then led her about the hall in the waltz.

"A penny for your thoughts," Rikkar said as they danced.

"I was just remembering the ball two weeks ago," Lainie answered morosely.

"Ah, you're a sentimentalist too. I shall always remember that ball for it was there that you consented to be my bride."

"Only because I had no choice," Lainie reminded him.

"Didn't you?" Rikkar asked, his gray eyes searching hers.

"You know I didn't," she snapped.

"If you are honest with yourself, you know you had other options than to marry me. If you had told your father what had happened when you were kidnapped he would have taken steps to help you get past the bad memories. Furthermore, if you had told your father about Miles Wentworth, he would have horsewhipped the fellow. Why didn't you?"

"I tried to tell him but he was too busy to see me that day," she said bitterly.

"I can't imagine that he would ever be too busy to see you," Rikkar commented.

"Then you don't know my father as well as you think you do," Lainie snapped. "Besides, I don't need my father to fight for me, I can do it myself. I—," she paused.

"Yes," Rikkar prompted gently. "You what?"

"Nothing," Lainie muttered and turning out of his arms, left the dance floor.

"Lainie," Rikkar called as he moved to catch up with her. An arm at her elbow guided her outdoors. A soft twilight had fallen. Silently they strolled along the verandah while she strove to regain her composure. Her heart was beating against the walls of her chest and her hands were trembling.

"Lainie, tomorrow, we leave for Greenwood," Rikkar said, steering her to a bench. He paused, waiting for Lainie to respond, but she kept her face expressionless. "I've just finished the building of the main house. Only the master bedroom and my study and the kitchen have been furnished, so when you arrive, you'll have a free hand with the decorating." He paused, then: "Greenwood will be our home for the rest of our lives and the home of our children. I want you to make it a place that we can be proud of and yet a place where our children can run and play and grow up happy.''

"We will never have children," Lainie said wearily. "Our agreement was that our marriage would never be consummated.''

"I never agreed to that, Lainie and I won't abide by it.''

"You—you—,'' Lainie sputtered. "You led me to believe that you agreed to it.''

"No, I've told you from the beginning what I want from this marriage. You believed what you wanted to. I agreed only that I wouldn't force you into consummating this marriage against your will and I won't. I also agreed to give you access to all my financial resources. I've given you a freedom that few married women have.''

"Am I expected to be grateful?" Lainie asked sarcastically.

"Some women would be," Rikkar answered, "but no, I neither expect nor want your gratitude. I do want you to recognize my action as an attempt to show you how much faith I place in you and in our union.''

"And what if I take advantage of that trust and try to hurt you?''

"I'm gambling you won't.''

"Then you lose," Lainie said, "for I will take every opportunity to hurt you as you've hurt me.''

"I will gladly take any punishment you offer, if it will erase the bitterness and pain you feel," Rikkar said, then he reached inside the breast pocket of his elegantly cut suit jacket and brought out a long white envelope.

"This is the letter we discussed," Rikkar told her. "It gives you all rights to my properties and money. It's addressed to my banker and lawyer.''

Lainie read the letter through then raised her head, a

smile on her lips. "You've just put yourself into my hands," she said. "Aren't you worried?"

"No, Lainie, I'm not."

"You should be. I promise you I'll make you sorry for the day you gave me this."

"I don't think you will," and before Lainie was aware of what he was about to do, he settled his lips firmly on hers. Involuntarily, her soft lips parted so that his hot, moist tongue touched hers. Lainie felt a fire flare up in her loins and breasts and race along her veins. Her hand pushed weakly at his chest, then he released her and she drew a long breath. Before she could begin a tirade of protests against his assault, they were interrupted.

"Well, look at the newlyweds, all lovey and sweet," Miles Wentworth sneered. Lainie turned to face him and she felt Rikkar's body stiffen beside her. Miles lolled against the railing, his cravat askew, his hair mussed. As they stared at him, he raised a bottle to his lips and took a long drink.

"What are you doing here, Miles?" Rikkar demanded.

"Oh, I came to kiss the bride," Miles laughed and straightening himself, wove his way to them. "She never let me kiss her once all those weeks she led me on and let me court her. She always held her body away as if she were a scared virgin. If I had only known." He laughed bitterly.

"Be careful what you say, Wentworth. You're talking about my wife," Rikkar warned.

"Oh, your wife." Miles's loud voice was attracting the attention of others. "You didn't have to marry her, you know. You could have had her without marrying her. You did on—"

Rikkar's fist cut off anything else Miles might have said. Miles fell sprawling against the side of the house and slid to the broad boards of the verandah. The sound of the scuffle brought people out onto the verandah.

"I don't want to see you around my wife ever again, Wentworth," Rikkar said. "Don't ever talk to her or about her again."

Impulse made Lainie move forward and put a hand on Rikkar's sleeve. "Darling, don't be too hard on him. You can't blame him for being bitter about it all. He had hoped to sweep me up and marry me before I heard those horrid rumors about his mother, the poor man." Rikkar looked at her, startled, but she turned an angelic smile upon Miles.

"I do understand, Miles, and I bear you no ill will, in spite of the rude advances you have made upon me. But you must understand that after hearing about your mother, I could never have married you even if Rikkar hadn't come along when he did. I am so sorry," Lainie ended with her voice full of sympathy.

"What rumors about my mother?" Miles snarled, rising to his feet.

"The rumor that your mother wasn't as white as she should have been, Miles Wentworth, and her trying to pass herself off as real gentility," Millicent Southfield stated, striding to stand in front of Miles.

"It's a lie!" Wentworth shouted, his face devoid of color, his eyes casting about wildly at the people who circled him. Taking Lainie's arm, Rikkar turned to the people gathered about. "Why don't we go back to our dancing." Reluctantly people left the spectacle on the porch.

"Well, you've paid one back, haven't you?" Rikkar asked as they danced, an amused smile on his lips.

"I don't know what you're talking about," Lainie said primly, avoiding his knowing eyes.

"Yes you do." Lainie glanced up into his coldly smiling eyes. "I also heard talk this afternoon of the men who came to rob your father's safe. They say you shot one of them.''

"Yes, I did," Lainie said. "He was an animal. He tried to—"

"What?" Rikkar asked, and this time his eyes held no amusement.

"He tried to force himself on me and I was able to get his gun and shoot him with it. He deserved it and more." She stopped dancing and stood looking up into Rikkar's eyes.

"You might remember him when you plan to claim your nuptial rights," she said, running from the room.

She wasn't aware of how long she stayed in her father's study, but eventually Millicent Southfield found her.

"My dear," she gushed, "here you are. We've all been looking for you. Your father and your new husband want you and I told them I would help find you."

"Here she is, right here," Millicent proudly directed the two men into the study. "I told you I would be able to find her. I'm very good at that sort of thing. I just think of where I might like to be myself, if I were a young bride, exhausted by all the excitement of the biggest day of my life."

"Lainie," her father said, "I've been looking every place for Elizabeth. Do you know where she is?"

Chapter 17

The room pitched for a moment, then righted itself as Lainie looked at her father. She struggled to maintain a calm she did not feel.

"I asked in the kitchen, but they didn't tell me anything. Is Elizabeth ill?" her father asked.

Lainie remained silent. Her eyes darted wildly from her father to Rikkar and finally to Millicent Southfield who stood listening. Rikkar turned to the woman.

"Mrs. Southfield, thank you so much for finding my bride for me." He took her arm and firmly escorted her to the door. "You have been so helpful. I forgot to mention to you," he said as she began to protest, "Pauline Butler was looking for you. She said she had something quite important to tell you about Emily Crawford."

"Elizabeth has been sold," Lainie said finally when the gossipy woman was gone.

"What are you saying, Lainie?" her father gasped.

"The men wouldn't accept Clay and I had to substitute someone."

"But why on earth Elizabeth? I never sell off my female slaves. They can be mistreated too badly." He looked at his daughter as if she were a stranger.

"They say you shot one of the men," he went on.

"Yes, he came back to try to steal the money he had paid for the slaves. Eli shot at his partner and wounded him, but he got away. The sheriff was going to search the area, but we haven't heard anything yet."

"And you gave my Elizabeth to such men?" Her father's face was filled with anger and he glared at Lainie. Suddenly, he was the same stern man who had come to her school months before and ordered her home to America.

"I'm truly sorry, Papa. I didn't know what else to do. I was just trying to give them a slave they would be happy with so they would pay the money as agreed." Her voice broke slightly.

"I know I shouldn't blame you, Lainie. I would never have involved you in this if I hadn't been needed so desperately for that petition. But surely you knew I wouldn't want to sell Elizabeth. Why Lainie, she was a friend to you."

"I know, Papa, I know," Lainie whispered. "I tried to get her back, but Jackson said it was too late, that the bill of sale had already been signed and she was his."

"But why did you let him have her in the first place?"

"I don't know. I—I know you loved her, that you didn't want her sold."

"Then why Lainie, why?" her father cried in despair. Her heart seemed to turn to stone. Had he ever cried like that over her and Marie when they left Belle Fleur?

"I gave her to him because . . ." defiantly Lainie raised her tear stained face and glared into his eyes, "because I know how you loved Elizabeth, more than you ever loved Mama or me."

"Loved her more?" He looked at her in shock. "Lainie, you're wrong, so wrong," Jean Gautier said.

"But why wouldn't you let me come back here? Wasn't it because of Elizabeth?"

"I tried to get you back, Lainie. God knows I tried. But

Marie heard I'd come to the school to see you and she threatened to take you away again, this time to a place where I would never find you. At least while you were at the school, I could be sure you were being cared for.''

"I was never happy away from you and Belle Fleur!"

"My poor child." Jean Gautier held his daughter in his arms.

"I'm sorry, Papa," Lainie cried. "So sorry."

"I must get her back." Jean said. "He must have headed for New Orleans, or would he have gone to Savannah? Yes, Savannah. We'll go there first. How many days ago did he leave?" Her father turned feverishly to her and Lainie told him.

"That means he only has a two day head start on me," Jean said eagerly. "I can catch him! He's wounded and he's driving a wagon. That'll slow him down. Eli! Eli! Damn it where are you when I ne—"

"You can't go out tonight looking for her. You've pushed yourself too far now," Rikkar protested. "Get some sleep and we'll leave tomorrow. I'll go with you."

"No, David, you must get back to Greenwood and start your own planting."

"It can wait a few more days," Rikkar brushed away his objections, "but you must rest tonight. You're nearly ill as it is."

"I can't, David. I have to go, can't you see? Elizabeth needs me. I can't abandon her when she needs me. Eli!" he shouted.

"Papa, don't go," Lainie cried. "Elizabeth was only a slave. There are others."

"No, you don't understand, she wasn't just a slave. She was . . . special." His voice grew weak and he struggled for breath.

"Papa, you're ill. Please don't go," Lainie pleaded again.

"I have to," Jean Gautier roared. "Eli, Eli!" His voice thundered down the hall and the Negro butler came running. "Saddle my horse immediately, and make up a sack of provisions for me."

"Yessir," the black man said. "But, sir, you don't look well enough to travel."

"Don't back talk to me," Gautier shouted as his hand clutched his chest, and his knees buckled. Rikkar's strong arms caught him.

"Eli, turn back his bed," Rikkar ordered and her father's distraught servant hurried to comply. At the door Rikkar turned back to Lainie.

"You stay here. I want to talk to you when I come back down."

She had tired of pacing when the door flew open. On trembling legs Lainie rose to meet Rikkar.

"Lainie, when will all this be finished?" he asked wearily.

"I don't know what you're talking about," Lainie replied evenly.

"Don't pretend innocence with me, I'm not in the mood for it," he snapped. "You know what I'm referring to. This need of yours for revenge. You sold off that woman deliberately."

"I don't know what you're talking about," Lainie repeated.

"I'm talking about a girl," Rikkar said, gripping her shoulders, "a girl so eaten up with hatred and the need for revenge that she strikes out at everyone."

"All right," Lainie blazed at him. "I saw him with Elizabeth the afternoon of the ball. I went to see about the wine and the door was open. I saw them together. They were making love. I—I thought she was the reason Mama left Belle Fleur, the reason I had to stay away from the only home I could ever love. I hated Elizabeth with all my heart, but I didn't mean to sell her.''

"How can you sell someone, a human being, without meaning to?" Rikkar rasped.

"Those men insisted," she cried in defense.

"And of course you've just killed one of them and the other is wounded. How convenient for your story."

"Surely you don't believe I murdered that man in cold blood," she asked, barely able to say the words. "It was self-defense," she cried, her voice shrill, "self-defense!" Rikkar remained silent, his eyes boring into hers.

"I didn't mean to sell Elizabeth," she said, "and I didn't mean to kill that man. I was only trying to escape."

"For someone whose intentions were so innocent, you've brought a lot of pain to others," Rikkar said levelly.

"I told you, from now on I'm going to pay back every man who does me a wrong."

"And so far you're doing it, aren't you?" Rikkar asked.

"You're the only one left, so beware," Lainie snapped.

"No, Lainie, you beware." Once again he gripped her arms. "Beware that as you strike at others, you don't do yourself irreparable harm."

"I won't," she said smugly.

"You already have and you're too big a fool to realize it," he said, letting go of her. "We better try to get through the rest of the evening. The guests know your father has taken ill and are preparing to leave. We'll go out and bid them goodnight." Rikkar looked at her for a brief moment, his mouth grim.

"Brides traditionally smile and are happy on their wedding day. Try to act as if you're a happy bride."

"Ladies and Gentlemen," Rikkar announced when they returned to their guests. "I believe there is still some champagne and food left and you must each of you help yourselves. Eli will see to any other needs you have this evening. In the meantime, if you will excuse me, my bride and I will retire.''

A cheer rose from the remaining guests as Rikkar scooped Lainie up in his arms.

"What are you doing?" Lainie squealed. "Put me down!" She struggled in his arms but to no avail and worse, his lips sealed off any further protests.

"Keep quiet, you little fool," he commanded and Lainie complied until he stopped at his door long enough to open it and dump her unceremoniously on the bed.

"I have no desire for you tonight. We'll stay in here together until all the guests have settled down into their own beds and then I'll leave you."

"Leave me?" Lainie questioned.

"Yes, I'll spend the night in your father's room."

"Is he that bad?" Lainie questioned fearfully.

"He is exhausted," Rikkar said, "and I'm afraid he'll try to leave during the night before he's had a chance to rest properly."

"I see," Lainie said softly.

"Eli has already put a cot in there for me. You, Madame, may steal away to your own room sometime in the morning, but you must spend the night here in this room. We must at least create an impression of a loving couple. We have provided enough gossip for one day, so we will maintain this farce over the next weeks, months, years, if necessary. Is that clear?"

His steely eyes glared into hers and although Lainie would have liked to deny what he said, the common sense of it made her nod her head meekly.

"Why don't you get undressed and get into bed?"

"There is no dressing room and you are in the room," she said calmly although her heart was beating far too fast.

"You don't need a dressing room. You're no virgin, Lainie, and we are no strangers to each other."

"I can't undo the buttons in the back," she said finally. Rikkar moved across the room to aid her. The brush of his fingers against her skin was hurried and impersonal. When she felt the last button give, she spun around, allowing the silk gown to fall to her waist, exposing her breasts covered only by her sheer camisole. She watched as Rikkar's eyes dropped to rest on the curved half moons. There was no flicker of desire in his gray eyes.

"I'll need help unlacing my corset," Lainie said softly.

As Rikkar's nimble fingers loosened the last hook and it fell to the floor, Lainie turned to face him. She pushed down the thin camisole slowly, provocatively, baring her firm young breasts, her nipples, taut in her anticipation to humiliate him. She smiled as her hands slid the soft material past the curve of her waist and hips and halted just below the slight swell of her stomach. Her eyes sought Rikkar's and held them as she ran her hands softly over her skin and brought them up to cup her breasts from beneath.

Rikkar's lips curved into a smile as he reached forward and removed her hands from her breasts. Lainie's heart thudded in her chest. Then his hands were at her hips, pulling the thin, silk material back up over her hips and up over her breasts.

"Go to bed, Lainie, there is nothing here for me tonight," Rikkar said, and turning, left the room.

"Why you—" Lainie began, stung by his rejection. Then she climbed into bed and huddled beneath the covers.

It was late in the morning when the stamping of horses awakened her. Knotting one of Rikkar's dressing gowns around her slim waist, Lainie stepped into the hall to cross to her own room.

"My dear, you've finally awakened," Millicent Southfield's voice assailed her. "Did you have a good night?

Oh, I shouldn't have asked that!'' the woman giggled. ''It's such a shame your husband has to leave his little bride after only one night,'' she continued.

''What do you mean?'' Lainie asked, startled.

''Why, my dear, didn't he tell you? Oh my, men can be such insensitive beasts at times,'' she said. ''Your father had to return to Savannah on some urgent business and David was afraid he was too ill for the trip, so he went along. I must say it was strange that he didn't tell you,'' Millicent said, her birdlike eyes watching Lainie closely.

''He mentioned last night that he might do so,'' Lainie said weakly, then began to edge along the hall seeking to escape the woman. ''I really must go get dressed, Mrs. Southfield. If you'll excuse me.''

Rikkar could have at least come to awaken her and tell her where they were going, Lainie thought angrily as she dressed. She would certainly give him a piece of her mind when he returned.

Five days later, they had not returned and Lainie was beside herself. By the end of the week she was seriously considering sending out Jenkins to look for them when they rode into the drive, their horses stumbling in an effort to stay on their feet. Her father slumped pitifully in his saddle and Lainie, who had run to the side verandah when Eli summoned her, felt her heart constrict with guilt and pity.

Her father, the man who had strolled into the school in France months before, confident of himself and his place in the world, was little more than a child-like figure huddled in his saddle. A rope had been tied to his horse's halter and Rikkar held the other end as he rode side by side with the sick man.

One of the slaves was sent to fetch the doctor who pronounced that nothing was wrong with the patient except extreme exhaustion and deep depression.

Later, Rikhov found Lainie in the parlor, idly playing the piano. "Lainie," Rikkar's cold voice stopped her. "If you can halt your playing for a moment there are a few things I wish to discuss with you."

"Yes, what is it?" she asked, striving to make her voice as cold and aloof as his.

"Since the doctor has said your father has no real physical ailment except fatigue and depression, for which he must stay in bed, I am returning to Greenwood to begin my planting. Please see to the packing of your belongings. We'll leave in the morning."

"You must be mad to think I would go away and leave my father now when he needs me."

"What he needs is to know that Elizabeth and the baby she is carrying are well and back here at Belle Fleur."

"Baby?" Lainie asked, stunned by the news. "Elizabeth was expecting a child?"

"Yes, didn't you know?" Rikkar asked.

Lainie made no answer but turned away from him, her mind registering his words. Yes, she had known, although she'd tried hard to deny it to herself. Elizabeth had told her that day the slavers took her away but Lainie had willed her words into forgetfulness.

"You dealt your father a terrible blow, Lainie. I'm going to see that you don't do him more harm. You will leave with me tomorrow morning, like it or not." He turned on his heel and stalked out of the room.

Lainie stood where she was, seething with anger at his tone. How dare he speak to her like that, how dare he dictate to her what she would and would not do. She would show him! But even as she moved toward the hall, she heard horse's hoofs thunder away.

A perfect opportunity, she thought. He had gone to fetch the wagon. Now was her chance. She would leave Belle Fleur and he would be forced to go to Greenwood without her. But where to go? She certainly couldn't go to her nearest neighbor, Miles Wentworth. She knew so few of her father's neighbors and she had no other relatives here. The image of Millicent Southfield crossed her mind and immediately she knew she could seek refuge with the gossipy woman for a few days until Rikkar had gone and she could return to Belle Fleur.

"Eli!" she called, heading for the stairs. "Have a horse saddled for me immediately," she told the butler when he appeared. She ran to her room and stuffed a few things into a small bag that could be tied to the back of a horse, then quickly shrugged out of the printed day gown she was wearing and into her riding habit.

Breathless with her haste, she rushed down the stairs. Eli was already holding a horse ready for her. Quickly, Lainie mounted and Eli tied her bag on the back, then she dug her spurs into the horse's sides and she was flying down the driveway. She would have to hurry if she were to make the Southfield plantation by nightfall. Her short experience in this sparsely settled land told her she didn't want to be caught on the road at night.

She had acted so swiftly on her impulse that she'd had no time to think of the foolishness of a woman travelling alone, but now all those reminders of what could happen came back to haunt her and she pushed the horse harder.

She was almost half way there and the sun had already set, leaving behind its red-orange trail to stain the clouds. Shadows were gathering in the trees and the bushes along the road, and Lainie pushed her mount still harder. Above the frantic rush of her horse's hoofs, she didn't notice the hoof beats of another horse until the rider was almost upon her. Looking back over her shoulder, Lainie saw that it was Rikkar who was rapidly closing the distance between them, his cloak billowing behind.

Leaning forward in her saddle, Lainie urged her horse

onward, but the valiant little mare had already ridden too far too fast and was slowing. Lainie shouted at her mount, urging it onward, and even resorted to the whip, but to no avail. Rikkar was already drawing abreast of her.

"Lainie, this won't do you any good," Rikkar shouted.

The only answer Lainie gave was to spur her horse forward. For a moment the little mare made a final effort and surged ahead, leaving Rikkar behind, then Lainie heard his horse's hoofs thunder close again and a strong arm wrapped about her waist, lifting her from her saddle. Wildly she kicked out, and struggling, pulled Rikkar from his saddle.

They fell into the roadway, rolling over and over, Rikkar holding her tightly to him. When at last they came to a stop Lainie fought against Rikkar's restraining arm. Over his shoulder she saw that their horses had stopped a few feet away. If only she could get free and reach her horse or better yet, Rikkar's mount, she might still get away. Wildly she struck out with her hands, but Rikkar grabbed them and pinned them beneath her. Using his body to hold her down, he used his free hand to grasp a handful of her hair and pull her face to his.

"Listen, you little wildcat, you might as well stop struggling. You're not going to get away," he exclaimed as Lainie continued to twist and turn in his grasp.

"Let go of me. You can't make me go with you!" Lainie gasped.

"You'll go and you'll stop this fighting. You'll go quietly or—"

"Or what? What horrible thing will you do to me that you haven't done already?"

"I'll think of something," Rikkar grated and suddenly, his mouth came down punishing and grinding against her own. At first Lainie fought against the contact, but her body acted of its own accord and she stopped struggling and arched against him. There was no love in their embrace, only two passions seeking to still the hungry flames that consumed them.

Rikkar's lips were brutal and his body heavy on hers, but she didn't notice. When at last he raised his mouth from hers, Lainie could taste the blood of her lips, swollen and bruised by the kiss, but her senses were too inflamed for her to care. Her eyes, smoky with unquenched passion, looked into his as he lifted himself from her. Every nerve of her body cried out in protest at the loss of contact between them. She lay in the road and stared up at this man she hated and desired with equal intensity, and knew that if he wished to take her now, she would offer no resistance. Indeed, she would be a willing participant.

Their eyes locked and it seemed as if things were said between them that would forever bind them. Not words of love, but an acknowledgement of a need for each other that surpassed all other emotions. Slowly, Rikkar held out his hand and pulled Lainie to her feet. They stood looking deep into each other's eyes for a moment more, then Rikkar turned away and got their horses.

She made no protest as they started back to Belle Fleur. The darkness fell around them and Lainie gave no thought to the danger of being on the road after dark. It seemed always to be like that. She felt safe when she knew Rikkar was nearby.

A stable boy ran forward to take their horses when they arrived back at the plantation. Rikkar went to see if the wagon had returned. He told her in clipped tones that he had sent one of the stable boys to town for it. So that was why he had been able to come after her so quickly. Her plan had been thwarted and now Lainie wondered if she had really wanted to flee from him.

Wearily she mounted the stairs to her room. She ordered

bath water and while she waited, nibbled a light supper from the tray May brought, then went to see her father.

He was sleeping deeply, as if too weary to ever wake up. There were lines in his face that had never been there before and he seemed to have aged in a matter of a few days. Lainie sat with him a while, holding his limp hand. The sleeping draught the doctor had given him had conquered his body but not his subconscious mind, for he stirred frequently and called out in his sleep for Elizabeth. Lainie sat with tears in her eyes until late in the night.

Chapter 18

She opened her eyes to see Rikkar standing over her bed.

"It's morning." Rikkar's voice was cool and impersonal. "It's time to get up and get dressed. I want to get an early start."

"What?" Lainie pushed heavy golden locks away from her face.

"We're leaving today for Greenwood, had you forgotten?"

"Yes, yes I had," Lainie said, her voice husky from sleep.

"I want to leave in an hour. Eli already has your trunks packed. You need only to put the last of your belongings in these small bags."

"I have no intention of leaving my father," Lainie protested. "You can go ahead without me." She lay back against the pillows and pulled the covers close.

"Your father is in no danger. He only needs to rest. I think he could do that better without your being here."

"Are you implying that my presence would disturb my father?" Lainie asked indignantly.

"Your actions have brought him a great deal of grief," Rikkar reminded her. "I think if you weren't here for a while, he might get over the loss of Elizabeth a little easier. We leave in one hour, whether you're ready to go or not," he finished.

"I won't be."

"Then, Madame, you will travel in your night clothes," Rikkar said quietly and went out, closing the door behind him.

One hour later all her bags were packed, she had dressed and breakfasted lightly, and was sitting in her father's bedroom, his hand in hers.

"I don't want to leave you," Lainie protested petulantly, hoping he would say he wanted her to stay. Rikkar could hardly refuse if her father insisted he wanted her at his sick bed.

"Lainie, my child, you are not to worry about me. I will rest and regain my strength soon. Rikkar must return to his planation or it will be too late for him to have a crop this year. He must get his planting done."

"He could go without me," Lainie offered.

"A wife's place is with her husband. Your married life has already been interrupted enough by me. I can't allow you to stay with me, when you should be with your husband."

"Papa," Lainie cried lowering her head to his chest. There was so much she longed to tell him, but as she opened her mouth to speak, Rikkar stepped into the room.

"It's time to go," he said.

"I hate to see you go, David," her father said wistfully, "but I know you must. Don't worry about me. I'll soon be on my feet again."

"I have no doubt of it," Rikkar said. "As soon as the crops are in, I'll bring Lainie back for a visit."

"Why don't you leave me here and come for me later, when the crops are in?"

"That's impossible," Rikkar said, then a mocking light

appeared in his eyes. "I couldn't bear to be parted from my new bride that long."

"I'm not going," she said stubbornly, sure that Rikkar would not create a scene in front of her father.

"Kiss your father good-bye," Rikkar said, gripping her elbow tightly, and Lainie gently touched her lips to her father's forehead.

"Papa," she whispered softly. "Papa, there was something that Elizabeth said just before she—she—left." His eyes stared into hers.

"She said to tell you that the name would be Jean as you wished." Lainie repeated the words she had remembered. Her eyes searched her father's for any sign of comprehension of what she had said, but the lids lowered and he breathed deeply. The doctor's medication was at work again.

Rikkar helped her into the buggy he had borrowed from her father, and May settled herself in the opposite seat, baggage piled around her. When they reached the harbor at St. Johns where the *Sea Hawk* lay, he would send the buggy and wagon back. As they bumped over the dirt drive leading away from Belle Fleur, Lainie did not look back.

St. Johns was a rough little sea side town, with buildings knocked together to warehouse the cotton the planters brought to ship out to Northern and European markets. They went directly to the wharf where Caloosa materialized from nowhere.

"Caloosa," Lainie cried, delighted to see him again, but the tall Indian only nodded his head at her then turned back to supervise the loading of the *Sea Hawk*. Lainie might have been hurt at one time by the Indian's austere countenance, but she had caught the gleam in his eyes and knew he was happy to see her again.

Once on deck, she was loathe to go below so she

walked about and unwelcomed memories crowded around her, bringing tears to her eyes.

Angrily she brushed them away and looked up to find Rikkar standing before her, his gray eyes dark.

"Lainie," he said, his voice filled with anguish as he reached forward and gripped her arms. His warm breath fanned her cheek.

"Don't touch me," Lainie said stonily, not bothering to struggle against him. With a sigh, Rikkar let her go.

"One thing you must acknowledge, there is that between us which cannot be denied. No matter what has passed, we will always be drawn to each other. You can't deny it, Lainie."

"What has passed between us is finished. It will never be repeated," Lainie told him.

"Won't it? What if I had come to your room last night?" Rikkar asked.

"But you didn't, and today I am stronger. I can resist you." She glanced up at him in time to see his head lowering to hers, but not in time to pull away before his lips settled over hers. Of their own accord, her lips parted to receive his probing tongue.

Lainie's knees grew weak and a trembling seized her body. Everything fell away but Rikkar and his mastery of her. When Rikkar lifted his hot mouth from hers, his eyes glinted with an arrogance she hated. She brought up her hand to strike at the smug smile that creased his face. A vise-like grip closed around her wrist.

"You'll never be able to resist," he laughed.

"I hate you," Lainie spat out.

"Hate and love are two emotions that are so close they are sometimes confused," he said softly.

"Be assured that is not the case with me, Rikkar," she breathed angrily. "I hate you with all my being and one day I swear I will show you just how much. You'll curse the day you ever met me.''

Lainie spent the hours it took to reach Tampa Bay above deck, glorying in the sense of freedom sailing gave her. The sun was setting when they tacked about into the wind and headed into the bay. Soon they weighed anchor near Fort Brooks; Greenwood lay not too far away.

Boats took them to the wharves at Fort Brooks at Tampa where Rikkar escorted her to the home of Commander Payne who would be their host for the night. Their supplies and luggage would be unloaded in the morning and they would make the short trip to Greenwood.

In the meantime, Lainie was settled into a comfortable room where she had time to rest briefly before dressing for dinner. As she moved about the room, grooming herself and donning a fresh gown, she cast troubled glances at the double bed that dominated the room.

She was just putting the finishing touches to her toiletry when there was a knock at her door. ''Hello,'' Lainie said to the young woman standing there.

''Hello,'' the woman returned her greeting absently, stepping into the room. ''I thought these were David Rikkar's rooms,'' she said, her eyes sweeping up and down Lainie's gown, taking in every detail.

''They are,'' Lainie assured the woman. ''I am Mrs. Rikkar.''

''*Mrs*. Rikkar?'' The woman's voice rose an octave. ''I didn't realize David was married.''

''We were just married a week ago,'' Lainie explained.

''I see.'' Once again her eyes swept over Lainie. ''This is quite a surprise. We didn't know David was considering marriage. Have you known him long?''

''Several months.''

"Where did you meet him?" the woman wanted to know.

"We met on a ship on the way from France," Lainie said, "and before I answer any more questions from you, I would like to know who you are?"

"I am Denise Payne, Commander Payne's daughter," the woman stated, her dark head held regally.

"I am Elaine Gautier Rikkar," she said graciously, a smile curving her lips. "I'm glad to meet another woman so soon here at Fort Brooks. I had thought there would be few."

"Oh, we are not so wild and uncivilized as you might imagine," Denise Payne assured her airily. "We're a small community, but we do observe the social amenities."

"I'm glad to hear that," Lainie said. "I won't be lonely then."

"That depends on you," Denise answered ungraciously. "In such a small community, not everyone fits."

"I shall do my best," Lainie refused to be baited. "Well, was there a message you would like me to give my husband when he returns?"

"No, I think not," Denise said. "This is a message I must give him myself." Her full lips curved in a sensuous smile and Lainie felt her face flush in anger.

"I'll give Rikkar the message later this evening," she purred.

"Oh, then you'll be joining us for dinner?" Lainie asked blandly.

"But of course," Denise smiled. "I'm looking forward to seeing David again." The door closed on the woman, although her cloying scent remained in the room.

Impulsively, Lainie picked up a hairbrush and threw it. How dare he put her in this position, she thought, bringing her to the very house of his previous mistress. How she would have liked to scratch out the woman's eyes and

Rikkar's as well. Angrily she paced her room. Only the thought of having to join everyone for dinner made Lainie calm herself.

When she descended the stairs and smiled graciously at her host, gracefully extending her hand, one would never have guessed that just minutes before she had been in a rage. Even the sight of Rikkar, his dark head bent near Denise as he listened to something she was saying, did not crack Lainie's façade of calmness.

There were several officers on hand and as Lainie was introduced to them, she flirted from beneath her lashes, allowing her French accent to become a little more pronounced as she answered their questions. Lainie made a conscientious effort to charm the men and women alike. When Rikkar took her round the room to introduce her to Denise, Lainie smiled warmly and put out her hand to the pouting woman.

"Denise and I have already met," she told Rikkar gaily, "and I'm sure we will become great friends."

"How on earth did you manage that?" Rikkar asked, perplexed.

"I came to your room to see you," Denise answered softly, her voice insinuating itself between Lainie and Rikkar as smoothly as if the woman were pushing them apart, "and that is when I discovered you had a wife. You should have told me when you left that you were going to be married."

"I didn't know when I left," Rikkar explained.

"But how can that be?" Denise asked. "Your wife tells me that you have known each other for several months."

"We have," Lainie laughed, "but the poor darling didn't know that I would accept his proposal of marriage. In fact, I must confess I held out until the night of the ball at my father's house, then I knew I must make a choice between the two men who had asked me, and of course, how could I refuse Rikkar?'' She smiled sweetly up into his eyes.

"Rikkar insisted that we must be married immediately since he had to get back to Greenwood and plant his crops and he didn't want to delay our marriage any longer than he had to. Isn't that right darling?'' She snuggled her arm in his possessively and deliberately led him away.

After dinner, everyone moved back to the parlor for a brief visit, but the party broke up much more quickly than Lainie would have anticipated.

"Everyone rises early here to take advantage of the cool morning hours,'' the Commander informed her, "and I know your husband wants to be on his way at first light. You must be very tired,'' he added noting the droop of her eyelids.

"Yes, we started out early this morning,'' Lainie explained. They bid the guests goodnight, then Denise turned to Rikkar and Lainie.

"I understand David won't be spending the night with you,'' she said smugly. "If you'll wait a moment, Rikkar, I'll get my cloak and accompany you. I need a bit of fresh air.'' She whirled away and ran lightly up the stairs.

"Denise, surely you are not going out after dark,'' her father remonstrated. "It would be unwise and it is unseemly for you to walk with Rikkar. He is a married man.'' His sharp tone brought Denise to a halt. Lainie turned to Rikkar with questioning eyes.

"I'm sleeping on the boat tonight,'' he explained. Lainie railed inside at the picture he was creating for Denise and her father. As if reading her thoughts, he pulled her to him.

"I'm sorry I didn't tell you sooner, darling. I hope you won't mind, but I felt it best to be on board so I can see to the unloading of my supplies the first thing in the morning.''

"Of course, I understand," she said lightly. "I shall miss you though."

Rikkar's eyes darkened until they were almost black in the candlelight. Before she could turn her head away, he was kissing her thoroughly. Behind him, Commander Payne cleared his throat and turned toward the stairs. At last Rikkar let her go.

"That will have to hold us both until morning," he murmured. "Goodnight, Sir! Denise!" he said, nodding his head at each of them before stepping out into the night.

"Well, I expect we'd best all get to bed ourselves," Denise said brightly and waited as Lainie and Commander Payne climbed the stairs.

"Are you a light sleeper, Lainie?" she asked as she held the lamp for them to see their way down the hall.

"I don't know," Lainie replied. "I never gave it much thought."

"Well, if you are, you mustn't mind the sounds you hear in this house. These old wooden houses dry out in the tropical wind and sun, and they creak and groan. Just ignore them." She smiled sweetly. Lainie was puzzled by Denise's sudden shift in attitude but smiled in return and offered her goodnights before closing her bedroom door behind her.

Once she had settled into bed, she found she couldn't sleep. The thought of Denise and Rikkar, their two dark heads close together as they shared some amusing anecdote, made her restless. She threw aside the covers and groped her way to the window.

Below her, a movement caught her eye. In the bright moonlight it was easy to make out the slender figure of Denise Payne and even as Lainie watched a tall figure stepped out of the shadows. The two embraced then disappeared into the shadows.

Lainie's heart beat like a drum in her ears. She suspected that Rikkar and Denise had been lovers, but she hadn't thought that they would remain so now. Anger made her blood race. She would make him pay, she vowed. Oh how she would make him pay.

Her temper was hardly improved the next morning when she descended the stairs to find that Denise was already seated at the breakfast table, her lovely eyes rimmed with dark circles. Rikkar was also there, and greeted her with a mere nod.

Only Commander Payne seemed predisposed to talk in the early morning and his bluff, hearty voice filled the air. Lainie played with the food on her plate, pushing it about with her fork, unable to down any of it.

Finally, in exasperation, she let her fork fall against the china plate, causing a clatter that halted the Commander's conversation and brought Rikkar's head up inquiringly.

"I'm sorry," Lainie said. "I guess I'm just not very hungry this morning. I'm rather anxious to get under way."

"Well, of course you are," Commander Payne blustered. "Any bride would be in a hurry to see her new home."

"Yes, I can hardly wait," Lainie said lamely and they all rose. Commander Payne continued to dominate the conversation as they walked to the carriages. A servant stepped forward to give Lainie a lovely bouquet of freshly picked, tropical flowers.

"You'll be at the dinner party at Greenwood tonight?" Rikkar asked. "I've sent word ahead to my servants and to the other planters in the area."

"Denise and I'll look forward to joining you for your first evening in your new home, Mrs. Rikkar," the Commander said gallantly and Lainie smiled warmly at him. "Just know that you are not as cut off from civilization as you might think. There are ships in and out of this harbor regularly and we can have just about anything shipped in that you might want." Rikkar handed her into the carriage and closed the door.

"Thank you, Commander Payne," Lainie leaned out the window, extending her gloved hand, "and thank you for your hospitality. It was very kind of you. Thank you also, Denise," Lainie called back to the woman who still stood on the porch step.

Denise Payne's eyes were riveted on David Rikkar who was swinging into the saddle of his horse. Suddenly she darted forward, throwing herself against the side of his mount, gripping his thigh with frenzied hands.

"Good-bye, David," she cried, tears welling in her lovely blue eyes.

"Denise, stop this." Rikkar's voice cracked like a whip in the morning air and slowly she let go of him.

Lainie seethed as they left Fort Brooks behind. How dare he have taken her to the home of his former and, it seemed, present mistress? The tears that rolled down her cheek were not from hurt or jealousy, she told herself, but from anger. Whatever their cause, her vision was blinded by them for most of the way to her new home.

Chapter 19

Greenwood, Lainie discovered, was well on its way to becoming an estate that would rival any in Florida or in the entire South for that matter. The clean majestic lines of the main house added a grace and charm to the imposing grandeur of it. Large, round, white pillars, as tall as the two-story structure, supported the front portico, while two-storied wings swept out on either side of the main structure. The whole was painted white and shone pristine in the morning sun.

Lainie knew Rikkar was proud of his estate as he rode back to join her and point out the additional buildings which made up the plantation. Only the red slate of their roofs and the shutters at the windows broke the brilliant white. The carriage swept around the circular driveway and Rikkar helped Lainie to the front steps of the portico. Up close she was even more impressed with the building's architecture. Taking her hand, Rikkar guided her to the large double doors which had been thrown open upon their arrival.

Rikkar swooped her up into his arms and stepped across the threshold into the great hall.

"Welcome to Greenwood, Mrs. Rikkar," he said and his gray eyes held dark glints of light.

"Thank you," Lainie responded aloofly. "You may put me down now."

She turned to look about her and caught her breath with delight and approval. She had been in some elegant dwellings in France and her father's plantation had been a show place, but Greenwood surpassed them all. The curving stairway sweeping down to the spacious entrance hall was truly majestic. Lainie had little time to study the interior of her new home for Rikkar was leading her forward to meet her servants and to present her as their new mistress at Greenwood. The house servants smiled and shyly dropped quick curtsies.

"Next, you must be presented to the field hands," Rikkar said. "They're anxious to see what their new mistress will look like."

He led her through the parlor, only half furnished, she noted quickly as they passed through. The slaves were gathered on the side lawn. Rikkar presented his new bride, then said, "Today will be a holiday so rest and ready yourselves for the celebration tonight. Even now the cooking has begun and the rum is being brought around." The slaves cheered.

"Tomorrow, we must begin to plant our crops. The work will be hard and long, but first we will celebrate, for Greenwood has a great and beautiful lady for its mistress."

"Smile at them," Rikkar told Lainie as he pulled her close to him. "They want to know that you'll be a kind mistress," he added.

"Of course, I will be," she answered.

"There won't be any slaves sold out of turn here, Lainie," Rikkar said harshly.

"Am I to assume then that there is an Elizabeth here for you as well? I should have known, since you were so sympathetic to my father." Her eyes flashed angrily as she spoke.

"There are no Elizabeths here," Rikkar's reassuring voice sounded softly in her ear.

"Only Denises," Lainie said and impulsively raised the bouquet that Commander Payne had given her. With a smile she threw it into the crowd on the lawn, then with a wave of her hand she turned and left the verandah. Rikkar's booted footsteps sounded on the polished floor behind her.

"I'm tired now and I wish to go to my room," Lainie told him.

"Certainly, I'll show you there myself," Rikkar said taking her elbow and leading her up the stairs to her room.

"I'll leave you to rest and refresh yourself," Rikkar said, remaining in the doorway of his room. "I'll be occupied with the festivities for tonight's party, but I trust you'll find something to take up this afternoon."

"I'll look over the house. Perhaps I'll begin planning some of the decorating. You needn't concern yourself with me," Lainie said.

"I'll always concern myself with you, Lainie," Rikkar said softly and her heart constricted at the intimacy of his pledge. Quickly she turned away from him and then heard the sound of the door closing.

The rest of the morning was spent in unpacking her cases and making room in the spacious chests and closets. This was easily done by packing up all of Rikkar's belongings and consigning them to the hall until he could decide where he wanted them. In the afternoon Lainie wandered about the house, and as she looked at each room, her mind began to race ahead to the changes she would make, thinking of how she would preserve the special moods created by the superior architecture.

The morning room, with its bay windows and the doors opening onto the verandah, fairly cried to be left free of the heavy cumbersome drapes and ornate furniture so many homes used. She would hang pots of plants about the room much as the house on the island had been decorated. She would leave the doors open as much as possible and retain the feel of light, cool airiness.

In the long formal dining room and the formal parlors, she would bow to convention, but still strive to keep a light touch.

She wandered back upstairs to the bedrooms and saw that there was no wallpaper or carpeting. She might leave them that way, using only a bright throw rug here and there on the highly polished wood. Each bedroom sported its own fireplace, but she knew enough of the climate to guess that a fire would seldom be needed.

The hours passed quickly and she was startled to see that she had to hurry to get dressed. Their guests would be arriving soon.

She bathed leisurely, washing the dust of travel from her hair, then rose and stepped from the tub.

Her hand froze as she reached for a towel, for the door opened and Rikkar entered. His dark eyes swept over her body, drops of water still clinging to her skin. He took in her lovely figure with its tiny waist and high round breasts. Quickly, Lainie picked up the towel and wrapped it about herself.

"What do you want?" she demanded harshly and was rewarded with a sardonic quirk of his lips.

"I should think that would be rather obvious," he commented, a smile sparking lights in his eyes.

"In the future, I'll thank you to please knock before you enter my room," Lainie said coldly. Taking another towel she began to dry her long golden tresses.

"Not just your room, Lainie," Rikkar spoke softly. "*Our* room. I came in to get some clothes so I can change for the party."

"Your clothes are no longer in here. They've been put

in trunks. You'll find them in the hall. I wasn't sure which bedroom you would choose for your own.''

''I've already chosen my room,'' Rikkar said implacably, his eyes holding that special glint she had come to know meant he would brook no argument. ''We won't discuss it now, our guests will soon be here.'' Turning about, he left the room.

Lainie stared after him angrily. Rikkar would soon learn that she would not be bossed around. If he was the master of Greenwood, she was the mistress and as such carried some weight as well.

''May,'' she called. ''During the party tonight, you are to take all my things and transfer them to another bedroom, one down the hall as far away from this one as you can get.''

''And be sure there is a bed made up for me,'' she warned the maid and turned back to her dressing table. She would show Rikkar that she was a match for him. As the maid hurried off to do Lainie's bidding, the door opened and Rikkar entered. He was dressed now in a dark suit coat, and Lainie was caught by the warm glow in his eyes as he crossed the room to stand behind her.

''You look very beautiful,'' he said softly, capturing a golden curl around his finger. Lainie had pulled the golden strands on top of her head, leaving only a curl or two to trail down at the nape of her neck. Now Rikkar's warm hand brushed across the sensitive, exposed skin, leaving a warm brand wherever he touched. Lainie drew in a quick breath and rose from the chair.

''I'm not yet dressed,'' she said, indicating the loose wrapper that covered her undergarments.

''I'll only take a moment of your time,'' Rikkar said, crossing the room to a painting which hung above a small chest. Gripping the frame at one corner, he pulled it away from the wall, revealing a small safe. He spun the dial and the door sprang open. Laying aside some papers, he took out a velvet case and turned back to Lainie.

"This is something I thought you might like to wear tonight," he said, opening the lid. Lainie gasped at the beautiful necklace that lay against the red velvet. It was a delicate scroll work interlaced with magnificent diamonds and emeralds. The jewels glimmered up at her like a mixture of white fire and ice.

"It's beautiful," she murmured.

"It belonged to my mother," Rikkar said, removing the necklace. Lainie turned around so that he could fasten it, but then Rikkar removed it.

"What's wrong?" she asked.

"The clasp seems to be broken," he said, examining the delicate chain. "I'll see if I can repair it for you." His annoyance was plain.

When he left, Lainie quickly donned her gown. She would feel less vulnerable with Rikkar if she could greet him completely dressed. She smoothed the green silk skirts about her and fluffed out the ribbons and bows. The pale green against her honey-toned skin and blonde fairness made her look cool and inaccessible, a message she hoped Rikkar would get. Rikkar returned, the necklace in his hand. His smile showed he had succeeded in repairing it.

"I think I have it now," he said, fastening the necklace about her slim throat. It lay against her smooth fair skin, striking sparks as it caught the light. She couldn't take her eyes off its loveliness.

"It's like you, Lainie," Rikkar murmured and Lainie was aware that his hands rested on her shoulders pulling her back against him. "Cool, green fire and white hot lightning that can sear a man's soul." His lips brushed against her cheekbone, his breath stirring the delicate curls at her temples. For one brief moment Lainie closed her eyes against the rush of sweet desire that swept over

242

her at his nearness, then angrily, she pushed away from him.

"We have guests waiting, remember?" she said tightly.

"They won't mind waiting a few moments more," Rikkar said, reaching for her.

"I mind." Lainie eluded his hands and headed for the door. With her hand on the knob, she turned and looked back at him. "Coming?" she asked, arching her brows.

Rikkar's dark brows lowered, then with a shrug he walked toward her. At the door he gripped the soft skin of her upper arm, left bare by the short sleeve of her gown and the long, elbow-length gloves she wore. His fingers seemed to burn their imprint into her skin.

"You can't run away forever, Lainie," he said lightly, and before she knew what he was doing he dropped a light kiss on her lips. "Shall we go?" he asked. His grip remained firm on her arm as he escorted her down the stairs and into the main hall to greet their guests.

The evening passed swiftly in a sea of new faces and Lainie was grateful when she recognized a couple she had met the night before at Commander Payne's dinner party. Denise Payne was there, sultry and alluring in a red satin gown cut daringly low.

During the evening the dark-haired woman stopped to chat with Lainie, her dislike for the new bride obvious in her expression and tone of voice. When she noticed the emerald and diamond necklace that Lainie wore, her lips grew tight, then she forced a smile on her face.

"I see Rikkar has repaired the clasp on that necklace," she said to Lainie, a malicious light in her blue eyes. "The last time I wore it, the poor dear couldn't get it unfastened and since he was in an impatient mood he just snapped it. He's *so* strong."

"Not strong enough, apparently," Lainie said cryptically and moved away from the woman. Anger made her eyes blaze and her cheeks flame with color.

She moved among her guests, smiling and nodding her head in acknowledgement of their good wishes. Rikkar, she saw, was doing the same, pausing now and then to join a discussion. Slowly she worked her way toward him, but as she reached him, she caught a flash of red and Denise was there clinging to his arm.

"We must protect ourselves from the opportunists who are taking advantage of the treaty to snap up already developed plantations," Rikkar was saying to the group of men about him, ignoring the woman on his arm.

"I heard last week that Jeb Cooper is losing his place because he can't prove he bought it before the treaty took place," another man said.

"That Jeb was always too careless of important papers and the like," still another man tendered his opinion.

"I've got my deed safely in my box and there's not a man who can take my plantation from me," the first man spoke again. "What about you, Rikkar?"

"Yes, I have my deed in a safe place," Rikkar said quietly.

"Rikkar, the music's playing and you promised me a dance," Denise pouted beside him.

"Yes, but I owe my first dance to my wife," he said, holding out his arm to Lainie.

"By all means," Lainie said, smiling flirtatiously.

Behind her smile, Lainie's eyes snapped with anger at the attitude Denise had taken toward her husband. She noticed that Rikkar's invitation to dance seemed to be more a duty than a pleasure. Lainie willed herself to relax as she followed him to the floor.

Lainie danced with almost every man there that night, and Rikkar was kept busy with the women. Once she saw Denise whirling about the floor with him, her bright dress like a flame as she moved in his arms. The woman was becoming a thorn in her side all too soon.

By the time the evening drew to a close, Lainie was weary of dancing and of forcing a smile on her face. Happily she bid her guests goodbye, smiling sweetly at Commander Payne and his daughter as they took their farewell. Secretly she longed to boot the woman down the steps.

When at last all had left and the servants were snuffing out the candles, Lainie climbed the stairs. She was aware that Rikkar was right behind her and tried to walk as straight and rigidly as possible, not wanting even the sway of a hip to be construed as an invitation. At the top of the stairs she turned away from the bedroom she had been in earlier and started to look for the room May had made up for her.

"Where are you going?" Rikkar asked.

"I'm going to my room," Lainie replied. "Since you've established that you don't intend to give up your room, I've asked May to make up another for me."

"I told May not to bother."

"How dare you!" Lainie cried. "Do you think you can force me to your will? You can't. I'm not a prisoner anymore. I'm not a frightened little girl, unsure of who she is and what her rights are. You can't do to me what you did on the *Sea Hawk* and what you allowed Tortugas to do to me." Lainie's wild tirade broke on a cry.

"Lainie, stop this." Rikkar moved forward and caught her in his arms. "What we had between us was not forced. It was beautiful and passionate. I want that passionate woman back in my arms."

"She no longer exists," Lainie cried, trying to twist away from him. "That woman died in Tortugas's cabin along with our baby. There can never be anything between us except lust and I don't want that."

"If lust is all that exists between us, at least it's something," Rikkar said clasping her to him. She could feel the heat of his hard body against hers and an answering surge began in her own body.

"You are my wife, and we are not going to waste the years hating each other and growing more bitter until we destroy each other." His hands caught in the curls at the back of her head, holding her so that she had to look directly into his smoldering eyes.

"We're going to try to build from this moment on. There's no room for hatred and vengeance. Put it aside, Lainie. Let's begin again, tonight." His voice beseeched her, his eyes held hers, asking her to forgive and forget, but Lainie could not.

"Never! I hate you with all my heart and I'm going to make you pay if it's the last thing I do!"

"Lainie," Rikkar's voice was an anguished cry as he buried his face in her hair, and then he was kissing her. His body pinned her to the wall, his broad chest flattening her breasts while his mouth moved against hers until she could taste blood on the soft, inner skin. She shut her eyes tightly, willing herself not to feel anything, striving to overcome the flash of fire that ignited in her veins. Lights danced behind her eyelids and her head swam dizzily until his mouth released hers and she was able to draw in a breath of air.

Her knees trembled beneath her and she feared she might fall if not for the weight of his body pinning her against the wall. Before she had a chance to regain her senses, Rikkar bent and swept her up into his arms.

"Put me down," Lainie insisted, beating at his shoulders, but he continued toward his room. A booted foot kicked open the door of the room, sending it crashing against the wall.

"Is it to be force them?" she cried. "Haven't you any pride? I don't want you. How can you justify this?"

"Lainie, I'm going to make love to you," Rikkar said, his voice rasping with anger, "and I'm certain I won't have to force you. I never have before." He tossed her on the bed and she landed in a heap of silk and petticoats.

"It won't be anything else," she told him. "I'll never participate in this. It isn't making love, because there is no love between us." She paused and looked at Rikkar, who was slowly undressing. As he unhooked his belt and trousers, she scrambled off the bed and raced toward the bedroom door, but he was quicker than she.

"Lainie, my little fighter," he said, allowing his hands to slid up her arms. When he touced the tender, sensitive flesh of her upper arms, she shivered and heard his low laughter.

"You despicable, egotistical oaf," she cried, pushing against the solid wall of his chest. He continued to hold her, bringing his hands up to cup each breast. Lowering his head, he blazed a path of fire along her neck, causing her to press against him. Fighting herself now more than him, she pushed away, raking across his chest with her fingernails.

"Lainie, stop this," Rikkar commanded, but she continued to strike out at him, scratching and kicking.

She heard the rip of silk and her gown fell to the floor around her, while Rikkar's fingers worked at the chemise that covered her breasts. The delicate material fell away and she felt the brush of wiry hair against her bared breasts as Rikkar clasped her to him.

"Stop fighting, Lainie," Rikkar's voice crooned in her ear. "Remember how we felt together? Remember? I haven't been able to think of anything else for weeks." He groaned as his lips found hers. A fiery, insatiable craving began in Lainie's body, and she clung weakly to him.

"No. I don't want this."

"Yes, you do, Lainie. You want it as much as I do. You may think you hate me, but you want me. Lainie, Lainie, don't fight it," his voice whispered near her ear, his hot breath fanning her cheek.

"I'll fight you until I die," Lainie sobbed, bringing up her fist to hit weakly at his chest, even as her mouth opened to receive his kiss once again. His hands came up to close around her breasts, his thumbs brushing across the sensitive nipples.

When at last all her clothes were removed, Rikkar carried her to the bed. With a sob, Lainie gave way to the passion that encompassed her, forgetting the horrors she had endured, the hatreds she had felt, giving in only to the feel of Rikkar and his body above hers and her own body's answering response, riding the crest of passion until it peaked and she cried out her delight before sliding back into the cradle of Rikkar's arms.

She awakened sometime in the night, pinned down by the heavy weight of Rikkar's body. The scratch of something beneath her made her shift around uncomfortably. Carefully, so as not to awaken him, she pushed Rikkar away, and feeling beneath the covers, she brought out the diamond and emerald necklace. Even in the pale light of dawn it twinkled at her. In her haste the night before she had forgotten to remove it and now it hung from her fingers in all its fire and glory, and with a broken clasp. The memory of Denise Payne's words came back to her and she had a clear picture of Denise and Rikkar together here in this very room, on this bed, making love as she and he had done.

Once again she had been made a fool of by her body, she thought, and flung the necklace across the room. Rising from the bed, she put on a robe, and in the growing light of the morning, paced first one way and then the other.

How dare he, she thought. How dare he flaunt his past mistress around her? How dare he give her his mistress's cast-off jewelry to wear? And how dare he force her to make love with him when he knew how she felt? Never again, she vowed, never again.

"May!" she called, rushing to the small room down the hall from her own. "May, I want you to go immediately to my room and pack all my clothes and bring them down the hall to the end bedroom."

"Now, Miz Lainie?" the little maid asked sleepily.

"Now," Lainie said and rushing out, went to the end bedroom and began feverishly to open windows and set it to rights for her occupancy.

"What is all this commotion?" Rikkar asked, following May as she carried the first bundle of clothes into the room and began putting them away in the closets.

"I'm moving," Lainie said. "I will not share a room with you."

"What brought this about?" Rikkar asked, puzzled.

"I won't sleep with a—a womanizer," Lainie burst out.

"A womanizer?" Rikkar repeated, stunned.

"Yes. I know all about your little friend, Denise. Do you think I'm blind? I know she was your mistress and still is if she has her way about it."

"Does that bother you, Lainie?" Rikkar asked softly as he moved toward her. His hair was still rumpled from sleep and she inhaled the warm scent of his body. It made her want to hold him in her arms and snuggle against his hardness. Quickly she turned away.

"Yes, it does bother me," she said, "but not the way you think. I won't be second in any man's life. You chose to marry me and you must tell that little tramp who throws herself so shamelessly at you that you will never see her again.''

"That might be a little difficult as Commander Payne is a good friend.''

"You know what I mean,'' Lainie stormed. "I will not have that woman usurping my place in any way. I know that you allowed her to wear that necklace you gave me and that you made love to her in the same bed you made love to me. Get rid of her or else.''

"Done,'' Rikkar said with a soft smile on his lips. "Now, why don't you come back to bed,'' he invited, the glint in his eyes telling her he had no intentions of sleeping when they returned to bed, but Lainie shook her head.

"There will be no more repeats of last night. I will be your wife in name only. That was our agreement.''

"That was *your* condition,'' Rikkar reminded her angrily. "I did not agree to it, nor will I ever. I told you last night what I expect from you and you will meet your obligations as my wife.''

"My obligations as your wife?'' Lainie stormed. "Very well, if you insist. You shall have what is rightfully yours. I will certainly do my duty as your wife,'' she cried. "Come, sir, I will return to your bed with you.'' She stalked out of the room and marched down the hall to his bedroom.

"Lainie, I didn't mean it to come out quite like that,'' Rikkar said as he followed her down the hall.

"Didn't you? What did you mean?'' she demanded. "Do you want me in your bed or don't you?''

"You know I do, but I want you there willingly.''

"That will never happen,'' Lainie cried furiously.

"It happened last night,'' he pointed out.

"It never will again,'' she cried.

"Perhaps, Madame, you will permit me to hope,'' he said mockingly and gave a slight bow from his waist. He moved toward her and lifted one strand of hair from her shoulder, letting it fall through his fingers in a silken gold web.

"Lainie," he whispered softly in her ear, running his hands lightly up and down her neck, each time dipping lower to her breasts, but Lainie steeled herself against the sensations he provoked within her. Rikkar lifted her in his arms and lay her on the bed. He flung open her robe so that her pale, honey-gold body lay slender and bare against the deep, brilliant blue satin.

"My God, you are so beautiful," he whispered, lowering his mouth to her breasts. He rained kisses across the sleek expanse of her stomach, taking little nips here and there. Lainie remained impassive, her eyes closed so that she need not look at him.

"Lainie, I grow tired of this game," Rikkar sighed wearily. "Must I subdue and seduce you each time?"

"And I, sir, grow tired of your ineffectual pawing, that would hardly elicit a response from a milkmaid," Lainie said scathingly. A sudden pain as he wound his fingers in her hair and pulled her head toward his, made her eyes fly open and she looked into his angry face.

"If I can't get your response one way, maybe I can in another," he grated as he lowered his lips to her in a punishing kiss. His hands on her breasts and body no longer sought to caress and seduce. He took her carelessly, not striving to elicit a ready response from her, not caring if she achieved satisfaction. But in the end her body betrayed her, as her hips lifted of their own accord in a churning answer to his plunging body. When at last they lay, heaving and sweating, their limbs entwined, their hearts and minds were far apart.

Pulling in one last great breath, Rikkar rose from the bed and stood looking down at Lainie who lay with one arm thrown across her eyes.

"I do not mistake what happened between us as an act of love," he said hoarsely. "It was lust, on both our parts, and if that's all you can give me, Lainie, then it will have to do."

"You animal!" Lainie's cry filled the room as she sat up and looked at him, allowing him to see all the hatred and revulsion she felt for him and for herself. After holding her gaze for a moment, Rikkar disappeared into his dressing room. Soon he was back, fully dressed.

"Whatever has occurred here between us," he said, pausing to look down on her with disdainful eyes, "will stay here in this bedroom. Outside this room, you will conduct yourself as a happily married woman who will be accorded every right and privilege that belongs to your rank. You may have a free hand with my home, but don't ever try to deny me what is my right. However it is given and taken, I will claim my rights as your husband. One of those rights is the conception of children."

"Even though you know how much I hate you?"

"Your feelings no longer concern me, only your conduct is of interest and I insist that it be impeccable."

"And if it is not?"

"You'll be happier if it is," Rikkar said coldly, and spun about on his heels and left the room.

Lainie lay back against the pillows and sobbed out her pain and unhappiness. The battle lines had been drawn, she realized, and Rikkar was a formidable enemy. But that didn't matter, she told herself. She was someone to be reckoned with, too. In the long run she would win. She would find a way to beat Rikkar and make him crawl for mercy.

A while later, she rose, put on the robe and went to the dressing table. A glitter of something at her feet caught her eye and she bent to pick up the diamond and emerald necklace that she had thrown away in the early morning hours. Common sense told her that it shouldn't be left lying about. It was far too valuable. She crossed to the safe and opened it as Rikkar had shown her the night before.

She would never wear the necklace again, she vowed, putting it back in the safe. Her hands brushed against the stack of papers, knocking them awry. She straightened them and was about to place them in the vault when a document caught her eye. It was Rikkar's deed to Greenwood. Curiously, she opened the paper and read through it. The date on it indicated that Rikkar had indeed purchased the plantation before the date on the Adams-Onis treaty. But what if he couldn't prove it?

Some thread of vengeance wound its way through Lainie's soul and without stopping to consider any of the moral issues involved, she made her decision. With this, she held a very strong weapon over Rikkar and for once she felt the odds were tipping in her favor. Closing the door of the safe and replacing the picture as Rikkar had done, she hid the document deep in the toe of one of her boots and pushed the boots far back into her armoire. Now it would be her turn!

Chapter 20

Lainie opened her eyes and looked about the room, her face petulant as she noted the gauzy curtains hanging limply at the window. Not a breeze stirred them. It was going to be another one of those wearisome days, where just breathing was a chore. She rolled onto her back and looked at the empty space beside her on the bed. As usual Rikkar had risen early and was out in the fields checking with his overseer about the fate of his young cotton plants. She lay thinking of the weeks that had passed since she first came to Greenwood.

Lainie had taken Rikkar at his word and had not spared any expense as she turned the raw, half-finished, half-furnished rooms into elegant showplaces. Within a month of her arrival, the first shipment of furniture had arrived from France and England.

Rikkar's steel gray eyes held lights of approval when she had her first dinner party. She had invited Denise Payne and had made a point of being a gracious hostess to the woman. There had been no doubt in the minds of anyone there that evening that Lainie was the new mistress of Greenwood. Her touch was everywhere, marking out the bounderies of her territory. Denise had been subdued by what she had seen and what she imagined existed between Lainie and Rikkar, but a flash of her eyes told Lainie that the battle was not to be won so easily.

Sometimes, Lainie wondered why she bothered to fight the battle at all, for she wouldn't allow herself to feel any love for Rikkar. Even at night, here in this bed, when he turned to her, she responded to him with a savagery that matched his own. It seemed to Lainie that each time they mated, it was done so in hate and lust. What was happening between them had become an ugly, bitter thing, but she could do nothing to change it. It was easier to drift along the way they were, each of them snarling at the other in private, and smiling and affectionate in public.

Lainie was beginning to feel the strain of their dual roles. More and more she thought of the time she had spent on the island with Rikkar. Many of those memories had returned because Metoo had come to join them again.

Lainie had joyfully greeted her friend and Rikkar, who had not told her of Metoo's arrival until the Indian stood on the threshold, had stood back with an enigmatic smile. Lainie and Metoo embraced each other and talked all day long, happy to be sharing their friendship again.

"You do not seem happy, my sister," Metoo said and Lainie had turned away, unable to answer, not wanting her to see the tears that had filled her eyes.

"It is very hard to deny that which our hearts want most of all," Metoo continued. Lainie had not answered.

Sighing, Lainie now threw aside the covers and rose from the bed. Crossing the room, she peered at her image in the mirror. Dark circles ringed her eyes and her hair was limp. Her appetite had been off lately and the subsequent loss of weight had shown itself in the hollows of her cheeks and the fine lines of her body. Even Rikkar had comented on it the night before, when he had taken her into his arms.

"Are you all right?" he had demanded, his gray eyes dark with concern. "You feel like you're losing weight."

"It only seems that way to you because you're used to Denise and all her over-blown cha—" His kiss, swift and punishing, had cut off the rest of her words. It seemed always to be like that. She would flail out at him with her words, fighting him and herself every step of the way, until in the end her body betrayed her and she rose to meet the crest of passion between them, hating him for arousing her and herself for responding. Shaking the memories, Lainie moved away from the mirror. A knock at the door made her raise her head and call out a response. Metoo entered, a tray balanced in one hand.

"I have brought you some food," the Indian woman said, a look of concern on her normally stoic features.

"I'm not hungry."

"You must try to eat something. It's not good for the baby that you do not eat," Metoo insisted.

"The baby?" Lainie looked at her in consternation, a growing awareness that what she said could be true. She had been nauseous several times in the past few weeks and she was tired all the time, even taking long naps in the middle of the afternoon. Lainie looked into her Indian friend's face and remembered that it was Metoo who had known when she was pregnant with the first baby. The first baby! All the grief Lainie had stored away from the loss of her first child came sweeping back over her.

"I can't be pregnant," she cried, pressing a shaking fist to her lips. "I can't be," she repeated, turning back to Metoo with eyes that seemed too wide in her thin face. "I will never give him a child, never!"

"You must not feel this way," Metoo said. "To have a child with the man you love is good. You give him a great gift. He will love you and honor you always for this."

"No!"

"You cannot change this thing," Metoo said, perplexed by Lainie's attitude. "This baby will make happiness between you and Rikkar. It is a good thing."

"No, you don't understand. I do not wish to give him a child. I don't love him. I'll find a way." Lainie looked about her feverishly. She paced the floor. "I'll ask May. In the slave quarters, they have potions," she said wildly.

"You would destroy this baby that you and Rikkar have made?"

"Yes!"

"But it is Rikkar's child too and he will want it."

"I don't care," Lainie said hotly.

"If you do this thing you cannot undo it," Metoo warned her.

Lainie reminded herself that Metoo was first Rikkar's friend and then hers. Metoo, Rikkar and Caloosa had grown up together. Metoo's loyalty was for Rikkar. Turning away from the woman, Lainie sought to gain control of her emotions, then turned back to Metoo allowing a humbled, shamed look to appear on her face.

"You're right, Metoo. It's just that for a moment I remembered the pain when I lost my first baby and I couldn't bear the thought of going through it again. Forgive me, I was just so frightened for a moment."

"I understand," Metoo said, placing a hand on Lainie's shoulder, "but you must not be afraid. There is no Tortugas to harm you now. Rikkar will never allow that to happen to you again."

"Yes, I know," Lainie said meekly. "Now I think I will lie down again. I don't feel very well."

"I will go to make a special drink for you that will help take away the morning stomach," Metoo said, picking up the tray.

"Metoo," Lainie called after her. "Don't tell Rikkar about the baby. I want to surprise him myself."

"It is your right to tell him," Metoo said with a nod of her head and moving gracefully, she left the room. Lainie found she hadn't lied when she said she didn't feel well. A lethargy crept over her limbs and she moved back to the bed to lay down. May, she thought, I must get May, but in the meantime her heavy lids closed wearily over her eyes. She was awakened much later by Rikkar bending over her, concern plain in his eyes.

"Are you ill?" he asked sitting on the side of the bed.

"No, no, it's just the heat," Lainie said quickly. "I'm afraid my system hasn't adjusted to it yet."

"It takes time. The best thing to do is move slowly at first. You've been working too hard on the house." He lifted one hand and wound a golden lock of hair about his finger.

"I want to get it finished," Lainie said, pushing away from him and rolling to the far side of the bed.

"I won't disturb you long. I just came to get the deed for Greenwood. The man from the federal government is here and wants to see it." His fingers worked swiftly at the dial of the safe while Lainie watched, frozen with fear.

She had forgotten that weeks ago she had taken the deed and hidden it. It was still stuffed in the toe of one of her boots in the armoire. All the color drained from her face as Rikkar thumbed through the packets of papers, a frown furrowing his brow. His look of perplexity increased as he went through them a second time. Lainie got out of bed and stood clutching the bedpost.

"I must have left it in the office safe," he said, placing the papers back into the vault. Turning to Lainie, his eyes swept across her face. "You don't look well at all," he told her. "I was hoping you could come downstairs and pour tea for us, but you should go back to bed."

"No, I'm quite all right," Lainie said. "I'll be happy to come down. I'll just get dressed. If you see May will you send her to me?'' Lainie moved across the room toward the armoire. Her fingers were stiff as she fumbled with the handle.

"Are you sure you're up to it?" Rikkar asked, pausing near the door.

"Certainly, it will be good for me to move around a bit," she said, keeping her back to him. The door closed behind him and she hurried to dress. May came to help her and as Lainie hurriedly pushed the last curls of her hair into a net, she turned to the maid.

"I want you to go to the old slave woman who makes potions," she whispered.

"I's afraid of her," May protested.

"You go, I tell you," Lainie whispered angrily, "and tell her I want a potion to stop a baby from growing."

"Yes, Ma'm," she said.

"I don't want to have this baby," Lainie said, "and I don't want anyone to know what I am doing, not yet, so do as I tell you, quickly."

"Yes, Ma'm," May repeated as she left the room.

Lainie went down the stairs to greet the government official who sat in the parlor, his speculative eyes noting every fine feature of the room. She had a feeling he had already moved himself into the mansion.

"How do you do?" she said, extending her hand. "I'm Mrs. Rikkar and you're Mr.—?"

"I'm William Shyler, Ma'm," the man said.

"I've had Mavis bring us some tea, and my husband will be with you shortly. Do you take tea, Mr. Shyler or would you prefer some lemonade?"

"I'd—ah—prefer something stronger," the man said.

"Certainly." Lainie didn't bat an eyelash at his breech of manners. "Mavis, will you tell Ben to bring Mr. Shyler a glass of sherry?" she instructed the servant who had brought the tea. She smiled charmingly at the man and suddenly he was aware that he was in the presence of a perfect example of Southern womanhood. He cleared his throat nervously.

David Rikkar, he knew, was a strong figure in the budding territory and he had been warned to approach him carefully. The sherry was brought and the man sipped gingerly at it, suppressing a shudder as the heavy, sweet wine filled his mouth. He really felt the need of some of that raw Southern whiskey most men kept in their private liquor cabinets. He smiled at the beautiful young woman sitting across from him as she chatted easily about the happenings in the area, the crops and the weather.

She sure was something to look at, he thought, surreptitiously eyeing her figure beneath the soft folds of her gown. She had a slight accent which sounded French to him. She didn't really look French, though, with all that blonde hair. He wondered suddenly what she looked like with all that hair spread out on a pillow and that slim body all naked and waiting for a man. The thought made him shift uncomfortably in his chair. He was even more ill-at-ease when David Rikkar walked into the room.

"I'm sorry to keep you waiting, Mr. Shyler," Rikkar said. "I'm afraid I haven't been able to locate my deed. I can assure you that the deed was dated well before the time specified in the treaty."

"I'm sure it is," Shyler said. My God, he thought, is it possible he doesn't have a deed to protect him? He could feel the blood rush to his face. He had never thought too highly of those men who took advantage of another man's misfortunes to further their own wealth, but by God he would in this case. He glanced about the magnificent room again. His eyes came back to rest on Lainie, still seated, a serene smile curving her lips, her eyes overly bright as she looked at her husband. Would she be persuaded to come with the plantation, Shyler wondered.

From under her lashes, Lainie watched the changing moods flash across the man's face. She knew exactly what he was thinking and she gave him a slight smile, not openly inviting but one that he would carry with him and remember in the days to come. From the tight-lipped expression on Rikkar's face Lainie could tell he was aware of the man's intent stare and she turned away discreetly.

"At any rate, Mr. Rikkar, my office requires that I see documented proof as to the purchase of your land. Unless you are able to prove the date of your purchase, you are in dire danger of losing what you have heretofore considered your exclusive property." The man paused, casting a look at the lovely, golden-haired woman whose large, dark eyes had widened as he spoke. Even now the lovely lips were pursing into a pretty pout.

"I assure you, sir, that my papers are in order and I am well within the law. You have no reason to make a claim against my estate."

"You have twenty-four hours to verify that, Rikkar," Shyler said. "If you cannot prove the validity of your deed, then you must be prepared to lose Greenwood."

"You will have your proof," Rikkar said tightly. "In the meantime, this is still my property, sir, so I'll ask you to leave." The dangerous glints in his steel gray eyes made the man turn hastily toward the door. A glance back over his shoulder at the woman showed him dark eyes peering after him, with a light of uncertainty in them and a tremble to her soft lips.

As Lainie watched the man depart, his words still rang in her ears. If Rikkar didn't show proof of the date of his deed he would lose Greenwood. Had she really meant to go this far? she asked herself. Did she really want to lose this magnificent plantation?

"Don't you have the deed, Rikkar?" she asked softly.

The cold steel of his glance penetrated her to the bone. Without answering, he stalked down the hall to his study.

It had begun, Lainie thought. At last she would bring Rikkar down. She would take the things that mattered most to him as he had once done to her. Then she would go away from him and never look back. She paused before a mirror over the mantle and stared at the serene face that looked back at her. Behind the innocent eyes and curving cheek was all the hate and vengeance she had kept locked away all these weeks. The woman in the glass wasn't her. She had changed. She was someone different now. She stood, one hand gripping the mantle, her face averted, while her heart pounded within her as if it would break the walls of her chest.

"Lainie," Rikkar's voice broke through her turbulent thoughts as he strode into the room.

"Metoo told me about the baby," Rikkar said, approaching her. His gray eyes were soft as they searched her face. "Is it true?" he asked.

"Yes, it's true," Lainie said, casting a look at Metoo who had entered the room.

"I did not mean to tell," Metoo said, "but he thought you had taken the deed to the plantation. He was very angry and blaming you. I told him a woman does not destroy the heritage of her child." Metoo's eyes asked forgiveness for betraying a confidence.

"It doesn't matter, my darling, who told me," Rikkar said, sweeping Lainie into his arms. "I'm sorry I doubted you." Over his shoulder Lainie could see Metoo leaving the room.

"Things will be so different between us, Lainie. I'm sorry for the way they've been, for the way I've acted toward you. We'll work it out, darling. We'll make it right between us, Lainie. We'll make it right between us. We have a baby to consider now.'' His voice was joyous as he spoke and he lowered his lips to hers in a kiss more tender than any she had received in all the weeks of their marriage. Lainie was impassive in his arms.

It was all too late, she thought. The wheels had been set in motion and she could not stop them, she could only pull a blanket of numbness about her to buffer herself from any feelings of anger or guilt. Only the bright light of her vengeance was before her now. Rikkar noted her passiveness and mistook its cause.

"Don't worry about Greenwood, darling. We won't lose it. I have that deed somewhere. I'll find it. Greenwood will be ours to pass on to our children. Nothing can stop me now." He pressed a kiss upon her lips, his strong arms cradling her gently.

"I'm going to the town clerk's office now to see what papers are filed there," he said. "I don't know if I'll have much luck, though. A suspicious amount of paperwork has disappeared over the last few years, but it's worth a try.''

He dropped another light kiss on her lips. "Why don't you lie down and rest until I get back," he suggested, the tender, protective light still in his eyes. "I won't be long."

"Yes, I think I will," Lainie said and moved toward the stairs. Rikkar watched her for a moment more, then with a happy smiled turned and left. Outside, Lainie could hear him shouting for a stable hand to bring him a horse. Slowly she climbed the stairs to her room.

May was waiting for her.

"Did you get the potion?" Lainie asked.

"No'm, she say she not givin' no potion to no slave girl. For all she know I might want it fo' myself. She say yo' come to her cabin after supper and she give yo' the potion. Ain't no other way.''

"All right," Lainie sighed wearily. "At least I'll have time to take a nap. I'm so tired."

She had no idea how long she slept but the sun had begun to set outside her window when she awakened. She called May who informed her that Rikkar had not yet returned. It was just as well, Lainie thought, rising from the bed. It gave her time to go to the slave woman's cabin. A strange tiredness had settled over her limbs and even her long nap had not helped. She seemed to be moving in slow motion as she dressed, her heart hammered anxiously.

She followed May down the back stairs and out into the night. The heat which had plagued them all day had not relented as evening set in. It lay over the hushed and exhausted land like a smothering blanket, making man, beast and plants wither under its onslaught. Lainie untied the strings of the summer cape she wore and pushed it away from her throat. Tendrils of hair clung damply to her cheeks and forehead, and she gasped for air as she followed May down the path.

The old woman's cabin was set away from the others as if signifying the specialness of its inhabitant. The dark woods pressed down menacingly on the small building. As they drew close, Lainie noticed a smell in the air and guessed it came from the smoke that poured from the chimney. They reached the rickety porch and May halted.

"Granny Mae, Granny Mae," she called softly and the door squeaked on its leather hinges as it swung inward.

"What yo' want?" the old woman's voice came to them weakly, then she shuffled forward and caught sight of May. She drew in her breath with a sharp hiss. "I tol' yo' I not give the potion to slaves," she said. "Get out o' here."

"I don't want your potion," May said quickly, "but my mistress here does."

"Eh?" The old woman shuffled closer and peered into the darkness beyond May's shoulder. "What yo' want?"

"May told you what I want," Lainie said, striving to keep her voice even.

"Yes, she to' me, but why yo' wan' it? The baby is Master Rikkar's. It give yo' much power in his house."

"It will give me more power not to have it," Lainie said.

"Mm," the old woman said, perplexed by Lainie's statement. "Come in," she said, shuffling backwards. "Not yo'," she pointed a bony finger at May.

"I'm not leaving my mistress," May said.

"Go back to the house. I can find my way," Lainie instructed. "And if anyone asks for me, tell them I'm still sleeping and will come down later."

The old woman led Lainie to a chair. Lainie glanced about her and was relieved to see the room was perfectly normal with a pallet neatly made up in one corner and a roaring fire in the fireplace. A kettle sat upon the hearth, its contents still bubbling and Lainie realized it was this which gave off such a pungent odor. In the back part of the room, bundles of herbs hung drying from the ceiling.

While Lainie studied the room, the old woman moved to a table that held several bowls and assorted jars and bottles. Most contained a dark liquid which was so dense that light couldn't penetrate it. The old woman stirred together ingredients from various bottles. As she worked, she droned words and snatches of songs. Suddenly, she stopped, fixing Lainie with her dark, penetrating eyes.

"The child within yo' lives, it is a boy and will be strong and healthy like his Papa." She returned to her stirring. Lainie tightened her hands into fists. She had never thought of the baby as a boy or a girl, or of looking like Rikkar.

A sudden vision of the baby as it grew into is childhood, racing about the fields and meadows of Greenwood, assailed her. She pushed away the thought and concentrated on the old woman. Once again the woman paused and looked at Lainie.

"Three, three, three," the old woman droned again. "Yo' have within yo'r belly only three babies. Yo' done los' one, yo' have only two left," the woman chanted as if she were in a trance. "Yo' have only this boy left and one more child which will be a girl. The girl will look like yo'."

Lainie's eyes moved restlessly from the woman's face to the mixture in the bowl as she listened to her words. Suddenly she clamped her hands over her ears. "Don't talk," she cried. "Just give me the potion."

The woman stopped stirring the mixture and brought it to Lainie. As she handed the bowl to Lainie, she set up a keening cry. The sound was so unnerving Lainie almost dropped the bowl of liquid, causing it to slosh over the sides and fall on her gown. It left a dark red stain that reminded her of blood. The old woman stood before her, her hands lifted toward the ceiling, her eyes closed as she continued the keening.

"Why are you doing that? Stop it!" Lainie cried.

The old woman stopped the noise and looked into Lainie's eyes. "Our master is dying, I mourn for the future of my people here on dis plantation. After Master Rikkar, there be nobody. Nobody!" The woman began the keening again.

"Stop it!" Lainie cried again, jumping to her feet. In her agitation the bowl slipped from her hands and fell to the floor. The old woman stopped and stared at her. Slowly, Lainie moved away from the dark spot on the ground, her eyes wide and wild. She couldn't do it. She couldn't kill her baby.

"I'll get yo' some more," the old woman said, bending to pick up the empty bowl, but Lainie hurried out into the night as if a thousand devils were hounding her. She ran, tripping and falling in her hurry to get back to the main house. Hastily she climbed the stairs, her breath coming in short jerks, and flung herself into her room. She sat on the edge of the bed, one hand gripping the bedpost as she drew in great shuddering breaths. Suddenly, the door was thrown open and Rikkar stood filling the doorway, his face dark with anger.

"Where have you been?" he asked quietly.

"I—I went for a walk," Lainie said. Aware of her dishevelment she continued, "I tripped and fell, but I'm all right, you don't have to worry."

"I'm not worried about you," Rikkar snarled, crossing the room in great strides and gripping her by the shoulders. He jerked her up, forcing her head to arch back so she had to meet his angry gaze.

"I don't care what happens to you," Rikkar said and his voice was bitter. "What about the baby?" One large hand gripped her chin and throat, the fingers biting into the tender skin. Lainie looked into his face, searching for any sign of tenderness about him.

"What about the baby?" he shouted, tightening his grip on her throat. "May told me what you were going to do. You didn't—you couldn't have killed our baby!" His words ricocheted around in her head. He didn't care about her. He was only concerned about the baby. Hysteria bubbled upward and she laughed harshly.

"There is no baby," she said. "The future master of Greenwood is no more, but that doesn't matter, because there will be no more Greenwood."

Rikkar shook her slightly. "What are you talking about?" he demanded. "What have you done?"

"I went to old Granny Mae and she gave me a potion to end the future of Greenwood. She keened the whole time I drank it," Lainie said.

"You lie," Rikkar exploded. "You couldn't have done something like that."

"I did. See, I even spilled it on my dress as I was drinking it. I told you I would never give you a child." Rikkar had stepped away from her as she held out her dress and was staring at her, disbelief on his face.

"And you're going to lose Greenwood, too," she went on. "I found the deed. It was here in the wall safe just as you thought, but I burned it. There's no way you can keep Greenwood. You've lost it, Rikkar. I told you that you would regret the day you met me. You've lost your plantation."

"Do you think that matters to me? Without a child, without you, none of that matters to me," he shouted, catching her arms in his strong hands, his fingers biting cruelly into her flesh. "I don't care about the plantation. It was something to build for you and for our children.

"I thought I could make you love me again. I thought I could take away the need for revenge. When I found out you were pregnant, nothing else really mattered to me. I love you, Lainie, I wanted you to love me too, but now . . ." He let go of her arms as if he couldn't bear the touch of her anymore.

"You've won!" he said quietly. "You've beaten me. I can't save the plantation without that deed, but I don't want to now. I wanted our child because I love you and thought it would bring us together. Now, none of it matters anymore." He crossed to the door and turned back to look at her again.

"Your need for revenge has hurt a lot of people. I wonder if you'll ever know the extent of suffering you've caused or if you even care. This afternoon I received a letter from the overseer at Belle Fleur. Your father's dying."

"Oh no!" Lainie cried, shocked out of her self-absorption.

"He found Elizabeth and her baby, but he was too late

to do much good for Elizabeth. She died in his arms. She wasn't able to survive the treatment and neglect she received from some very evil men.'' His words fell like blows on Lainie. Tears rolled unheeded down her cheeks.

''Your father killed the man who took her, but he was wounded himself. Jenkins doesn't expect him to live. He did manage to bring his son back to Belle Fleur. The new heir of Belle Fleur! Tell me, Lainie, is that another male for you to destroy? How far does your need for revenge go?''

''Rikkar!'' Lainie cried out as he turned and walked down the hall. Elizabeth dead, her father dying and an innocent baby about to be orphaned because of her, because of her blind hatred.

The clatter of a horse's hooves in the driveway made her jerk her head up. Rikkar couldn't be leaving. She had to tell him that she had lied, that their baby wasn't dead. She still carried it safely within her. Blindly she ran down the hall toward the stairs. She had to tell him that she loved him, that she always had and had never stopped.

''Rikkar!'' she screamed, starting down the stairs, the hem of her skirts tangling in her feet. Reaching out, she frantically grabbed the balustrade, clinging to it as she stumbled down the stairs.

''Rikkar,'' she cried again, one hand going to her trembling mouth as through the tears she watched the tall, broad-shouldered figure of her husband ride away on his horse.

''Rikkar,'' she whimpered and continued to watch as his figure disappeared from sight. She fell to her knees beside one of the soaring pillars of Greenwood as great wrenching sobs tore from her throat. All around her the world was empty and silent. The only sound was the wind sighing through the trees, and her sobs.

Chapter 21

Lainie wiped the damp tendrils of hair back from her forehead. Casting a glance at the sun, she quickly redonned the straw hat she wore when she was riding through the fields. It was not yet noon and the sun was already ferocious. The hot, humid air settled on her like a second skin. Sighing, she slapped the reins against the back of the horse.

Very soon now, she realized, she would have to start using a carriage. Metoo was already predicting dire consequences if she continued to ride in her condition. Lainie pulled to a stop near the corner of the new field and breathed in deeply. Today the heat and the ride bothered her more than it usually did.

She looked out over the new field with its mature cotton plants. White, fluffy cotton bolls hung from them ready for picking. In spite of the discomfort of the heat, Lainie hoped the weather would hold until the pickers could get through the rest of the fields.

A look of satisfaction settled over her features. Who would ever have thought that she, Lainie Gautier Rikkar, would be sitting here on a horse in the middle of a cotton field overseeing the harvesting of her husband's crops. The thought of Rikkar brought a shadow of pain across her face.

It had been almost three months since Rikkar had left; she had neither seen or heard from him since. Caloosa, too, had disappeared with his master. Metoo had remained behind and Lainie had been eternally grateful for her presence.

The two women had become even closer and Lainie truly felt herself a sister to the Indian girl. She remembered how staunchly Metoo had stood by her since that night Rikkar rode away from Greenwood without even looking back. Lainie had thought her world had ended. She had lain in a miserable huddle, too spent to cry anymore, not knowing what to do next and not caring. Then Metoo had come with strong arms and strong words to lift her to her feet. Lainie had leaned against the sinewy strength of the Indian girl and together they had gone up the stairs.

"He'll come back, he cannot stay away. When the hurt has let up a little he will come back and you can tell him you still carry his child. You can tell him why you did not kill this baby the two of you made," Metoo had said as she helped Lainie back to bed.

"Oh, Metoo, I love him, I love him," Lainie had sobbed. "I want to have his child. The old woman said it is a boy and that it will look like Rikkar. I wanted to tell him, but it was too late. I drove him away."

"He'll be back," Metoo repeated and Lainie found herself clinging to that hope.

The past three months had been busy ones for Lainie, weeks of triumph and of sadness. She thought again of the scene with William Shyler the day after Rikkar had left. The man was shown to the same parlor he'd occupied the day before and there he had sat waiting until Lainie had arrived. But before she met him, she gave Metoo a message. She also gave the house butler instructions and a sheaf of papers.

"Mr. Shyler, how good to see you again," she had said graciously. The man looked at her with bright, bold eyes. Lainie smiled demurely, keeping her eyes down while she made polite conversation about the weather. Tea was brought and set up near her chair so that she could pour. Deliberately she did not offer him sherry as she had the day before. Several times the man shifted restlessly on his seat and cleared his throat nervously. But each time he opened his mouth to speak of his purpose there, Lainie would offer a light, intentionally innocuous remark, until time passed and Metoo opened the door slightly to nod her head in a prearranged signal.

"Well, Mr. Shyler," Lainie said, placing her cup back on the tray. "This has been a delightful visit, but I'm sure you didn't come all this way to have tea."

"I came to speak to Mr. Rikkar," Shyler said stridently.

"I'm afraid my husband is not at home today," she said evenly. "Perhaps I can help you."

"I doubt it," Shyler said, fighting hard to keep his elation from showing. If Rikkar wasn't here, then it must mean he couldn't find his deed. "You may have heard that we need to see Mr. Rikkar's deed showing the date of purchase on this land."

"I'm surprised that you don't simply look at the records with the city clerk."

"I'm afraid some of those records have disappeared," Shyler told her. "Has Mr. Rikkar found his copy of the deed?"

"No, he hasn't," Lainie said softly, lowering her lashes. "But I found some papers that look like a deed to me." She lifted her lashes and smiled into Shyler's eyes, laughing within herself at the dismay she saw there. "Perhaps if you look at them, you could tell me if they are what you need?''

"All right," the man agreed, and Lainie rang the bell on the table beside her and when the butler entered, asked him to bring the papers she had given him earlier. Ben left the room, but suddenly the door was pushed opened and Jed Thompson, the overseer, entered the room with Metoo behind him.

"Sorry to bother you, Ma'm," Jed said, "but we need you down at the barn. One of your colts is crippled and since I know it's your favorite, I wasn't sure whether to put it out of its misery or not."

"Oh dear," Lainie said, her eyes wide. She opened her mouth to say more, but Ben reentered the room carrying the papers she had given him.

"Oh, just a minute, Jed," she said to the overseer. "I'll go right with you." Turning to Ben she took the papers and opened them up. Ben remained in the room as did Metoo. Lainie handed the papers to William Shyler and watched with some amusement as he opened the packet and read the words written there.

"Are they the papers you needed to see?" she asked softly.

"No, I'm afraid they're not," Shyler said, his eyes refusing to meet hers. Lainie gathered up her skirts and moved closer, peering over his sleeve.

"But it says right there that it is the deed for this property and there is the date which proves that my husband bought the property before the deadline set by the treaty."

"Ah, yes, I see it," Shyler said as if seeing it for the first time. "However, I'm not sure if these papers are enough. I'll just take them with me and check them out at my office." He refolded the papers and returned them to their envelope.

"I'd prefer you leave the papers with me," Lainie said and held out her hand. The steely look was back in her eyes and Shyler held the papers uncertainly. He was aware that the overseer, the Indian woman and the butler still stood in the room, all watching him intently. Meeting the dark eyes of the petite woman before him, he realized that she had set this up on purpose. She knew these papers were the proper ones and that they were all in order and she had surrounded herself with witnesses in case he refused to give them back. The bubble burst for him and with a sigh he handed back the papers. He hadn't really believed this magnificent place could be his anyway.

With the deed safely in her hands once again, Lainie smiled graciously, again the helpless, womanly mistress of Greenwood.

"You will excuse me, I hope, Mr. Shyler? As you heard, my attention is required elsewhere."

William Shyler nodded and bent to retrieve his hat from the table nearby. With one last glance at the people in the room, he moved toward the door. The butler followed behind to let him out.

"Good day, Mr. Shyler," the soft voice of the plantation's mistress called after him. It had been a moment of triumph for Lainie and she had shared it with the three other people in the room. Their smiles were conspiratorial and happy as they filed out of the room and went back to their duties. Greenwood had been saved. None of them knew that it was Lainie herself who had put the plantation in jeopardy, but they had been proud of their mistress when she had stood before the towering figure of the government agent and demanded the papers back. They all felt happier knowing she was the mistress of Greenwood.

But Lainie had had only a short time to savor her victory against William Shyler, for she remembered Rikkar's words about her father and over Metoo's protestations about her condition, had gone back to her father's plantation. She arrived only a few hours before he died and as she held his thin body in her arms, she wept against his shoulder.

"Papa, forgive me," she cried.

"There, there, my little girl. It doesn't matter. Elizabeth is dead, you see, and I don't mind going, too. Soon I will be with her again. Don't judge me too harshly, Lainie," the dying man said.

"Lainie, you must accept this and you must not blame yourself for it. You must not carry a guilt such as this with you or you will distort your life even more, my child. Put away the revenge and the guilt. It can only harm you." Lainie looked at him in amazement, her mind reeling. He knew, he knew all that had happened to her.

"Papa, was Rikkar here?"

"Yes, my child, he was," her father said weakly.

"Where is he Papa?" she asked urgently.

"He has gone away, Lainie. He told me everything, and I have cried such tears for you and the pain you are enduring."

"But Papa, I lied to him. I told him I had killed our baby, but I haven't. I still carry it. I couldn't do it, because I love Rikkar."

"Lainie," he whispered and his brow furrowed from the effort.

"What is it, Papa?" Lainie's smile vanished as she gripped her father's hand anxiously.

"I have a request, which you must honor."

"What is it, Papa? Anything, I'll do anything for you."

"You must take my son, you and Rikkar, and raise it as your own. His name is Jean," he whispered. The memory of Elizabeth's message returned to Lainie with a jolt.

"Promise me, Lainie, promise me."

"I promise, Papa. I will love him and care for him as I will my own son." Her father eased his grip on her hand

and lay back on the pillow. Lainie watched him anxiously, tears running down her cheeks as her father's face convulsed for a moment, each muscle bulging, then suddenly, the features relaxed and he looked almost young again as he smiled, his eyes gazing off into the distance.

"Elizabeth," he whispered, then his eyes closed slowly. It took Lainie a moment to realize that he was dead.

After her father's funeral, Lainie had taken the little baby, Jean, and left Belle Fleur, deciding that the overseer would remain in charge until she could decide what to do. She had to keep the plantation for her little brother. It was his rightful inheritance, but she couldn't stay there. She had to return to Greenwood and wait for Rikkar.

Lainie now thought that perhaps she would return to the house earlier today and lay down. The overseer, Jed, had proven to be very reliable in bringing in the crops, but she felt her presence was needed every day to let the slaves know that someone from the big house was in charge. It made Rikkar's absence less obvious and it eased her mind a little. She preferred to ride about the plantation, feeling she was aiding in its prosperity, than to sit passively in her room, praying for Rikkar's return. It seemed his presence was everywhere, but she felt closest to him here in the fields of Greenwood. Her hand fell against her rounding stomach for a moment. He had to come back, she thought.

Clucking at her bay, she moved on down around the fields. She would just ride through this field and check on the cotton picking before going back to the house, she decided. A cool bath and a nap would revive her for the party tonight at the Fort. Denise Payne had driven all the way out to the plantation a few days ago to invite Lainie to her dinner and ball. At first Lainie had declined, but Denise had been uncharacteristically friendly, insisting she needed to get away from the plantation for a while. Lainie had finally accepted.

If Denise were willing to make attempts at a friendlier relationship, then she should meet her halfway, Lainie thought. There was also the hope that she might learn something about Rikkar. She had ridden over to talk to Commander Payne on her way to her father's plantation, but he knew nothing of Rikkar's whereabouts and Lainie hated to probe for fear Denise would guess at the trouble she and Rikkar were having.

Lainie brought her horse to a stand near the wagon that had been pulled to the center of the field and was already piled high with the fluffy, white cotton. Slaves were making their way to the wagon, their stuffed sacks dragging heavily on the ground behind them. Once the sacks had been emptied, they were hung once again around the shoulders of the pickers until picked full again. One man sat in the shade of the wagon, an injured foot extended before him, a pad and a piece of charcoal held in his hands as he made marks to indicate the number of sacks being emptied into the wagon. Jed Thompson rode up on his own horse.

"Good morning, Miz Rikkar," he said, touching his hat.

"Good morning, Jed. How's it going?" she asked.

"Very well, Ma'm. We'll have it all finished and stored inside by tonight."

"And tomorrow, we celebrate," Lainie said, smiling at a little boy who walked by pulling a cut-down version of the adult sacks. During this time, everyone was pressed into service in an effort to get the crops in before a rain or winds ruined them.

"Are the barrels ready?" she asked referring to the rum that would be given tomorrow.

"Yes, Ma'm," Jed said.

With a nod of encouragement, Lainie moved on down the path toward the house. She knew the overseer had a lot to do that day and her presence for too long a period would be distracting to him as well as the workers.

"How is little Jean doing today?" Lainie asked Metoo when she had arrived back home.

"He never cries," Metoo said. "He will make a good Indian brave."

Lainie picked up the dark-eyed child from his crib. In three months he had grown from a thin, sickly infant into a chubby cherub with somber, dark eyes and dark hair. Lainie thought he looked more French than anything. There was no sign of Elizabeth's parentage.

"We won't tell anyone," she crooned, holding his fat little cheek to hers. She knew that the laws governing people of mixed blood were as harsh as those for full-blooded blacks. Somehow, she would have to protect Jean and save him from the prejudice that had already begun to erode Southern morals. Jean Paul Gautier would inherit Belle Fleur one day and she would see to it that he got that inheritance. If only he were a more cheerful baby, she thought, laying him back in his crib and straightening the gold chain and medallion which had belonged to her father.

Her father had always worn it and had explained to her once that the emblems on the medallion were the coat of arms for the once powerful Gautier family. On an impulse, Lainie had removed the medallion from her father's neck and placed it around her brother's. He was the new master of Belle Fleur. Somehow, the small gesture had comforted her and helped ease some of her guilt.

"Oh, you are a precious baby," Lainie said to him, taking hold of one of his fat little feet and wagging it playfully. The baby's eyes looked into hers as if he understood what she said.

"One day soon, you're going to have a playmate," she said to him and incredibly the baby's mouth opened in a gurgling laugh. Merry lights twinkled in his eyes.

"He laughed, Metoo," Lainie said, calling the Indian woman to the crib. Together they played and talked to the baby until at last he tired and fell asleep. With a smile on her face, Lainie moved down the hall to her own room. What a delight Jean Paul was. She could hardly wait for her own baby to be born.

Gratefully, she sank into a tub of water, easing her weary muscles in its fragrant warmth. Looking down the length of her once slim body, she gloried in the curve of her rounded stomach and wondered what Rikkar would think of her if he could see her now. She remembered the wonder and adoration in his eyes the morning he had stripped away her blue robe and gazed at her slim body. It had been the morning after they had first made love as man and wife, and after that everything had gone wrong between them.

It had all been her fault, Lainie acknowledged to herself, but it was no less difficult for her now. She thought of the weeks when she and Rikkar had made love as if they hated each other. For the thousandth time she wished back those early weeks of her marriage. She would do things so differently, she thought, if she were ever given a second chance.

Sighing softly she rose from the water and toweled herself dry, then lay across the bed and fell into a light sleep. The hot afternoon passed swiftly and she awoke feeling refreshed. She even looked forward to the party that night.

Lainie chose a soft dress that fell from the ribbons and gathers beneath her bosom. The style hid the slight swell of her stomach. It was only when she moved quickly that the folds of the gown molded themselves to her figure, giving away her condition.

Commander Payne's home was brightly lit when Ben halted the carriage at the front door.

Denise and her father were in the main hall greeting their guests, and the woman's blue eyes sparkled maliciously when she saw Lainie. Servants moved about the parlor bearing trays of drinks and hors d'oeuvres, a practice recently brought over from France. Lainie took a glass of wine and waved aside the offer of sweetmeats.

The first people she saw were the Wilsons, a couple she had met at Commander Payne's dinner party when she first came to Tampa. The Wilsons had also been her guests at Greenwood.

"My dear, how are you?" Mrs. Wilson asked, pressing her cheek against Lainie's, then stepping back to look at her. "You've become a hermit since Rikkar left," she reprimanded. "Do you have any idea when he'll be back?" Most of the neighbors believed that Rikkar had gone away on business, but as time passed and he hadn't returned, their questions had become more persistent.

"No, I haven't," she said faintly. "His business is taking longer than he thought. Would you excuse me? I've had a long drive and I want to get some more wine and some of those delicious looking little snacks."

"Jack can get some," the woman said and not giving Lainie a chance to make her escape, turned to her husband and sent him off for refreshments. While she waited for the unwanted food and wine, Lainie searched for something to talk about to the woman. Mrs. Wilson filled the space with empty, friendly chatter. Lainie paid attention to her ramblings with only half a mind, until the woman began on a new topic.

"Have you heard? The Indians are making attacks on some of the outlying plantations again. You must be very careful while Rikkar is away."

"Are they that much of a threat to us?" Lainie asked.

"Jack thinks so. He brought extra men along tonight. He said he didn't want to be scalped on the road going to some party." Mrs. Wilson smiled cheerfully. Obviously she was unconcerned about the threat.

"Oh, my dear," the woman said suddenly, gripping Lainie's arm, her face beaming as she looked at Lainie. "Your husband has returned."

Lainie looked in the direction she was pointing and her heart seemed to stop beating as she caught sight of her tall, dark-haired husband. He was dressed in formal evening clothes and the white of his shirt made his tanned skin look even darker.

Her face lit up in anticipation and she took a step toward him. "Rikkar," she called out, but her voice died in her throat as Denise Payne came through the crowd and put her arm possessively through Rikkar's. She signalled to the orchestra and turned, smiling confidently at Rikkar, then he swept her into his arms and swung her around the floor in a lilting waltz.

"He didn't see you here, my dear," Mrs. Wilson said, but her eyes looked troubled. Another woman came to join them and Mrs. Wilson soon became immersed in conversation with her. Lainie could hear their excited voices exclaiming over something, but she paid no attention. Her eyes were on the couple on the floor. As they glided by, Denise Payne shot Lainie a triumphant look.

"Oh, Lainie dear, I didn't want to hurt you, but Sarah just told me that Rikkar has been at the fort for several days. He has been staying here with Commander Payne." Mrs. Wilson's kind eyes held many questions.

Unable to stand the pity and speculation of those around her, Lainie gathered up her skirts to make her way through the dancers and milling people. It became a nightmare for her. People were looking at Denise and Rikkar on the dance floor, smiling knowingly. Denise had done her work well.

Lainie had almost made it to the door when she pushed

her way through a knot of people and went sprawling on the floor. A woman screamed and there was a stir of voices as all eyes turned toward her. Lainie could feel scalding tears, then she was pushing herself up as people crowded around her. She looked wildly around the room.

She had to get away before Rikkar saw her, but even now he was moving toward them, his brows drawn down over his eyes in a way so familiar to her. His eyes locked with hers and she saw his lips part as he called her name. Frantically she pushed against the people who were helping her to her feet. She tried to move toward the door, but the filmy folds of her skirt caught under the heel of one of the men and as she moved, the material tightened about her body, then ripped, making her condition obvious.

Without pausing to collect her cloak, she ran out the main door, down the steps and across the lawn to the carriage, calling Ben's name as she went.

"Take me home, Ben, as quickly as you can," she cried and sat back against the cushions. Ben scrambled into his seat and whipped up the horse. They went careening out of the drive, through the square and toward the road back to Greenwood. Lainie sat huddled in the corner, fighting back the tears. She thought she heard her name called, but she didn't look back as the carriage bounced along.

The evening air was chilling through her thin gown, but she gave it little thought as she wrapped her arms about herself. Her mind was too occupied with the scene back in the Payne's parlor for her present misery to register. Rikkar had been back for several days and he had come not to Greenwood, but to Commander Payne's house. He had made his choice and Lainie was not it.

Lainie had cried herself out by the time they reached the big house. She shouldn't have run away, she thought. She should have stayed and told Rikkar that Greenwood was still his and that his crops this year had been all he had hoped. She should have told him that and more.

Tomorrow, she thought, she would tell him tomorrow, then she would take Jean and they would go back to Belle Fleur. She would devote her life to the two babies and people could think what they liked about her, a lone woman with two children and no man.

Wearily she climbed the stairs to her room. She was so tired. But once she was ready for bed she found she could only lie awake wide-eyed while visions of Denise in Rikkar's arms tormented her. The woman had moved with such assurance. She had known Rikkar was hers for the taking and she had wanted Lainie to know it, too.

Restlessly, she rose from the bed and wandered about the room. Tomorrow, she would send him a message that the plantation was his and she would leave. She could at least start packing now, she thought, and called to May to bring her trunks. She wouldn't take everything, just enough for herself and Jean Paul. She would send for the rest later.

She was distracted from what she was doing by shouting. As she opened the window and looked out, she heard a woman scream. What on earth was happening? she wondered as she leaned out. The moon was certainly bright tonight, she noted as she looked around at several people running about. With a start she realized it wasn't the moon casting such a glow, it was the warehouses at the back of the slave's quarters. They were on fire! And the figures running about were smeared with brightly colored paint and wore feathers in their hair.

Indians! Her heart shook with dread. Pulling back inside she closed her window, then without thinking about danger to herself, turned and headed for the stairs. She knew the slaves must be cowering in their cabins, while outside the

Indains were firing the warehouses that held the product of their labor.

No one was going to burn that cotton if she could help it. She ran through the kitchen, rousing the house servants as she went, then raced across the back toward the slave quarters. The Indians would move toward these buildings soon, she knew. She ran from one cabin to another hammering upon the doors and calling the slaves out.

"Get buckets," she called. "Go to the warehouses and put out the fire." The loyal men and women quickly took up their pails and formed a brigade.

Jed Thompson was there, his rifle at the ready as he fired on any Indians that threatened to break the brigade. They swarmed around the slaves now and then, striking one down with their tomahawks, while others swooped up the children that ran shrieking, trying to find their mothers.

Lainie gathered up a broom and running to the nearest barn began beating at the flames that had jumped across from one burning building. One storage barn was already lost, but they were making some headway with the others and finally she began to believe they could be saved. Then a cry went up and she turned to see that the east wing of the main house was on fire.

"Bring some men and follow me," she shouted at one of the field hands. Another brigade was formed to the main house and they worked frantically to save it. Again they were hampered by the flying arrows and the flailing tomahawks of the Indians. Lainie coughed as smoke filled her lungs so that she could hardly breathe. Her face was scorched by the heat of the flames, but she worked on doggedly, beating at the flames, carrying water, whatever she could do. Suddenly she saw Metoo emerge from the burning house, Jean Paul cradled in her arms. She raced toward the orchard and as Lainie watched, an Indian brave stepped forward, his tomahawk at the ready.

"Metoo!" Lainie screamed, but she was too weak. She watched with horror as the Indian's club came down on Metoo's head and the Indian woman slumped to the ground, Jean Paul still clutched in her arms.

"Metoo," Lainie shouted and this time her voice came out in a piercing scream as she ran toward the fallen woman. Even as she ran, she could see another Indian brave pick up the wiggling bundle that was her baby brother. The Indian held the baby by his heels as if he would dash the child against the tree.

"No!" Lainie screamed, rushing up and tearing at the Indian's arm. He pushed her away and she stumbled backwards nearly falling to the ground, but she regained her footing and tore at the Indian again. The Indian who had struck down Metoo stepped forward with his tomahawk raised. Lainie saw the flash of its blade in the air and ducked to one side just in time. The Indian with the baby shoved her and she fell forward.

Stunned, she twisted around to see the Indian with the tomahawk wrestling with Rikkar! Beyond them, Caloosa was kneeling over the still form of his sister. He raised his voice in a terrible cry and Lainie knew that Metoo, her Indian sister, was dead. Thankfully, she sank into the darkness that swept over her.

Lainie slowly opened her eyes and looked around her. She was back in a room that was vaguely familiar. Obviously, the fire hadn't damaged her bedroom, she thought, and then she remembered Metoo and Jean Paul, but the dark shadows were there to reclaim her.

She drifted in a world of red-hot lights peopled with flitting shadows that reached out and delivered swift, sure death. She woke and found she was in a soft bed with a cool clean pillow beneath her head. She looked about the strange room and finally realized that she was back in the bedroom she had shared with Rikkar on the island. He had brought her back to the key! Her head hurt dreadfully and she turned her eyes away from the bright sunlight that poured through the windows. Her closed lids brought the darkness back and the memory of Metoo's body lying crumpled on the ground.

"Metoo," she cried out and her voice shattered the stillness of the room. The door opened and Rikkar crossed the room to wrap his arms about her and cradle her against him.

"It's all right, Lainie, it's all right," he crooned, rocking her slowly.

"Jean Paul" Lainie gasped, pulling away from the comfort of Rikkar's shoulder. "Is he all right?"

"He was taken by the Indians and we haven't been able to recover him yet. Caloosa is out with scouting parties looking for him now."

"Is there any hope?" Lainie asked anxiously and the look on Rikkar's face told her there was not. She put her head back against his shoulder and gave way to her tears. She had lost too much in the past few months. Rikkar let her cry, holding her tightly until she slept again.

Later in the day when she had awakened and eaten some of the broth Rikkar brought her, she was able to talk to him about all that had happened.

"What about Greenwood?" she asked and tears stung the back of her eyes as she thought of the beautiful house with flames shooting from its windows.

"One wing was damaged. The workmen are rebuilding it now. We'll stay here until they have it ready," he said and Lainie's heart seemed to stop beating at the implication of what he had said. Was he back for good? But that question brought her to another, a question she was afraid to ask. She asked instead about the crops.

"How much damage was done to the storage barns?"

"We lost two, but two remained and the cotton is good, if a little scorched around the edges." A light of humor twinkled briefly in his eyes.

"Oh no," she lamented. "It was such a good crop this year and now we've lost half of it. We worked so hard to get it into the barn early, so you wouldn't lose any. It would have been better if it had been left in the fields."

"We have no way of knowing these things, Lainie," Rikkar said gently. "Besides, you've obviously never seen a field of cotton burning. It's just as devastating. Don't fret about it now. Go back to sleep. You need to rest."

She did as he told her and the next time she awoke she told him about Greenwood.

"It's still yours," she said. "I didn't burn the deed. I hid it on an impulse, then, when the government agent came I . . . I—"

"I know, Lainie. I went to Belle Fleur to find you. I thought you had gone back to live with your father. Jenkins told me you were still at Greenwood. I guessed then what had happened."

"I didn't do it for myself," Lainie said, suddenly afraid he had misunderstood her motives.

"I know, Lainie," he said, bending to place a light kiss on her hand. "Stop worrying and go to sleep," he ordered smilingly and his hand held hers in a warm, sure grip. Lainie closed her eyes and weak tears rolled down her cheeks. There was something else she wanted to tell him, something important, but the memory of his words blocked everything else out. He had gone to Belle Fleur looking for her. She held that thought in her mind while she drifted off to sleep.

In the morning when she had finished with as much breakfast as she could eat, Rikkar lifted her in his arms and carried her to the verandah where he settled her into a cushioned chair. He sat beside her, saying nothing. His patience astounded her, but then she remembered his kindness on the boat when she had been a captive. And now she could see it as a kindness. His own life had been in danger, but he had risked it to save her.

"I didn't kill the baby, Rikkar," she finally said timidly. "I still carry it."

"I know," Rikkar replied softly. "I've known for a long time." Lainie met his gray eyes questioningly.

"After I got over my rage at what you'd told me, I began to think more clearly," he told her, "and I realized you couldn't have killed the baby. You had suffered too much over the loss of the first one. I went to see Granny Mae."

"Then why did you—?"

"Stay away? I wasn't sure of your feelings. Your hate for me nearly drove you to destroy our child. I couldn't take the chance it could still happen."

"Oh, Rikkar," Lainie cried, thinking of all the months of pain and loneliness. "I don't hate you."

"I know, Lainie, I know," he replied and his hand came out to hold hers. They sat side by side, letting the healing begin between them.

A week had passed since the Indian raid and now Lainie went every day to the verandah. She had also walked about in the yard a bit, although Rikkar forbade her to go further and she was strangely content to follow his orders. The baby moved often within her, reassuring her it was unharmed by the trauma its mother had endured. Each time she felt the flutter of life, she mourned for the loss of her baby brother.

They had received word that Caloosa had been unable to find the Indians. Indeed, his fierce assaults on them had driven the tribes deeper into the Green Swamp. Lainie knew it was hopeless. Too many children had disappeared forever once they were snatched by the Indian tribes. She could only hope that he was alive and being treated well. Metoo had said once that he would make a brave Indian. Perhaps she had had some premonition of how things would turn out.

One day, restless with her bounderies, Lainie decided to walk down to the lagoon and it was there that Rikkar found her. He called out her name as he caught sight of her. Lainie remembered the last time they had been here in this spot together. He had crossed the clearing with long strides, his broad-shouldered figure taut and compelling as he approached and she had felt such a wave of love for him. She had meant to tell him of the child she carried, but he had hurried her away to the ship and taken her to Tortugas.

What had Metoo said of him? His temper was his worst enemy. It had caused them both much pain and great loss and she, because she had been unable to forgive, had almost cost them more.

"I couldn't find you," Rikkar said and Lainie saw his fear.

"We have to talk," she said.

"I love you, Lainie." His words touched her deeply. There were many things they must have straight between them. She wanted no more shadows, no more misunderstandings.

"What about Denise Payne?" she asked hesitantly.

"What about her?"

"When you came back you stayed with her. She was your mistress."

"Was," Rikkar said, "but that was over long before I met you. I knew Denise wasn't what I was looking for. I took that special assignment with the Navy to help get rid of the pirates in the Keys because I thought the distance would discourage Denise."

"But when you came back from your trip, you went back to her," Lainie said.

"I went to stay with Commander Payne because he has the room for extra visitors and because I had business with him. Denise did not figure in the reason for my staying there."

"The night you brought me to the fort, I saw Denise running out to meet you. She stayed on board the ship with you."

"Lainie," Rikkar said with a sigh, "I don't want to answer every suspicion that Denise arouses in you. That's no way for us to have our marriage, but I will answer all your questions this time and you must believe me. I did not meet Denise that night or any night. She tried very hard to take up again with me, but I couldn't bear to have another woman when all my thoughts and senses were full of you. Denise Payne has the morals of an alley cat. It has been a source of concern for her father for some time. Denise did come to the boat that night, but I told her I was married and I loved my wife very much. There would never be anything between us."

"But you let her wear your mother's jewelry," Lainie said. "Denise knew about the broken clasp!"

"Let me explain about the broken clasp. Commander Payne came to see me about some business once and Denise tagged along. When I took some papers out of the safe in the study, I inadvertently took out some of my mother's jewels. Denise put on the diamond and emerald necklace. I was angry and when I removed the necklace, I broke the clasp."

If she had only asked him, Lainie thought, or believed in him, so much heartache could have been avoided.

"Denise tried again when I was staying with her father, but I didn't know to what extent she had gone until I saw you at the ball. The pain on your face made me realize that Denise had contrived to make our relationship seem more than it was. But more than that, when I saw your pain I realized you still cared, that there was still some hope for me.''

"Oh, Rikkar," Lainie cried, moving toward him. "I thought I had lost you. I thought there was no hope for me.''

"I ran after you but you were already in your carriage and Ben was careening down the road. Caloosa and I left for Greenwood. Thank God we made it when we did.'' He pulled her to him fiercely. "If I had lost you, I couldn't have lived myself,'' he murmured hoarsely and his voice broke on the words.

Tears rolled down Lainie's cheeks, but they were tears of happiness. She had lost so much, most of it because of her own willfulness, but she hadn't lost Rikkar. She raised her mouth to meet his and her arms wound around his neck tightly.

"Beauty?" he said softly and his voice beseeched and demanded at the same time. Her kisses gave him his answer.

"I love you, I want you," she whispered breathlessly against his mouth.

"Come on, I want to show you something," Rikkar said and led her up the trail toward the house. "Look," he commanded when they reached the clearing.

A bubble of laughter rose from Lainie. Arranged all around the lawn were sticks holding Conch shells, the time honored way the people of the Keys announced the coming birth of a child.

"It's a new beginning for us, Lainie," he whispered and she raised her radiant face to his.

"Yes, a new beginning," she agreed softly. New beginnings were usually built on old ashes of past dreams, and perhaps because of that they would be stronger.

Epilogue

The ship skimmed the waves gracefully. It rode just over the rim of the horizon, its great sail billowing above its sleek, dark hull like some great bird of the sea. Indeed, the ship's bow carried the name, *Sea Hawk*, and on its bow was a great hawk, its fierce beak and eyes no less menacing for all that they were carved of wood.

Men scurried about the deck, silent and purposeful in their actions. Little direction was needed for they had been through this many times before.

The captain stood tall and certain on the rolling deck, his gray eyes intent upon the horizon. About his legs clung a small boy, just old enough to take his first steps. With a laugh the tall captain lifted the small boy in his arms and pointed out something at sea. The little boy followed his father's hand, then laughed and clapped his own hands as he watched the silver flash of dolphins leaping among the waves.

Rikkar turned and smiled at Lainie over the dark head of his son. His eyes glittered with appreciation at the sight of his golden-haired wife and the tiny bundle that was his daughter. Even as young as she was the baby looked like her beautiful mother and Rikkar's heart swelled with pride as he gazed at his family.

Briskly he ruffled the hair of his son, set him back on his feet, and took the wheel again. They were returning to Greenwood after spending the golden summer on their Key. The months ahead would be filled with planting crops and the business of their plantation and of Belle Fleur. Although her brother had never been found, Lainie still insisted upon keeping the large plantation in operation.

Sometimes she still grieved for him. He had probably been adopted by some Indian family and was even now being raised as an Indian, not knowing he was the owner of one of Florida's most prosperous plantations.

A nursemaid came from the cabin below and took the sleeping bundle from Lainie and now she came to stand beside Rikkar at the wheel. The Gulf breeze stirred the tendrils of her hair, blowing them about her face and he remembered her years before when she had stood like this, letting the wind blow about her, a smile on her face that had told him of her joy in being here. He had let his own anger blind him to what he had seen there and had betrayed her, but now it was behind them.

Rikkar put an arm about his wife, pulling her closer to him. Above them the sails flapped briefly, then filled once again and the ship skimmed over the waves as if it were flying.

Peggy Hanchar was inspired to write DESIRE'S DREAM by a plaque she saw in a Key West, Florida, churchyard. She is the mother of four and lives in Wisconsin with her husband, a mechanical engineer. This is her first novel.

Patricia Matthews

America's leading lady of historical romance.
Over 20,000,000 copies in print!

☐ 42223-7 **LOVE, FOREVER MORE** $3.50
   The tumultuous story of spirited Serena Foster and her determination to survive the raw, untamed West.

☐ 42364-0 **LOVE'S AVENGING HEART** $3.50
   Life with her brutal stepfather in colonial Williamsburg was cruel, but Hannah McCambridge would survive—and learn to love with a consuming passion.

☐ 42365-9 **LOVE'S BOLD JOURNEY** $3.50
   Beautiful Rachel Bonner forged a new life for herself in the savage West—but can she surrender to the man who won her heart?

☐ 42012-9 **LOVE'S DARING DREAM** $3.50
   The turbulent story of indomitable Maggie Donnevan, who fled the poverty of Ireland to begin a new life in the American Northwest.

☐ 42464-7 **LOVE'S GOLDEN DESTINY** $3.50
   It was a lust for gold that brought Belinda Lee together with three men in the Klondike, only to be trapped by the wildest of passions.

☐ 42463-3 **LOVE'S MAGIC MOMENT** $3.50
   Evil and ecstasy are entwined in the steaming jungles of Mexico, where Meredith Longley searches for a lost city but finds greed, lust, and seduction.

☐ 42222-9 **LOVE'S PAGAN HEART** $3.50
   An exquisite Hawaiian princess is torn between love for her homeland and the only may who can tame her pagan heart.

☐ 42462-0 **LOVE'S RAGING TIDE** $3.50
   Melissa Huntoon seethed with humiliation as her ancestral plantation home was auctioned away—then learned to survive the lust and greed of a man's world.

☐ 40660-6 **LOVE'S SWEET AGONY** $2.75
   Amid the colorful world of thoroughbred farms that gave birth to the first Kentucky Derby, Rebecca Hawkins learns that horses are more easily handled then men.

☐ 42465-5 **LOVE'S WILDEST PROMISE** $3.50
   Abducted aboard a ship bound for the Colonies, innocent Sarah Moody faces a dark voyage of violence and unbridled lust.

Buy them at your local bookstore or use this handy coupon
Clip and mail this page with your order

◎ **PINNACLE BOOKS, INC.**
Post Office Box 690
Rockville Centre, NY 11571

Please send me the book(s) I have checked above I am enclosing $_____ (please add $1 to cover postage and handling). Send check or money order only—no cash or C.O.D.'s

Mr./Mrs./Miss_____

Address_____

City_____ State Zip_____

Please allow six weeks for delivery. Prices subject to change without notice

Voyage to Rom

Win A Romantic Caribbean Cruise!

On November 9, 1985, the luxury liner *Carla Costa* will embark on a special romance theme cruise to the deep Caribbean's most exotic ports of call, and you can be on board! Four lucky Pinnacle romance readers and their guests will set sail with us as winners of the *Voyage to Romance* Sweepstakes. Sponsored by Pinnacle Books and Costa Cruises, the *Voyage to Romance* theme cruise will visit San Juan, Curaçao, Caracas, Grenada, Martinique, and St. Thomas. Top romance authors, like Heather Graham Pozzessere, will be on board to conduct writing workshops and give island tours. And to get our guests ready for romance, there will be fitness and nutrition experts, cosmetic and fashion demonstrations on board. So, enter today and get ready for romance on Pinnacle Books' *Voyage to Romance!*

1. NO PURCHASE NECESSARY. On an official entry blank or plain 3" x 5" piece of paper, print your name, address and zip code. Mail your entry to: VOYAGE TO ROMANCE SWEEPSTAKES, Post Office Box 5, New York, NY 10046. Enter as often as you like but each entry must be mailed in a separate envelope.

2. One (1) winner of a cruise for two will be selected on a monthly basis, May through August, for a total of four cruises. These winners will be selected in random drawings from entries received under the supervision of Marden-Kane, Inc., an independent

ance *Sweepstakes*

judging organization whose decisions are final and binding. All entries received by the last day of the month will be eligible for that month's drawing, with the final receipt date being August 31, 1985.

3. *PRIZES:* (4) GRAND PRIZES of a 7 day cruise for two to the Caribbean aboard the ms *Carla Costa*. Cruise includes round trip air transportation from winners' home to point of embarkation. Cruises must be taken on dates to be specified by sponsor. No substitution or transfer of prizes. Winner consents to use his/her name and/or photograph for publicity purposes. One prize per family. Winners will be required to execute an Affidavit of Eligibility and Release. Odds of winning will depend upon the total number of entries received.

4. Sweepstakes are open to residents of the United States, 18 years of age or older, except employees and their families of Pinnacle Books, their affiliates and subsidiaries, advertising agencies and Marden-Kane, Inc. Void where prohibited or restricted by law. All Federal, State and local laws apply.

5. Winners will be notified by mail. For a list of Grand Prize Winners, send a stamped self-addressed envelope to: VOYAGE TO ROMANCE WINNERS, c/o Marden-Kane, Inc., Post Office Box 106, New York, NY 10046.

Name_____

Address_____(No. P.O. Box)

City_____ State_____ Zip_____

Name of Bookstore_____

City_____ State_____

We've got a job so important, it takes a retired person to do it.

We want you to help give new lives to the 27 million Americans who are functionally illiterate.

Today, illiteracy has become an epidemic that has reached one out of five adults. But you can help stop it by joining the fight against illiteracy.

Call the Coalition for Literacy at toll-free **1-800-228-8813** and volunteer.

Volunteer Against Illiteracy. The only degree you need is a degree of caring.

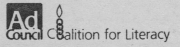

Ad Council Coalition for Literacy

Join Pinnacle in the fight against illiteracy!